Miranda Inside and Out

David A. Thyfault

ISBN 978-1-957077-94-9

Cover design by Jeff Ruiz, Just Right Productions

Published by BookCrafters, Parker, Colorado.
www.bookcrafters.net

This book may be ordered from online bookstores.

Somebody said that this book is based on a true story that resembles an adult version of the Wizard of Oz. But on the other hand, you can't believe everything you read.

ACKNOWLEDGEMENTS

Sounding Board: Patricia Thyfault
Cover Girls: Julie Kemp, Kasey Bourque
Photographer: Stacie Thyfault
Remaining Cover: Jeff Ruiz
Editor: Liz Netzel
Publisher: BookCrafters

1

How the hell am I supposed to soar like an eagle when I'm surrounded by stupid turkeys? The particular turkey that I'm speaking of weighed a hundred-and-sixty pounds and brought a gun inside our minimum-security prison for women, known as the Lighthouse.

Glendale, California was a perfect place for our facility because it looked more like a well-kept dormitory than a prison.

I am among the few who are allowed to go off-campus in street clothes from time to time. The rest of the time, all thirty-seven of us were anxious to serve out our sentences and get out of that place, so we were usually on our best behavior, but I should have known that something had to go wrong. Sure enough, Turkey-Boy put it all in jeopardy.

As for me, a lot of people thought I shouldn't be there in the first place, even though my original sentence required a minimum of forty-one years behind bars in the Bakersfield Penitentiary, ostensibly because I had played a role in three murders.

After serving ten years for those bogus crimes, I was able to prove my innocence by committing several misdemeanors.

Once that was completed, the original sentence was waived then I was moved to the Lighthouse for five additional years for the misdemeanors. Thankfully, I had served all but three months of that sentence and was scheduled to be released for good.

That's when gobble-head inserted himself in everybody else's business. That idiot's behavior had the potential to derail both my appointment with freedom and the other thing I'd always wanted more than anything else – to meet my teenaged son for the very first time.

The chaos all started after dinner. Our very pregnant receptionist needed a paper from the kitchen area. Her given name was Kathy Pratt, but when she was a toddler, her father began calling her "Kandi." A generation later, her hubby's last name was Barr, making her "Kandi Barr."

Anyway, it was chilly in the Lighthouse and I wanted to change into my casual jeans, so I agreed to retrieve the paper that Kandi needed.

When I returned, I dropped said paper on her desk and noticed a familiar mustached visitor with a long black ponytail and a dingy red baseball cap coming toward the building. Unfortunately for me, Lenny Canosa was the husband of my cellmate, Neeva.

Lenny reached for the entry bell at the same time that I turned my back on the reception area. Then I heard the buzzer go off, indicating that guard Donna had authorized Kandi to let Lenny in, but before Donna could pat Lenny down, he stepped deeper into the main room, produced a huge gun, pulled the trigger, and shattered the window off to my side.

I wrapped my arms around my head and ducked down while others screamed and glass shards pinged off the table beside me.

Given that there was only one gunshot, and it shattered the window, I assumed that nobody was hit, but Kandi was at the greatest risk, partly because she had a baby to think about and partly because Lenny's gun was just a few feet from her head.

"Except for Kandi," Lenny said into the room, "I want all the rest of youse guys to lay on the floor, face down, hands behind your back so I can see them."

The majority of us had already made a voluntary trip to the carpet, but the remainder of our group did what he said.

Lenny turned to Kandi and showed her his gun, presumably to intimidate her and to keep her under control. "Where is Neeva, honey?" he asked.

As I said, Neeva was my cellmate. She'd earned two years in the Lighthouse when she hit an obnoxious drunk over the head with a beer bottle, knocking him out and destroying some of his eyesight.

Nearly crying, Kandi pointed toward the center hall. "I think Neeva is back in the kitchen."

"Alright then. I want you to stand by your desk so you don't get hurt."

With trembling fingers, Kandi nodded and wiped a tear from her eye.

While Lenny moved toward the center hall, one of the other inmates yelled at a guard. "Dammit, Brandon. Get your gun and take him out before he kills somebody."

But instead, Lenny's gun popped a second bullet into the far wall. "I told youse people to keep your hands behind your backs. If I see either of you guards going for a phone or gun, I won't be so friendly."

Everybody tightened up as Lenny turned his attention toward the hall. "Come on out, Neeva," he yelled.

After a few seconds of shuffling, my thin Hispanic cellmate made her way up the hall. "I'm coming, Lenny," she said in a highly irritated tone. "What are you doing?"

That was when I got a glimpse at Lenny's shaking hands.

"Stop this, Lenny," Neeva barked. "You're scaring everybody."

"Shut up. I know what I'm doing. Now get the guards' guns, then join Kandi by her desk."

Lenny turned to Kandi. "How you doing? Is your baby alright?"

The receptionist squared her glasses and wiped her cheeks. "I guess I'm okay."

"Good"

"Got 'em," Neeva said, referring to the guards' guns.

"Bring 'em to me."

"Okay, okay, I will, but don't shoot that gun no more. Okay?"

"I see Miranda by the window," Lenny said, ignoring Neeva. "I want you to stand up and walk toward Kandi and the door."

My stomach tightened. The last thing I needed was drama. On the other hand, this loon was trigger-happy and when an angry person points his gun right at you, you take him seriously. "Alright, alright," I said standing and revealing my hands. "Can't you take somebody else? Maybe they'd like to go with you?"

"Stop talking and do what I say."

"Okay, Lenny, alright," I said as I eased toward the reception area. "Just be careful with that gun."

A minute later, we scooted outside, where Lenny pointed toward his SUV. "Over there, youse guys, and hurry."

As we rushed along, I heard chaotic scrambling behind us. Presumably somebody was calling the local police and the off-site warden.

At that moment my pregnant and scared counterpart whispered to me, "Are we going to be okay, Miranda?"

How the hell would I know? I was just as scared as she was. "I sure hope so," I said in the calmest voice I could muster.

Lenny made Neeva take the driver's seat while I rode shotgun, leaving the back seat to Lenny and Kandi.

"This way, I'll be right behind you, where I can keep my eyes on everybody," he said.

Like it or not, I was "in the wind" for the second time in five years and I prayed that turkey-man's stupidity would not infringe on my release.

2

Barely out of the parking lot, Neeva glanced over her shoulder toward her husband. "Now what, big shot?"

"For now, drive the speed limit so we don't draw no attention." He turned to Kandi. "I hope your seatbelt isn't too uncomfortable."

"Of course it is, you idiot. I'm expecting a baby. Everything is uncomfortable."

"That's why I brought Miranda with us. Neeva likes her and she's the only one who has had a baby."

That was true. I was also the only one who wanted to yank the steering wheel, crash the car and end all the nonsense, but Lenny was behind me and I couldn't tell if he still had his gun in hand. I wouldn't want to do anything to endanger Kandi's baby. "If you want my opinion, Lenny, I said, "we should go back before somebody gets hurt."

Neeva nodded. "I second that."

"I don't need no opinions; I just want youse guys to help Kandi when she needs it."

Suddenly Kandi freaked out. "Oh no, I left my cellphone at my desk. How am I gonna call my husband?"

"You can't," Lenny said softly. "None of us have phones. I planned it that way so the police couldn't track us."

He was correct about that, too. Inmates weren't allowed to

have phones because they could use the phone to coordinate breakouts.

"And just so everybody else knows," he resumed, "I got more weapons and some food and water if you want anything."

"Oh, my God, Lenny," Neeva said. "Where'd you get weapons? That's not like you."

"We just got two extra guns from the guards and I already had some things I borrowed from Victor at work."

"That crazy Victor? What kind of weapons?"

"The gun I came in with and a big knife, and some handcuffs. And I have some duct tape."

"This is nuts, Lenny. What are you going to do with those things? Kill us all?"

"I don't know yet, but I've got a hiding place a few hours north. We can stay there until it's completely dark."

It was times like that when I missed my boring prison life. "I don't like the sound of that," I said. "I still think we should go back and turn ourselves in. Otherwise, there's no telling what will happen to us."

"Me too," Kandi said, through constant sniffles. "If you hurt my baby, you'll rot in—"

"Nobody is going to hurt your baby. Why don't you unbuckle your seatbelt? I'll roll up a sweatshirt; you can use it for a pillow."

"No, no, no. Don't you get it, you freak? I just want to go back to my job."

"Me too," Neeva said emphatically.

"Me three," I added.

Lenny waved his gun in the air. "This ain't no vote, damn it. I'm trying to be nice to youse guys, but you're making me mad. If I have to shoot this gun—"

Kandi's jittery hand cupped her mouth.

"That's better," Lenny said. "Now I want to talk to Kandi." He smiled at her. "Your baby-girl is due next week, right?"

"Yes. How'd you know that?"

"I asked you a while back. You said you were having a little girl. I guess you forgot about our talk."

"I'm sorry, I don't remember that. Everybody asks me things like that. I just don't remember who all I've spoken with."

"That's okay. You're probably really looking forward to it?" His tone was calmer.

While Lenny asked Kandi more questions about her pregnancy, we were getting farther and farther from the Lighthouse, which prompted Neeva to butt in. "C'mon Lenny. We should turn around."

"Not yet, I'm talking with Kandi." He returned to his questions. "So, what you gonna name her?"

"We like the name Serene. It means peace."

"That's a pretty name. What about you, Neeva? Do you like that name?"

"Huh? Me? Yes, of course. We are going too far."

"Be quiet. I want to know how long it took to get pregnant."

"Just a few months," Kandi said. "I hate to say it, but I really need a restroom."

"Oh, yeah, I hear that happens a lot to pregnant ladies."

"We can all use a break," I pleaded.

"C'mon, Lenny," Neeva added. "Show us some mercy."

"Not now. There are too many people around here. You guys might tell somebody else to call the police. That would ruin everything. Besides, you'll have your chance pretty soon… Now let's all be nice to each other."

Neeva glanced in her mirror, then tried something else. "If you really want everybody to be nice, you should at least put that damn gun away."

Lenny ignored the plea and all the rest of our complaints for nearly two hours.

Finally, we reached the southern end of San Jose, where the sun tapped at the horizon. "See that long black fence on the right?" Lenny said. "Pull in there."

We all looked in that direction.

"A cemetery?" Neeva said. "Now I know you're out of your mind."

"No, I'm not. It's Hillsdale Cemetery. I've already checked it out. It's quiet and there's a place we can hang out and rest 'til it gets dark. Plus, youse guys can take care of business without talking to anybody else."

Just inside the entrance area, a tranquil blend of mature trees, a small lake and flower gardens contradicted the tension in our vehicle.

"Take the road on the right," Lenny ordered.

We meandered around a slew of headstones and past a little porch-like shelter that was likely used for funeral services.

Just past that, the road and fence eased down a back hill where a cluster of very old and stout trees and some bushes provided a perfect spot for grown women to pee.

"Stop here," Lenny said at the base of the trees. "Youse ladies can go behind the bushes, one at a time. And remember, I still have my gun."

Since he'd already nixed the idea of a public restroom, we employed the better-than-nothing lavatory.

Thereafter, Lenny removed the keys to his car and whizzed behind the vehicle, where he could make sure none of us bolted. When back in the car, Neeva spoke to her husband. "What are we going to do now?" she asked.

"I'm not sure. We might go to Portland, but first I have another question for Ms. Kandi." He turned his head in her direction. "Would you consider selling me and Neeva your baby?"

Kandi covered her ears while Neeva turned her head. "You're out of your ever-loving mind, Lenny. Take that back."

"I'm serious," he interrupted. "I want to make an offer. What will it take? I can sell my car and give you all the money."

"No!" Kandi screamed. "Nobody would do that."

"Sure, they do. They put babies up for adoption all the time. In fact, Miranda gave up a baby, didn't you, Miranda?"

Obviously, Neeva had told Lenny about the worst day of my life, which was fifteen years earlier. I was incarcerated and gave birth to Trevor in prison. Trouble was, I didn't have a sister or friend who could raise him, so I put him up for adoption.

"It was a lot different situation, Lenny," I said.

3

The idea of buying Kandi's baby was repugnant and completely rebuked, but Lenny wasn't ready to give up. "Well then," he said to Kandi, "if you won't sell your baby to me, I can just wait a week and when the baby comes, I can give her to Neeva."

Spine, meet ice-water.

Neeva's head spun his way. "What the hell are you talking about, you crazy man? That's the most ridiculous thing you've ever said."

"Too bad," he blurted back. "And stop ridiculing me. I did all of this for you."

"For me? That's crazy. I'd rather make a baby later than deal with this shit."

"But what about your miscarriages?"

"What about them?"

"You know. Every time you get pregnant, you have a miscarriage and cry your eyes out. I don't like it when you feel sad. I thought if I could get you a baby, you'd be grateful and happy, but you're being mean."

"Damn right. I'd be more grateful if you'd take us back."

"I'm sorry, lover. I can't do that."

It seemed like my turn. "Can I say something, Lenny? Five years ago, I was on the lam and scared to go back, so I know how you feel. But it worked out. Now, I'm scheduled to be released and I'm the happiest I've been in a long time."

"Well, I ain't you, and I'd like Kandi to give her baby to Neeva. Then Kandi can make another one. She already said it was easy for her."

Neeva turned her head toward her husband. "Listen to me, you nut job. In a yucky sort of way, that's the most romantic thing you've ever said. I love that you love me that much, but we can't take somebody else's baby. You get that, right?"

He hesitated a few seconds, then spoke softly. "Maybe I should shoot myself for being so stupid."

Neeva shook her head. "That's not the answer either. I don't want to lose you. Let's just go back and face the consequences. At least nobody will be hurt."

"No way. I ain't going to jail."

"What if we compromise?" she asked. "We can turn Miranda and Kandi loose, then you and me can go wherever you want."

"Yeah," Kandi said. "I saw a grocery store on the way in. You can take us there and drop us off."

"I already told youse. I ain't taking you where people are all over the place. Somebody will call the cops."

Then, I had an idea. "Lenny, you can use those handcuffs you mentioned to hook Kandi and me together at the ankles. That'll take us a long time to walk out of here. By then you'll be a long way off and we won't know where you went."

His silence suggested he was thinking it over. Then he said, "I have a better idea. Neeva, give me the keys to the car and youse guys stay in the car while I take my bag to the back of the car. Then, I'll tell you what to do. Remember, I have all the weapons in my bag."

At least we were making some progress, but I was still petrified. The man was unstable--lovey-dovey one minute and wielding weapons and threatening people the next. In fact, Neeva once said that he occasionally forgot to take his meds. This appeared to be one of those days.

While he was out of the vehicle, we reminded each other to stay calm, so that everybody got out of there alive.

"Okay," Lenny said. "I want Neeva to hand me the sweatshirt in the back seat and stay in the car while Miranda and Kandi come back here."

At the back of his vehicle, he offered Kandi his sweatshirt. "Just in case you get chilly."

She and I traded glances. "Go ahead," I said. My jeans are warmer than your dress is."

"All right," he said, motioning toward a nearby tree.

He pulled out the handcuffs, which were connected by a long chain. Standing under a stout branch, he threw one end of the chain over the top and instructed Kandi to hold out one hand. She looked at me then back to him. "Why? What are you gonna do to me?"

His red face suggested he'd just about reached his limit with all the back-talk. "Look," he said loudly, "youse guys want to go back and I ain't gonna do that. So, youse can either come with me and Neeva or put up with a little inconvenience. What the hell is it gonna be?"

Kandi hesitated and looked at me again.

Having previously been at somebody's mercy in a similar situation, I knew the best thing to do was to separate ourselves from an irrational man with weapons. "Go ahead," I said to Kandi. "We'll be better off here than in the car."

Lenny jingled the cuff of the chain at her. "You gonna listen to Miranda or what?"

With trembling lips and chin, Kandi began to cry. Seconds later, Lenny clicked one of the cuffs to her wrist. "All right," he turned toward me. "Your turn."

I still believed that our best bet was to get Lenny out of there, so I let him cuff my wrist.

4

I DON'T KNOW HOW OR WHY I got into bizarre situations, but Lenny-the-turkey had Kandi and me standing face-to-face with one arm extended over our heads like stand-up riders in a subway.

Unfortunately, neither of us had the strength to pull ourselves up and over the branch. On the plus side, we each had a free hand and a bottle of water.

As unpleasant as it was, Lenny had one additional rabbit to pull from his hat. He grabbed a roll of duct tape from the back of his vehicle and came toward us.

"What you gonna do with that?" Kandi asked in a quivering voice.

"I'm sorry I have to do this to youse guys, but this should keep youse quiet for a while. It's the only way Neeva and me will have enough time to get away."

Suddenly, Kandi freaked out. "Help! Help!" she screamed, in hopes of getting some attention from anybody else.

Angered, Lenny slapped her face. "Looky here, Kandi, I've been nice to you; I gave youse guys a fair chance to come with us. Now, I'm going to cover your mouths, but not your noses, this way you can breathe but can't scream for a while."

I could see the terror in Kandi's eyes, but I realized that

we could use our free hands to remove the tape as soon as he and Neeva drove off. "You can tape me first, Lenny."

That done, it was Kandi's turn. "I'm sorry I slapped you," he said, "but you'd better listen to Miranda."

"Screw you, Lenny," she barked while he taped her mouth. "I hope you get caught."

Just before they drove off, Neeva laid some more water at our feet. "Here you go. I hope we all get what we want."

Moments later, Kandi and I were alone and taped like a couple of drunk mummies. Nonetheless, we could see and breathe and I was glad that we'd been separated from a nutcase and his guns.

I quickly raised my free hand so that Kandi could see me reach for the tape. She nodded and duplicated the exercise. We began slowly spinning around and peeling off each other's tape. It was more challenging than I had expected, but eventually we were able to speak with each other until the last piece of tape found the ground.

After we caught our breath, I said, "Lenny was right. He and Neeva gotta be twenty-five miles away by now."

The next thing we did was scream for help, but nobody came for us. "It's no use," Kandi said. "This is all your fault, Miranda, for putting us in this situation."

I was tempted to bark back, but it seemed imprudent. "I'm sorry you feel that way, but can we focus on getting out of here first?"

"It's no use. Nobody else is around. We might have to spend the whole night, or longer, standing up. We shoulda gone with Neeva and Lenny. At least we'd be out of the elements."

"I get that, Kandi, but I've been in a situation like this before. There's no telling what would happen if we went with them. Lenny is unstable and armed. We're better off here. The police are probably looking for us right now. Sooner or later, somebody will drive by and baby Serene will be out of harm's way."

"You don't know that, and nobody goes to a cemetery at night."

"Fair enough, but it's still our best chance. We don't want to depend on a guy like that."

She shook her head. "All right, I guess that makes sense, but my husband is going to go crazy if our baby—"

"First off," I said quickly, to prevent her from finishing that horrible thought, "we should try to break the branch or scoot to the end of it."

Just then, a hornet buzzed over our heads and caught Kandi's attention. "Don't be alarmed," I said. "I think we'll be okay if we don't get near their nest."

"Okay, I just hope they leave us alone."

For the next half-hour we tried everything we could think of to either break the branch or to slide our chain out to the end of the branch, but the main branch was sturdy and stubborn and the side-branches were as big as a baseball bat. "Face it, we're stuck," Kandi eventually moaned.

By that time, we could barely see each other in the moonlight. "I have another idea," I said. "We can distract ourselves by getting to know each other better. Worse case, a groundskeeper will find us in the morning."

She sorta nodded. "I sure hope so, but I'm used to sitting at a desk all day. My feet are not used to standing up a whole lot."

"We're just got to tough it out. In the meantime, we can rest against the trunk or stand back-to-back and keep each other warm."

"And pray."

"You got that right, girl."

Just then another hornet landed in the branches of the next tree over. Mercifully, the nest was behind Kandi's back so she didn't see it, but I sure as hell did.

5

AFTER SUGGESTING THAT WE STAY CALM by telling each other some stories, Kandi wanted me to go first.

"Okay, then," I said, while checking my watch. "I guess the best place to start is at the beginning."

I told her about my deceased, mentally-challenged twin brother and the twins' conventions that we'd attended. Before long, Kandi asked some questions, which distracted us a bit.

After exhausting that topic, I moved on to my school days and the blackouts I'd had whenever I was stressed out, such as during the school play. "All of these things combined," I said, "landed me in prison for three homicides that I didn't commit."

By the time I explained all of that, I'd chased off the remainder of any daylight. "What about you?" I asked. "What roads have you traveled?"

"Me? I don't know what to say."

"Anything is ok. We're just trying to kill time. What about your family?"

"Well, okay. Daddy has always said that if my mom dies before him, he wants to be buried in the same hole, face down."

"Why was that?" I asked.

She went on to reveal that her parents still held hands and

engaged in other romantic gestures. "Daddy loves looking into Mom's eyes when they dance, so he wants to be buried upside down, so that he can see her beautiful eyes forever. Now you talk some more. You're better at it than I am."

We kept trading little stories like that to keep our minds off our situation. An hour passed, then two. It was very dark and getting colder. Mercifully, the hornets left us alone.

Sometime around eleven o'clock I spoke of another weird crime that I'd endured. "I was also convicted of a thought crime," I said.

"What's that?"

"Well, before my brother died, he needed some high-priced meds that I couldn't afford. My boyfriend knew of an elderly woman who had a lot of money in a trust. He figured we could steal enough money for Mickey's treatments. I didn't want to take the woman's money, but Don said she had insurance and would get all her money back. It was Mickey's only chance, so I was willing to steal the money for his meds."

"And you got arrested for that?" Kandi said. "I bet a lot of people would have done the same thing."

"It seems like that to me too, but 'planning' to defraud somebody amounts to a 'conspiracy,' whether you carry it out or not."

She looked me in the eyes, presumably to find out if I was telling the truth. Then, "I'm sorry for you, Miranda."

"Thank you, but the Good Book tells us that each life gets some rain."

"That's for sure. Now that I think of it, my mom has a fun quirk, if you'd like to hear it?"

"That would be nice."

"When I was a kid and my sisters and I fought and screamed at each other, she made us kneel down in the living room floor, nose to nose, and sing Christmas carols, even if it was the middle of the summer."

"That's interesting. Why'd she do that?"

"Couple reasons. She loves Christmas and it was so silly

we'd start giggling. Did you know that you can't be angry while you're laughing with somebody?"

I almost laughed.

"I also have a funny story about my uncle Johnny. One day he wanted to trim the enormous rose bush that grew up a trellis on the side of his house. But he kept getting stuck by the thorns so he got a blow torch from his garage and tried to burn the branches. Trouble was, it got out of control and the fire department had to put out the fire. My aunt was so mad about losing her beautiful roses that she made him paint the whole house as punishment."

That too was a good tale. "It must be nice to have a big family."

"I can tell you this. When we get out of this place, my mom will want me to quit my job and come home, with or without my husband."

We continued to distract ourselves by sharing stories. Every once in a while, we stopped and yelled for help even though there was nobody around.

It was at that time that a pair of hornets buzzed past Kandi's head and toward the nest. This time she saw them and pressed the fingers of her free hand to her mouth. "Oh, my God. Bees. That's the last thing we need."

"They're hornets," I said. "They won't bother us if we leave them alone. Just stay calm."

"Okay, but I don't know how much longer I can take this. My feet and back hurt and I gotta pee."

So did I, but there wasn't a simple solution to that problem. To distract myself, I checked my watch. "We've got to be strong. You can do it. There are lots of people who stand up all day. Why don't I tell you how I met Phillip?"

She nodded her head. "Your husband? I like him. When he comes to visit you, he's always nice to me."

"Yep. That's my Phillip. It was a couple weeks after I escaped from a hospital. He was cruising across the country on one of those three-wheeled motorcycles. He even had a tiny dog for a traveling companion. It was so cute, I nearly melted in his arms."

"I can understand that."

"After a month of floating around the Midwest I told Phillip who I really was."

"Oh, my God. That was risky. What did he say?"

"First, he said that he loved me, then he called his godmother, who proved to be an extraordinary attorney, near San Francisco. She's the one who got a huge part of my original sentence overturned – course she couldn't erase the fact that I'd escaped the hospital and was in the wind."

"And that's when you were taken to the Lighthouse. At least you're getting out in a few months. Thank God for that."

"I hope so, because Phillip and I are going to meet my son. I just hope that the Department of Corrections won't think you and I were involved in Lenny's scheme. I sure don't need more conspiracy charges."

"You're a good woman, Miranda. You've always been nice to me. I'm sorry you've been through so much just because you wanted to help your brother."

Unexpectedly, I heard some buzzing at my own ear, then a lone hornet landed on the back of my neck. I swished my hand behind my head in hopes that my unwanted visitor would fly away but instead the motion opened a crack at the back of my collar and the wasp fell inside my shirt and flipped around.

I shrieked and it fell a few inches down my back before it planted its stinger just above my bra.

I yelped and swatted at it with my loose arm but then a second one stung me, followed by a third. I panicked and pivoted. "Oh my God, Kandi, there are a bunch of them inside my shirt, attacking me. You gotta squish them." I turned so she could get to my back.

"I don't see any," she said. "Wait, there's one."

She hit it with her fist. It plunged the stinger deeper into my skin as it fluttered and died. "Hurry, get the others. Get the others."

"I'm looking, but I don't see any more of them."

"They are a lot of them in there. Get 'em out. Please hurry."

"Okay. I gotta lift your shirt so they'll fly out."

"Hurry! My back's on fire. Hurry!

"There aren't any more."

"There have to be more of them. I've been stung a million times."

"Believe me, there aren't any more."

"Okay, okay," I said, while blowing out a deep breath and rubbing the wounds the best I could with my free hand. "I just hope they don't come back"

Suddenly, I heard a new voice. "I told you," somebody said. "There's some ladies over here."

Stunned, I lifted my head.

"Over here!" Kandi yelled. "Over here!"

6

TRUTHFULLY, WHEN IT GOT DARK, I thought Kandi and I would be stuck to our tree until the next morning, but when a pair of middle-schoolers showed up, I could barely believe my eyes and ears. "Do either of you have a cell phone?" I asked. "We need to call 911."

The girl shook her head. "Not me. My mom took mine away."

"What about you?" I asked the young man. "You've got a phone, don't ya?"

"Sure, but it needed charged so I left it at home. I heard you screaming. What's going on?"

I sighed. "Some bad people did this to us. I got stung by a lot of hornets. We need you to get somebody who can get us down."

"I don't know. You might be bad guys."

Kandi snapped. "Do we look like bad guys? I'm pregnant and there's a dangerous hornet's nest behind us. My friend has been stung a lot. Can't you see that?"

"She's right," I said. "At least three of them got down my back and stung me. We have to get out of here. You can be heroes."

"Not likely," the young fellow said. "Three hornets wouldn't get down your shirt at the exact same time unless you were messing around in their nest. It's more like one hornet stinging you three times. They're different from bees; bees can only sting you once because they lose their stingers and die, but hornets can sting you more than once."

The girl grinned from the darkness. "Clinton is the smartest boy in school."

Frustrated, I took a deep breath and smiled at the young lady. "I believe you. What's your name?"

"I'm Jackie. I'm thirteen, and Clinton is fourteen. We're going to get married someday. We already kiss like movie stars. Wanna watch us frenchy kiss?"

"No. That's okay, Jackie. Our arms are sore. We need you guys to get some help. Can you do that for us? Please!"

Clinton raised a finger. "Is there a reward?"

"I don't know about that," I said, "but you might be famous and end up on TV."

Kandi turned to the side. "Surely you can see how dangerous this is. If my baby comes, it's a life and death matter. If you don't do something those wasps could kill us and you'll probably go to jail."

"You ain't gonna die from no hornets," Clinton said. "You'd have to get stung a thousand times for that to happen. By the way, did you know that only girl-bees can sting you?"

"Please!" I said. "If you guys notify the police, you'll be big shots in school."

Clinton nodded. "I might be able to get a can of hornet killer. It's best to squirt them now because this is when they rest."

"Yeah, but by that time, you could get somebody to break this chain. It would be better if you called the police."

"Alright, I guess we could go home and call the cops."

"Thata boy. Please hurry. We'd be very, very grateful."

"Under one condition," he said to Kandi.

She blew out a deep breath of frustration. "Okay, what is it?"

"I've always wanted to feel a baby move around in the mama's belly."

A moment later, Clinton and Jackie oohed and aahed while they rubbed Kandi's belly as if it were a gypsy's crystal ball.

Eventually, they peddled off and Kandi spoke to me. "You were right, Miranda. We are going to be rescued. I gotta one-arm hug you."

"Me too. It's past midnight. Shouldn't be long now."

* * *

Just past a long section of headstones and out of hearing range of the dangling ladies, Clinton had moved ahead of Jackie. "Wait for me," she pleaded. "Stop a minute. I gotta tell you something."

Clinton spun around and waited until she reached him. "What's so important?"

"You're not really gonna call the police, are you?"

"Why not? Those ladies are desperate. The grandma is afraid of the hornets and prego-woman is hotter than all hell. You know how she got pregnant, right?"

"Sure, I do. A man put his penis in her vagina. But, if we call the cops, they'll find out that I snuck out of my house to be with you again. My mom would kill me. Not to mention that we're not supposed to be in the cemetery in the first place."

"So what? We're not hurting anything. And this is the only place we can be in private."

"But I'll get in super trouble."

"Well, that's your problem. I'm gonna get my phone and save that pregnant lady. If you don't want in on it, just go home to your mommy and daddy and I'll see you tomorrow, or the next day."

"No, Clinton. If you call the police, those ladies will tell them about me, and I will get grounded for a hundred-million years. Let's just go frenchy kiss, like we always do."

He shook his head. "Naw. We frenchy kiss all the time. It's boring."

"Well then, what if I let you do those other things to me that you talked about?"

"Really? Are you saying you'll let me touch your privates and you'll touch mine, cause the last time I asked, you said you didn't want—"

"I know, but things have changed and I'm ready now."

"Okay then, I guess I can go for that. We'll let somebody else find them."

7

After Clinton and Jackie peddled off, Kandi and I traded high-fives. "Thank God," she said. "Our husbands must be climbing the walls."

"I'm sure they've been notified and questioned about the escape," I said. "I just hope the authorities realize that you and me and Neeva were not involved in Lenny's plan."

Kandi turned slightly toward me. "You keep saying that, but why would they think that?"

"Trust me. They're trained to suspect everybody."

"Well, I hope they catch Lenny and send him to prison. Especially for trying to get me to give him my baby. What kind of idiot does that?"

"You don't have to worry about that. If they catch him, they'll charge him with kidnapping and endangerment and gun crimes and whatever else they can think of."

"He deserves it. What about your stings? Do they still hurt?"

I reached over my shoulder to rub a swollen bump. "It still feels like somebody burning me with a lit match but it's getting better."

"That has to be painful. I just hope they leave us alone from now on."

"Me, too. That kid was smart and intrigued by the hero-talk. I'm betting he's racing to his phone as fast as he can."

"It's no wonder that the girl idolizes him. Guys like him can be exciting to younger girls. I know because I lost my virginity to a so-called boyfriend who convinced me that we loved each other; but, after we made love, he admitted that he just wanted to add a member to his 4-F club."

"4-F club?" I asked while rubbing my sore back. "What's that?"

"Find'em, Feel'em, Fuck'em, Forget'em – it's vulgar but those turds don't care who they hurt as long as they conquer somebody."

"Yeah, I've met some guys like that too, but to be fair, when I was in the Bakersfield Prison, there were some women who were just as dreadful. They forced the weaker girls to get them off. In addition to the sex acts, they made the weaker ladies do their laundry and clean out the cells and give them money for the prison store."

"Really? I didn't know any of that."

"It's not the kind of thing that people want to talk about. For now, I'm anxious to get back to the Lighthouse and my safe bed."

"I can't wait for one of my mom's special dinners."

"I envy people who have large families," I said while glancing at my watch for the hundredth time. "It's been quite a while since those kids left. I'll be glad when I see some headlights coming toward us."

"Yeah. Neither one of us is in condition for something like this."

"At least when they remove your cuffs, they won't replace them with another pair."

Kandi tilted her head. "Oh, yeah, I hadn't thought of that. If they have any decency, they won't cuff you either. You haven't done anything wrong."

"Well thanks, but that's not how they look at it."

"I can tell you one thing. They better get here pretty soon cause I gotta pee."

"Hopefully, they'll let us go behind a bush, even though that's against the law."

"Really, I didn't know that, either."

"It's indecent exposure and can land you on a sex offender list."

"What the hell are we supposed to do? Wet our pants?"

"That's better than having a criminal record."

She looked like she was going to cry, but I suspected that we had a bigger problem.

If Clinton had called the police, as he promised, a mass of law enforcement officers would have already arrived. I needed to distract Kandi again. "I don't know about you," I said, "but my legs are getting stiff. I think we should march in place just to stay warm."

After killing more time by stretching, marching, and random small talk, Kandi nearly panicked. "It's no use," she said. "We're going to die here."

I looked into her reddened eyes, then laid my free hand on her shoulder. "It's not that dire, honey. Places like this have surveillance cameras and groundskeepers. Somebody will surely be here in the morning. I just know it."

"I hope so, but I still have to pee and I can't wait any longer."

That was okay for her. She was wearing a loose dress and could manipulate it enough to do the job, but I was wearing jeans and couldn't remove them with one hand or put them back on when done.

The exercise might have been funny in some other situation but neither one of us was in a laughing mood.

Eventually, while standing in urine-soaked grass, Kandi reached a breaking point. Crying and scared, she shot a familiar glare my way. "If we would have gone with Neeva, like I wanted, we'd be home now."

8

RATHER THAN ARGUE WITH KANDI, I took on a comforting, motherly tone and lowered my voice to a whisper.

"You know that isn't true, honey. Lenny had a gun and wanted to take your baby from you. Would you really want to ride around with that guy?"

She looked right at me then lowered her head. "No, of course not. I'm sorry."

"I understand your frustration, but while we're being honest with each other, it appears that Clinton and Jackie changed their minds about calling the police, so it looks like we're in for the entire night after all."

"I was thinking that too. Now what?"

"For one thing," I said while jiggling my upper arm. "We should take turns rubbing each other's arms to keep the blood flowing."

"And I'd like to lean up against the tree some more to take some of the weight off my feet."

"That's a good idea," I said, "Anything else?"

"No. I prefer we just keep talking to take our minds off our situation."

"That's okay by me. I talked the most last time. You go first this time. Say anything you wish."

"All right. When I wake up in the mornings and get out of

bed, Serene usually kicks me. It makes me smile, particularly when I imagine how my sisters will react when they get to hold the baby."

"I envy you. I only had one child and haven't held a baby for a long time."

"I also hate my name. It was okay when my last name was Pratt, but then I married Caleb and became Kandi Barr. It sounds like a stage name for a pole dancer."

"I get your point, but it shouldn't be too difficult to hyphenate it. Kandi Pratt-Barr is good. I've known a few prisoners who've changed their names to make it difficult for their exes or bill collectors to find them."

"I like that idea too, but would you mind taking over? I feel better when you're the one doing the talking."

"Alright. I have a secret for you about Phillip."

"What about him?"

I leaned up against the tree to take some of the weight off my feet.

"You'd think I'd be excited about getting out of prison after all these years, but I'm worried about acclimating. I haven't had a real job or paid rent or cooked for myself in a long time. It's a little spooky too."

"Spooky? How so?"

"Yeah. When a married person is behind bars, her spouse has an awful lot of freedom. There's nothing to stop him from having affairs."

"Has that happened to you?"

"Not that I know of, but Phillip used to come by twice a week; now, it's half of that and he always has excuses for the other times. What else could it be?"

"I see what you mean."

"There's something else. When I first met him, I was running from the law, and he was trying to escape an overly protective family and learn the ins and outs of relationships. We needed each other. But when I'm released, the dynamics will be completely different.

"We'll only have one car so he'll be in charge of transportation. Everything will be exciting to me, even if it's just getting gas for the car or going to the drug store or buying an ice-cream cone for the first time in fifteen years. I'll love all of it, but he'll be bored."

Kandi shook her hair from side to side. "I have to admit, when I put gas in my car or go to the grocery store, I can't wait 'til it's over. Now I feel sorry for the cashiers and other people who stand up for a living. I'm gonna be nicer to those people from now on."

"Well, that's one good thing that's come out of this situation."

"You know something, Miranda? I just remembered a secret of my own, that is if you want to hear it."

"Why not? The hornets are leaving us alone and we sure aren't going anywhere for a while."

"It has to do with Serene. I'm afraid of the delivery room."

"That's normal, particularly for first-time moms. I was scared too."

"This is different. Nobody else knows this, but I'm not sure who her daddy is."

"Uh-oh!"

"Before I got pregnant, Caleb and I had a rough patch. He started going to a bar and drinking and playing pool with his buddies. A little bit of that is okay, but he was coming home after midnight and wanting me to make love with him. But that wasn't exciting under those conditions."

"Sorry to hear that."

"I got tired of it, so one night I went down there and caught him playing kissy face with some bimbo who didn't even know he was married. I was super mad. We had a big fight and Caleb finally admitted he'd screwed that bitch more than once."

"Uh-oh, again."

"Well, I knew some people too, and I wanted to get even. One of my girlfriends has a sexy brother named Clarence. He's funny and I liked him, so I looked him up."

"Revenge sex," I said. "It probably happens more than we think."

"Yeah, but there's another problem. Clarence is African American."

"Even more uh-oh."

"Eventually Caleb and I made up, and I figured out that I was pregnant, but I've never told him what I did. If it's obvious that the baby is not his, things could get really sticky in a hurry."

"Couldn't you get a DNA test? Then you'd settle the matter once and for all."

"I guess I could call a doctor but I don't want him to know either."

"That is a dilemma, alright."

"If my Caleb is the daddy, then I get what I wanted, but I'll feel guilty either way. Do you think I should tell him what I did?"

"I'm no expert, but whatever you do, don't think of yourself as a bad person. Everybody makes mistakes."

"But what if it's obvious that Clarence is the father?"

"I guess you'll have to cross that bridge when you get to it," I said, while glancing at my watch. At just before 3:00 a.m., we were running out of stories.

Then I saw some movement up the road. I squinted.

"You guys are still here, I see."

"It's Clinton," I excitedly said to Kandi as he rolled up to us. "We gave up on you."

Kandi instantly pivoted toward him. "Where the hell have you been?"

I nudged her foot hoping she'd back off so that he wouldn't bolt away again.

9

"I wanted to call the police the last time we were here," Clinton said, "but Jackie snuck out of her house and was afraid that if the police came around that she'd get in trouble."

"But what about us?" Kandi asked. "Couldn't you have gone home and called on your own?"

"I hoped that somebody else would find you guys. Jackie and me did some private things until a little while ago. Then I helped her sneak back into her bedroom. After that I came back and saw you still here so I went home and got my cell phone. I have it now and it's all charged up."

"Are you stupid?" Kandi asked. "Didn't you see that this is a crisis? I could have lost my baby, just so you could get your rocks off, you dumb ass."

I nudged her foot again, hoping she wouldn't chase him away.

"To answer your question," Clinton said, "I knew that you'd be okay because it's no different than tying a dog to a tree for a while. Besides, how was I to know what you guys did?"

I decided to butt in. "The important thing now is, you can still be our hero."

"Yeah. Sure. That sounds good, I'll call for some help

right now if you promise you won't tell the police about Jackie. Okay?"

Once again, I took over. "Of course, Clinton, of course. That's very reasonable."

He nodded and then looked at Kandi, "What about you?"

"She agrees. Don't you, Kandi?"

She looked my way and seemed to get it. "Sure. I can't be mad at the hero who saved me and little Serene."

A few seconds later he had the 911 operator on the line, but we could only hear Clinton's side of the conversation. *"Yes, ma'am. My name is Clinton Cooper. I found two ladies handcuffed to a tree branch in the Hillsdale Cemetery.*

"Yes, ma'am. We're on the back road of the cemetery.

"Just two of them and me. One is real pregnant. The other one is old. They said to tell you that they are from the Lighthouse, whatever that means.

"Yeah, everybody is okay. There's no blood or anything, but they could use some water. I'll stay with them until you guys get here.

"No, ma'am, nobody has weapons, but they are chained to their handcuffs and can't get over the tree limb. You gotta send somebody who has really big bolt cutters; the kind that can break big padlocks.

"Cool. Tell the driver to turn right once he gets into the graveyard. I'll keep an eye out for you. Bye."

After ending the call, our extremely proud teenager walked around the tree and snapped a bunch of selfies with Kandi and me in the background.

Kandi couldn't hold back any longer. "Is this a fucking party to you?"

"Like you guys said, I'm a hero."

Indeed, he was. Off in the distance, a faint siren announced that somebody was coming for us. Giddy, I held still until I was certain that they entered the cemetery. Then I got a glimpse of the headlights. I hadn't been that excited to see an oncoming vehicle since the popsicle man roamed our street when I was a kid.

Another siren joined the first and they grew closer and louder until we could see treetops full of flashing red lights.

Not to miss his opportunity, Clinton stepped into the middle of the road and waved his arms at the approaching lights of two police cars that stopped with spotlights on Kandi and me.

"Over here," we yelled, waving our free arms.

Two officers popped out of one car, a young male and a younger female. An older guy from the other car went for Clinton.

"I'm the one who saved their lives," he bragged.

"You got any weapons?" the officer asked him.

"Me? No way. I don't need guns."

"Good, then let me pat you down before we do anything else."

After the pat down, Clinton and the officer went to the rear of the officer's car for an update.

Meanwhile the other two officers had eyes on Kandi and me. "I'm Kandi Barr," my young friend said to the policewoman. "You have to get me out of this."

The male officer turned his attention to me. "Any of you people got any weapons around here?"

"No sir. We've been here for hours and hours. I think you should get my friend to a hospital just to be safe," I said.

"I know who you are and I don't need your advice," he said as a new siren and additional flashing lights joined us from the other side of the cemetery.

"Where are your other gang members and the guns?" the officer asked me.

"We're not a gang. Lenny Canosa is your perp. He and Neeva dumped us off here and went north or east. They have three guns and some knives. That's all we know. I don't want any trouble. I'll do whatever you want. Just take care of my friend first."

Just then an ambulance joined the fray and the officer who'd been questioning Clinton produced a pair of extra-large bolt cutters.

Our chain was snipped, and our numb arms fell limply to our sides. The next snip removed Kandi's cuff completely and the ambulance crew lifted her onto a gurney.

The next thing I knew, my own handcuffs had been snipped and replaced by a fresh set, indicating that they knew I was an escaped prisoner. I happily sat at the base of the tree sipping water and rubbing my numb arm.

Given that the only con was under control, the officers all holstered their weapons.

"You know something, Miranda," Kandi said just as they started to wheel her toward the ambulance, "I understand why your son's parents don't want you to meet him."

"Huh? Really? Why?"

"You would be a wonderful mother and they're afraid they'll lose him to you."

"Oh, my God, Kandi. That's beautiful. Thank you."

Then it was my turn to move. The officers walked me slowly to the caged back seat of a patrol car. All I could think about was an extra-large featherless turkey named Lenny.

10

Up until the breakout, everybody thought the glass in the Lighthouse windows was bullet-proof, but Lenny's gun shattered that idea. It would take several weeks to get the new ones installed.

In the meantime, thirty-seven unhappy inmates had to be transferred to jails in nearby sheriffs' offices.

I landed in Riverside, California, and was placed in my own cell until detectives could determine my role in the breakout, if any, but that would take a while.

Additionally, I was due to be released in ten weeks so common sense indicated there was no way I would put that in peril. Nevertheless, a pregnant receptionist had been in serious danger and the badge-folks wanted explanations.

By this time, I'd been incarcerated for nearly fifteen years, so I knew a few things about interrogations. For instance, if I lied to them, they could charge me with new crimes such as "interfering in an investigation."

Regardless, I assumed that Kandi would have my back, so I agreed to meet with the detectives, sans my attorney.

In a stuffy conference room, they introduced themselves as Sergeant Cheryl Tallmeed and Detective Robert Hoyle.

After some feigned niceties, Tallmeed began the interview with an aggressive statement.

"We know it was your idea to attach Mrs. Barr to a tree. Do you deny that?"

"You've mischaracterized it. We did what we did because our only other choice was to stick with Neeva and Lenny, and that wild-eyed gun-toter wanted Kandi's baby."

"Elaborate on that."

"Like I said, he literally wanted Kandi to give her baby to him, like an unofficial adoption."

"Why would he do that?"

"It had something to do with Neeva's miscarriages. He argued that Kandi could always make another baby and might want a boy baby instead. When everybody nixed that idea, Lenny threatened to wait until the baby was born and then simply take it from Kandi. The dude is sick."

Hoyle butted in. "Alright, back to you and Mrs. Barr. What would you have done if she went into labor while she was incapable of getting to a hospital, or at least a phone?"

Yikes. Naturally I'd thought of that while Kandi and I danced with hornets, but this conversation was taking on an accusatory tone and I felt vulnerable.

Suddenly a young male deputy stepped into the room and handed the sergeant a phone. "It's a Ms. Breanne Hize. She claims to be your suspect's attorney."

Thank God. For once in my life, I caught a lucky break. I later learned that Phillip had gotten a call right after the breakout, so he'd called his godmother, my extremely talented attorney.

Not surprisingly, Breanne stopped the interview dead in its tracks and established that any additional questioning would be with her present or on FaceTime, where she could protect my interests.

After the air was let out of the detectives' balloons, I was returned to the Riverside cell block.

Unfortunately, a typical jail didn't have the same amenities as a minimum-security facility. There was no lounge area, no back porch with flowers, no going outdoors, no dining area, no private bathrooms, no trips to our off-site jobs, and no conjugal visits. To top it all off, regular visiting hours were reduced to two hours per week per inmate, unless an attorney was involved.

Along those lines, I later learned from Breanne that Tallmeed and Hoyle were seriously considering bringing reckless endangerment charges against me for putting Kandi in a predicament in which she couldn't reach medical attention should she need it.

Thankfully, Breanne convinced them that they'd never get a conviction because there was no way to know if it was safer to hang from a tree branch in a cemetery or stick with a gun-toting wild man who wanted Kandi's baby.

Completely thwarted, the detectives turned their attention to the remaining inmates and a handful of staff members at the Lighthouse, any one of whom could have some useful information regarding the breakout.

A few days later, and still packed in the sheriff's jail, I was led to a conference room and handed a phone. It was Breanne. *"It appears all your troubles regarding Kandi are over,"* she said.

"Thank goodness. What happened?"

"Two things; first off, Kandi had her baby. Six pounds and healthy."

Since Breanne didn't mention any other drama involving the baby, I assumed that Caleb was the biological father rather than Kandi's African-American friend. "What's the second thing?" I asked.

"That's a little more serious. Apparently, Lenny and Neeva were spotted with a broken tail-light. There was a high-speed chase. The police were able to spread spike strips across the road, which shredded Lenny's tires and sent their car into a spin."

"Oh my God! Is Neeva alright?"

"They're both going to be okay, but the investigators aren't willing to let Neeva off the hook just yet. But either way, you're cleared."

"Whew. I'm glad to hear that," I said. "I know a very good way to thank my husband for getting me out of this mess, but I have no idea how I can repay you for your part."

Breanne laughed out loud. *"We can discuss that at the party, when you get released."*

"Oh really? A party? This is the first time I've heard about a party."

"Uh-oh. Maybe it was supposed to be a surprise, but it was definitely Phillip's idea."

When we hung up, it occurred to me that my life was like that of a guinea pig in a cage; sometimes I had to run as fast as I could to stay in the same place. This was one of those times. After all of that unwanted drama, I was still a couple months away from my release date.

11

FIVE YEARS EARLIER

WHEN MIRANDA FIRST MET PHILLIP, he was thirty-two years old and practically a virgin. He lived in his grandmother Juju's rental home and spent most of his time in a small office, where he and a couple subordinates worked on a software program that amounted to a micro-GPS system. When perfected, the team hoped that the program could be worth millions.

Back then, all of that nerd-time limited Phillip in other traditional activities such as dating and interacting with other people.

After some encouragement from his younger sister and his grandmother, he bought a three-wheeled motorcycle and adopted a small dog as a traveling companion. The two of them headed toward the Midwest.

After a collection of lonely days on highways and back roads, Phillip found himself at a truckstop in Utah, where he'd observed a middle-aged woman rummaging through the trash cans. He'd never met anybody like that, so he coasted toward her and offered to buy her a meal and give her a ride.

The woman said her name was Eunice; however, that was an alias. Her real name was Miranda Munchak and she was an escaped convict who'd gotten away from a hospital after

44

donating part of her liver to her son--a son who was taken from her at birth.

In her mid-forties, Miranda had a little history. Over the years, she had had a few boyfriends and had been married and divorced.

Following her meeting with Phillip, they grew closer. After a romantic weekend at an incredible airb&b, Miranda revealed her true identity. When she claimed she had been wrongly convicted of three murders, Phillip said his godmother was a great attorney who might be able to help.

After a chain of phone calls, and some long months of legal wrangling, Miranda's life sentence was replaced by a five-year stint in a minimum-security facility in Glendale, California, known as the Lighthouse.

By that time, it was easy for Phillip to see that he and Miranda had a wonderful symbiotic relationship; specifically, he could help her deal with her legal matters, and she could help him to interact with other people. Then Phillip asked her to marry him, which she did, right there in the lounge of the Lighthouse.

In the early weeks of Miranda's stay there, Phillip drove to see her twice a week. The three-hour drive was worth it. He usually brought small gifts and they always ended their visits in her room-like cell.

As far as Phillip was concerned, all of that was the good part. But there was also a difficult part. After his visits with Miranda, Phillip returned home, where he was alone the majority of the time.

None of this was news to Phillip's grandmother. Right from the beginning, Juju warned him about women like Miranda.

"After all," Juju said, "the woman is thirteen years your senior and has been in a prison for a reason."

"You don't know her," Phillip argued. "After she was sent to prison, the doctors found some new evidence which proved that she didn't kill anybody."

"They don't keep innocent people in jail, buddy boy."

"I told you, before, Juju. She had to commit some minor crimes to prove that she wasn't guilty of those murders."

"And if you believe that, I've got a unicorn to sell you."

"Poke fun if you will, Juju, but when Miranda and I are together, I feel great - but I'm lonely the rest of the time."

"Didn't I warn you? A real marriage should be a full-time commitment. But you didn't believe me. How much longer before your girlfriend gets out?"

Phillip sighed. "She's not a 'girlfriend,' she's my wife."

"I know you think that, but you've never even lived with her or any other woman for that matter, so you don't know squat. Now, how much longer before she gets out?"

"A little less than four years."

"That's what I thought. You need to face the music once and for all; this relationship isn't going anywhere. You need to find somebody else who can give you a couple babies and then you can divorce Miranda."

"No way. That's cheating on her and I don't want to do that."

"Wake up and smell the bacon. That woman is going to be unstable as all hell when she gets out of that place. She won't need you anymore. She'll want to celebrate and that means nightclubs, drinking and dancing where a lady like that can pick up a different man every night. From there it's just a matter of time before she dumps you. Then what?"

"I dunno, Juju. I just wish I wasn't so friggin' lonely."

12

HALF-WAY THROUGH MIRANDA'S SENTENCE
AT THE LIGHTHOUSE

WHEN MIRANDA WAS TRANSFERRED to the Lighthouse, Phillip vowed to visit her as much as possible. There was only one problem: Those visits were limited to two hours, and no more than twice per week, after which Phillip had to drive home and wait for the next visitors' day.

Meanwhile, all he could do was call her in the evenings and look forward to the day she'd complete her sentence and they could get out of there.

After two-and-a-half years of long drives and short meetings, Phillip's perspective evolved. He still loved Miranda and vice versa but the routine was wearing thin. He lived more like a lonely bachelor than a husband.

But that wasn't the end of Phillip's learning curve. Since he had been home-schooled and relatively sheltered in his youth, he had never had a chance to play the field.

That caused Phillip and Miranda to have several serious conversations about his interactions with other female acquaintances.

On one of his weekly visits, Phillip brought some lovely pink roses for Miranda. "How's my favorite lady?" he asked.

She sighed. "To tell you the truth, I've been locked up for so long, I keep thinking that when my release day finally gets here, something will go wrong."

"Doesn't Breanne have all that worked out?" he asked.

"Yeah, she's awesome, but I've had a long string of bad luck, so I'm skeptical."

"That's understandable, but I'm certain that she's got everything under control."

"I hope so."

"Before we go to your room," Phillip said, "I'd like to talk with you about something else."

"Sure, honey," she said. "I always like our talks."

"You might not understand, but it's about all the time that we're not together."

"What about it?"

"Do you realize that you have more company and variety in your life than I do?"

"I guess I never really thought about it."

"It's simple. When it's visitors' day, I have a long, lonely drive back and forth. While I do that, you interact with your friends. If it's somebody's birthday, you all celebrate together. Then after all of the visitors leave, you guys get to eat together and watch movies, like a sorority."

"I see what you mean."

"There's more. When I have to leave, I miss you right away. I'm lonely before I get out of the parking lot. And the only people I see before my next visit are my two partners, my grandmother and sister and her kids. It's as if I'm the one in jail."

"If you're trying to make me feel guilty, it's working. Why don't you join a bowling league or something?"

"I'm thinking about getting a part-time job, but just being there isn't enough. If I see other couples having fun, I get jealous, and it makes me wish I had some normal activities too."

"I understand. I've known lots of inmates who have been separated too much. No doubt, loneliness screws up a lot of marriages around here. Sooner or later the free spouses wander and look for other outlets for their needs."

"What do those people do to get over it?"

"If you're as lonely as you say, I've heard of ladies who simply allowed their lovers to play around once in a while – since it's in the open, there's no cheating."

"Really? That would solve everything."

"It's counter-intuitive, but the inmate and spouse make a pact. The spouse is allowed to do a few physical things when the urges strike, but it's supposed to be strictly physical, with no emotional attachment."

"Are you serious? Because I've had thoughts like that. I'd would love to spend some time with other women without feeling guilty about it."

"That's the point. If you're authorized to play around a little, you can keep your sanity until I get released. But if we're going to do this, I have some rules."

"Such as?"

"First off, don't get emotionally involved. We're talking about having meaningless relationships, not falling in love, so there's no flowers or chocolates or lovey-dovey cards. Secondly, I don't want to know about any of it."

"Well, I don't know if I really would play around with another woman, but you've lifted a lot of weight off my shoulders."

"If you are discreet and don't fall in love, we can get by until I'm finally released in a couple years."

13

When Miranda and Phillip agreed that he could interact in meaningless fun with other women from time to time, it wasn't the kind of thing that a person ordinarily hears, but it made a lot of sense under the circumstances.

Then one day, after working on his app, Phillip drifted into the parking lot of Wilson's neighborhood bar. Inside, he took a seat and before long a brown-haired cocktail waitress, named Francie, engaged him in some friendly small talk.

"Do you live around here?" she asked, slipping him a beer.

By the time he'd finished a beer or two, he'd spoken of the software app he'd been developing, which had to do with getting around in large places like shopping malls, hospitals, campuses and sporting events.

More talk revealed his relationship with Miranda, and a trust that his grandparents had given him. Impressed, Francie put a friendly hand on his shoulder.

"You're an interesting fellow, my friend. If you ever need somebody to talk with, I'm here every night except Tuesdays."

Phillip knew that Francie was merely fishing for a larger tip, but it was nice to have somebody to talk to.

Weeks later he had been to the bar several times and

quickly determined that the place was frequented by both regulars and a blend of new folks. He even met a few friendly people of both genders.

Among that group, it was likely that a number of the ladies could be interested in dating. Thanks to Miranda, that idea felt less wrong than it previously had.

One night, a little tipsy, Phillip called Juju from the bar and mentioned his new friends. "Well, baby, you know that I'm not fond of your wife," she said, "but these other women are sending you a message."

"What message?"

"Think about it. Miranda was a very independent woman before she met you. She's had multiple partners, and done exciting things, some of which landed her in prison. For all we know, she's an alcoholic, too. A drama queen like that isn't going to be content with a low-key guy like you. It won't take her long to find some fun guy and run off with him."

"You keep saying that," Phillip said, "but Miranda is a good woman. I wouldn't want to leave her."

"Nonsense. You only know her as a prisoner, but your friends at the bar, there, prove that you don't have to settle for a loser like that. I still think you need to look for a more domestic partner, somebody who can give you babies. There are a lot of women like that. Try one of those dating sites if you want to or join a church."

As always, Juju made some good points, but Phillip didn't want to discard Miranda. He simply wanted to fill some of his free time with other people. Common sense dictated that there were definitely fun-seeking women right there in Wilson's bar. It wouldn't hurt to buy them a beer.

More weeks went by and Mr. Wilson fired one of the bartenders for giving away too much booze. That got Phillip to thinking.

He had seen first-hand how customers and cocktail waitresses buzzed around the bartenders. Those guys had status and always had somebody to talk to, not to mention the extracurricular activities that originated inside those walls and ended someplace else. He could fill lots of lonely hours if he could land a job like that.

He waited until Wilson was by himself and approached the owner. "Can I ask you something?" he asked.

"I guess I can take a few minutes. 'Sup?"

"I've been thinking about that bartender you fired."

"Yeah? What about him?"

"I was wondering if you needed somebody to replace him."

"You? I thought you were self-employed. You got any experience?"

"Not really, but I've been paying attention, and it couldn't be very difficult."

Wilson grinned. "You'd be surprised. When this joint is humming, it takes somebody with experience and a cool head and fast hands to keep it on track. Trust me. It's too much for a first-timer."

"I wouldn't need much money. Technically, I could work for free."

"Free? That's the first time I've heard anybody say that."

"It's true. I have a trust and all the money I need so I wouldn't need to steal money or anything else from you."

Wilson stared at Phillip for a few seconds.

"Are you serious about this or just messing with me?"

"I'm serious. I'd like to meet some new people, and you've got a bunch of them."

"Alright. Like I said, I can't put you behind the bar, but you can wait tables. A cocktail waiter meets more people than the bartender anyway. After you get more familiar with how a bar works, I might be able to use you behind the bar."

"That might work. You know about my wife, so I'd have to have a day or two each week so I can go see her."

"No problem. I was thinking of giving you the late shift anyway. I can pay you minimum wage. You'll also get some tips. Come back tomorrow, late morning, and we'll attend the paperwork and introduce you to a few people."

14

With his first shift just a couple days off, Phillip dropped into Wilson's one last time as a customer.

Mr. Wilson was mixing drinks and filling beer mugs while Francie buzzed around with a big grin. She appeared to be raking in some good tips.

Phillip watched the customers gulp down their snacks and drinks of choice while they engaged in conversation or played pool or worshipped their cell phones.

He witnessed multiple couples and groups of friends and non-ring-wearing women. He also knew from the dating sites that there were lots of women who weren't looking for a commitment but just wanted to have fun, which could mean just about anything.

Beyond that, some of those lady customers had to like an adult friend without getting serious about it.

With his basic strategy tucked away, he'd only addressed half his battle. Namely, he didn't know much about dating. Fortunately, he knew a lot about searching the internet.

He scoffed at some of the online recommendations, such as "Check for wedding rings," "Watch for flirty smiles," and "You can't pick women up with your first line because they don't want to be thought of as 'easy.'"

Clearly, that simplistic advice was best-suited to the

nightclubs where the twenty-somethings liked loud music, getting high and dancing past midnight.

But Wilson's catered to a more seasoned clientele. Both single people and married couples were likely to wander in as early as four in the afternoon. A number of those customers might have a burger or eat some pretzels or check on their kids. Others went home in time to get a decent night's sleep so they could get to their full-time jobs the next morning.

According to the internet, a number of the ladies among that group would subscribe to the three-date rule, or have a spontaneous one-nighter, or be involved in a casual friends-with-benefits arrangement – all of which were about casual fun, not falling in love and making babies.

Bottom-lining it, all of the single women in that group were perfect candidates for Phillip. They'd been in and out of enough relationships to know the ropes better than he did.

After his first few shifts, it was obvious to Phillip that he'd landed the correct job. There were lots of people coming and going and nearly everybody was in a good mood.

While he brought the drinks and snacks to the tables, he tried to remember as many names as he could - especially when ladies weren't with dates. There weren't any immediate sparks, but eventually a Saturday produced a potential playmate.

In her mid-forties, Tawny Jones came in on most Saturday nights and always sat at or near the bar. If a nice or interesting fellow were to buy her a few drinks, there was a chance she'd go home with him. Although she was a little older than Phillip, she seemed harmless and might just fill some lonely hours.

The following Saturday, Phillip made sure Tawny always had a drink. Along the way he told her about Miranda and explained his problem.

"I only get to be with her a few hours a week," he said. "The rest of the time I need some company without it turning into a complicated relationship."

"I get it," Tawny said. "Loneliness is a bummer."

After his shift, Phillip bought a bottle of wine and brought her to his house, where the wine and some small talk eventually led them to the bedroom.

The next morning, Phillip felt guilty, but he reminded himself that the hookup was a meaningless, one-time event with no implied obligations.

"I enjoyed your company," Tawny said, while Phillip drove her home. "We'll have to do it again sometime."

That wasn't likely to happen anytime soon, but Phillip had confirmed his theory: If lonely people had a companion once in a while, even a barfly or a guy with a prisoner for a wife, that was a good thing.

As the weeks unrolled, Phillip waited on his customers and concentrated on the dozens of ringless women.

A number of them expressed sympathy for his situation, especially when he stated he wasn't looking for a complicated relationship.

Over more weeks, people of either gender were actually intrigued by his marriage to a prisoner and how conjugal visits worked.

15

After several months working at Wilson's, Phillip met a lot of interesting women. Most of the time the interactions were benign, but every once in a while, he connected with somebody on a slightly more personal level.

He believed that the ladies who were open to spending time with him would consider him to be non-threatening because he wasn't on any sex-offender lists and the proprietor wouldn't have hired somebody who would put his customers in peril.

Throughout that time, brief conversations led to phone numbers of eligible ladies. In his time off, he called some of them and invited them to come back to the bar with a friend. "The first round is on me," he always said.

In a few short weeks he was like a happy pig in mud. He had a lot of fun conversations with a wide variety of available and flirty ladies. There were working ladies, women with roommates, unwed mothers, and everybody in between.

One of the early ones was Lydia Cornell. On a Friday during rush hour, she came in with a co-worker and the co-worker's boyfriend.

Lydia's cropped brown hair, classy pink blouse and dark slacks implied she held some sort of semi-formal job.

After they settled into a booth, Phillip dropped by. "Hello, everybody. I'm Phillip. What can I get you?"

"Margaritas all around," the boyfriend said.

"Not me," Lydia interrupted with a perfect smile. "I want something sweeter."

Phillip nodded. "How 'bout a cosmopolitan?"

"Yeah. That'll be good."

Phillip placed the order with the bartender and waited on another table before circling back for a brief chat with Lydia and her co-workers. "Are you guys related?" he asked.

"Not really," the other woman said. "Lydia and I work in a dental office. Jake is my beau."

Lydia nodded. "More specifically, I'm a dental hygienist."

For the next hour and a half, Phillip dropped by to make sure Lydia and her friends didn't run out of drinks and to learn about Lydia.

In her mid-thirties and twice-divorced, she had excellent people skills. "It's from sticking my fingers in everybody's mouths," she responded to one of Phillip's questions. "I have to carry the conversation most of the time."

That gave Phillip an idea. "Whenever I feel cramped up like that, I like to hit the road on a big trike."

"Really?" she said while tilting her head. "Do you own one of those? I've always wanted to ride one."

"We could definitely do that. All I gotta do is gas it up. If you're just fantasizing, that's fine, but to really get the cobwebs out, you have to make a day of it and do a little sightseeing."

"That sounds like a lot of fun."

"Like I said, if you're serious, I can pick you up Sunday morning. There are fewer people on the road at that time of day. We can eat lunch in a little café that is right on a lake that I know about."

"Really?" she said with her perfect toothy grin. "That's my day off. I'd love that."

Since Phillip had sold his trike a long time ago, he rented

one for the weekend with Lydia. By the time they returned, they had taken a very long ride on the trike and a very pleasant ride on each other - all of it, just for harmless fun.

16

ONE SATURDAY AFTERNOON, Phillip approached the table of an attractive, thirty-something woman and her scraggly-faced date.

"What can I get you guys?" Phillip asked.

"A couple of beers," the man said while looking the place over. "Where are all the hot babes?"

Phillip looked over his shoulder and back. "They come and go."

"You'll have to excuse Russell," the woman said to Phillip. "Sometimes he's uncouth."

"You mean 'forthright,' Jerrie Jean," Russell said. "I got the balls to say what everybody else is thinking – ain't that right, Phillip?"

Phillip grinned. "I try to stay out of conversations like that. For now, I've got you down for two beers."

When Phillip returned with the beers, Russell was off to the restroom. "Your husband is an interesting fellow," he said to Jerrie Jean.

She scoffed and held up her left hand. "Do you see any rings?"

"I guess not. I just thought—"

"We ain't married but we have a couple kids. Russell doesn't live with us. That's why we're here. He's late with child support again and trying to apologize."

"Sorry to hear that."

"It's his own fault. He won't take his meds. I never know if he's going to be all lovey-dovey, or depressed, but I can tell you one thing."

"Oh really? What's that?"

"I'm sick and tired of our part-time relationship. It's not good for the kids or me."

"Been there, done that," Phillip said before copying something that Francie often said. "If you ever want somebody to talk to, I'm here."

Jerrie Jean nodded. "I just might take you up on that someday, Phillip. I don't have any close friends to talk with, but between the housework and kids and all the disrespect, sometimes I just have to vent." She pulled her beer closer. "I'm sorry for unloading on you, Phillip. I know that you got better things to do than listen to me."

"It's part of the job. We all have to vent once in a while."

"I guess so. I see you have a ring. Does your wife get all freaked out and jealous when you talk to other women?"

He chuckled. "You wouldn't believe me if I told ya."

"Oh, yeah? Try me."

"What you guys talking about?" Russell asked while returning to the conversation.

Jerrie Jean glanced back and forth between Phillip and Russell. Then, she said, "Phillip was about to tell me a secret about his wife."

Russell looked at Phillip. "Oh, yeah, what about her?"

"Well, I guess I can tell you guys. Miranda is in a minimum-security prison called the Lighthouse. It's just over a hundred miles away. I don't get to see her as much as I'd like."

Russell grinned. "No shit? I bet those prison bitches get horny as all hell."

Phillip smirked. "It was erotic in the beginning, but it's always in the same room and same time every week with people coming and going up and down the halls. There's no wine or candles or soft music or anything romantic."

"I can relate to that," Jerrie Jean said.

Russell shook his head. "You and me don't got to play those games, sweetie. We can get it on whenever we want to."

Jerrie Jean rolled her eyes, "You mean anytime 'you' want to, but it's all sex, no romance."

Russell turned to Phillip. "Couldn't you get a guard to lend you some handcuffs? Bondage can be fun."

Phillip laughed. "Handcuffs? That's the last thing inmates want to see."

"That was obvious," Jerrie Jean said, shaking her head.

"Then what about videos or toys? Me and Jerrie Jean would die without our toys. You ever hear of a Rabbit vibrator? Best damn vibrator on the market. It does the trick for Jerrie Jean every time. Don't it, baby?"

Suddenly, a red-faced Jerrie Jean leapt to her feet. "What the hell's the matter with you, Russell? That kind of stuff is private. I want you to take me home right now."

"Calm down, baby. I'm just trying to cheer up this guy."

"No Russell, you're being an obnoxious asshole, and I don't like it. Are you going to take me home or do I have to call somebody else?"

Russell shrugged, then gulped down the rest of his beer and followed the mother of his kids out the door.

17

It didn't take Phillip long to learn there were hundreds of patrons who frequented Wilson's each month. Eventually, he became comfortable with nearly everybody, including available women.

In one scary situation, he spent the night with Valerie Mitchell, a foxy blonde from Australia with a pleasant accent and legs that went all the way to the top.

She'd drifted into Wilson's and had several drinks before plopping an interesting opportunity in Phillip's lap. She said that her husband had gone out of town on a hunting trip without consulting her and he did those kinds of things regularly, whether she liked it or not.

"Well, two could play that game," she proclaimed.

Phillip had heard of revenge sex, but this was the first time that it tapped him on the shoulder.

The next morning, after Phillip and his Australian bedmate went "down under" for the second time, Valerie glanced at her cellphone, where Google Maps revealed that her hubby's vehicle was just a few miles away and getting closer.

Fully aware that hunters carried guns, a completely naked Phillip found his clothes and got the hell out of there - just as a pick-up truck turned onto Valerie's block.

In another situation, Phillip and a female electrician made sparks, just for the fun of it.

Adding to that, he enjoyed the company of a fun-loving professor at a nearby medical school. Not long after that, he bumped uglies with a pudgy real estate broker who invited him to an open house in which they ended up entangled in the master bedroom.

Up to that point, all of Phillip's interactions were with mentally healthy partners who knew what they were doing, but one Sunday evening he met up with Marjorie, a thin chain smoker, whose boyfriend of six years had dumped her. She was ready to move on. That sounded promising to Phillip, so he suggested a nice dinner and some drinks, but he found out she was taking high doses of Prozac and Phillip called it off.

Another time, Phillip was busy serving drinks when a familiar pixie-faced woman walked in and quietly parked herself in a corner booth.

He strolled her way. "Hi, I see you're back. You're name's Jenny or something like that. Right?"

"Close. It's Jerrie Jean."

"Oh yeah. Sorry. I'd ask you where your husband is but the last time we talked, you told me that you guys weren't married, so I guess that makes him a boyfriend?"

"An asshole would be more accurate - and to answer your question, I don't know where he is, and I don't give a damn."

"Uh-oh! Perhaps I should buy you a drink to get your mind off your troubles."

"Thank you, Phillip. The last time I was in here, you said I could talk to you. I don't know anybody else I can trust with my secrets so—"

"I remember that," he said, looking over his shoulder. "It's slow in here. My co-worker can watch over things for a few minutes so you and I can have a little chat if you'd like."

She nodded. "I want to apologize to you."

"Apologize to me? For what?"

"For Russell's crude behavior the last time we were here. He shouldn't have commented about our private lives. He embarrasses me at times like that."

"Oh, that's no problem. There's a lot of big talk in bars."

"I guess so, but I'm mad at him and wanted to vent."

"I don't know if I can help, but I've got good ears."

"Thanks. To begin with, I do all the work with the house and kids, while Russell is a ghost."

"If it makes you feel any better, I've heard that from a number of other women."

"I spend a lot more time with our kids than he does so they should have my last name instead of his. Don't you agree?"

"Never thought of that. Sounds reasonable, though."

"I don't matter to Russell no more. He never hugs me or kisses me unless he wants, well, you know."

"I'm sorry to hear that," Phillip said, thinking of Miranda. "But we all take certain things and people for granted."

"I don't even know if I'm dating material anymore. What about you? Do you think I'm repulsive?"

"You? Repulsive? No way. A lot of guys would love to know you."

A tear formed in the corner of her eye, then rolled down her cheek.

"Thank you. I have to go home now because my kids will be back from school in a little while. Would you be willing to give me a good-bye hug?"

"Of course I would, Jerrie Jean. I don't see any harm in that."

"I hug my kids all the time," she said, "but I'd like somebody to hug me for a change."

"Well, let's take care of that right now. I don't think anybody will mind."

"Okay. I guess we should stand up."

Seconds later they wrapped their arms around each other, drew together and swayed like a couple of small trees entangled in a slow breeze.

Jerrie Jean whimpered slightly and squeezed him approvingly. "Thank you for that," she said. "I feel better now. Can I come back sometime?"

Phillip nodded. "But call first just to be sure it's not real busy."

18

With Miranda's release date a year off, Phillip had been having loads of harmless fun with various women, but he knew he'd abused the spirit of his understanding with Miranda.

She had said he could discreetly play around when he needed to fill some of his lonely time, but she didn't authorize him to become a man-whore. Now he felt guilty.

Miranda deserved better than that and it was time to trade in the rollercoaster for a much gentler ride.

While toweling off from a shower, he recalled his first get-together with the elder-but-sweet Tawny Jones. He found her calm demeaner to be comforting, which was more in line with what Miranda intended. Thereafter, Phillip and Tawny hooked up a couple other times and it was always a pleasant, low-key exercise.

Since they hadn't been together for a while, he called to ask if she'd like to get together. "I can pick you up," he offered.

"I'd like to see you, Phillip," she said, *"but I need to meet at my place this time."*

"Okay by me," he said. "Does Sunday work? That's my day off."

Phillip had assumed that Tawny lived in a modest home of some type, but when he turned into her neighborhood, all he could see was a long row of two-story mini-mansions. He wondered how such a humble woman could afford to live like that.

Nonetheless, he grabbed the bottle of wine that he'd purchased and strolled to the front door, where a blend of foul scents caught him off guard. Sour wine, fermented flowers or a cat box might be to blame. He scrunched his nose and rang the bell.

When Tawny opened the door, it became immediately evident that scented candles or bathroom spray or both were employed to diminish the effects of the unidentified stench.

Tawny wrapped her arms around his neck. "I'm sorry about the smell. If you can hold your nose for a few seconds, we can hurry through the house to the back porch. It's nice back there."

He smiled. "If you can do it, I can too."

Tawny took his hand and tugged him through the plush living room and around a large dining room, complete with a classy chandelier, and out to a cozy back porch, where his nostrils scooped up enough fresh air to fill his lungs.

Against the exterior wall, a large wooden table was home to a bright yellow tablecloth and an active aquarium with plastic flowers and live fish.

On the far end of the room under a window, a lone twin bed hid behind a bamboo curtain, affording absolute privacy and an abundance of much-welcome fresh air.

"This is very nice," Phillip said.

Tawny shrugged and pointed toward two lounge chairs that faced the well-groomed yard. "I don't usually like to bring people to my house," she said. "It's too stinky."

Phillip shrugged. "It's not bad back here, but we could go to my place or a nice hotel if you'd like."

"I can't do that, but if you'd rather leave, I'd understand."

"I don't think that's necessary," he said, smiling flirtatiously.

She kissed him on the cheek. "Can you pour us a glass of wine?"

"Sure. What's the problem, anyway? Do you have a sick cat or something?"

"No, but you're close. My husband is the one who is sick."

Phillip's spine straightened. "A husband? You've never said anything about a husband."

"Don't worry. It's not what you're thinking. Thirteen years ago, I was in my twenties, on my own and having tough times financially. Then I found a part-time job, in a nice Greek restaurant.

"One day the owner of the place introduced me to a very nice gentleman from Greece, named Gando.

"Come to find out, Gando's wife had passed away from breast cancer and he needed somebody to help him raise their two daughters."

Phillip nodded, "I think I can see where this is going."

Tawny nodded. "The boss of the restaurant recommended that Gando and I unite. It was my job to help his girls get by, and to take care of his home. For doing that, I got room and board and a modest salary, plus some time off when Gando was with his girls or lady friends."

"I get it completely," Phillip said, "When Miranda and I met, we had a relationship of convenience too."

"I know. You've always been very forthright about that. Anyhow, Gando's girls were young teenagers when their mother died. So Gando wanted them to think of me as a nice step-mother, so that they could preserve a sense of family.

"We all knew that I couldn't replace their mother, but it was still important for them to have a woman around who they could relate to when they needed it. Similarly, Gando and I have always called each other 'husband and wife,' even though he's a lot older and we're more like brother and sister than husband and wife."

"That's a very touching story," Phillip said. "Where do things stand today?"

"Well, both of the girls have moved out of state. Jaycie has a baby of her own and Jewell is in college. Gando was grateful for my help, so we stuck with our arrangement after they left the nest. That way I could live in a better home than I could afford on my own and he had a built-in caregiver, some company and a housekeeper."

"That explains a couple things."

"Everything was running smoothly for a few years there—"

"What changed?" Phillip asked.

"Well, a little over a year ago, Gando had a terrible stroke. He's had a few more since then. Now he's bed-ridden and barely a fraction of who he once was. It's sad."

"I'm sorry to hear that, Tawny. You clearly love him on some level."

"After that first stroke, he got frustrated and refused to be connected to catheters and tubes, and I don't blame him."

"That's why he uses adult diapers and that's what smells so bad. The medications in his urine can get raunchy.

"That explains a lot. What do his daughters think of all this?"

"Naturally, they are sad about his condition, but they can't be here so they're thankful for my involvement. I've thought about moving on, but I can't abandon him. It just wouldn't be right."

19

Intrigued by Tawny's story, Phillip poured another round of drinks.

"I've known you quite a while now, and never knew any of this information about Gando. I'm very impressed by your loyalty to the man."

"I don't know about that, Phillip. Gando's daughters hired another woman for Saturdays, but this weekend Kaylynn couldn't make it, so I had to work a double shift. You don't know how glad I was when you were willing to come visit me."

"It's the least I can do, Tawny."

"If you mean that, there is something else you can help me with."

"If you can take care of the man full-time for so long, I ought to be able to help with a single chore."

"Are you sure, because it's time to change his diaper and the sheets. I can do it by myself when I have to, but it's safer if you'd stand beside the bed so he won't roll out."

"Okay," Phillip said, "I think I can handle the job, but I'd like another sip of wine first."

After a half-bottle of courage wine, Tawny handed Phillip a white lab coat and a pair of rubber gloves. "Here, put these on. You're going to be a doctor."

Upstairs and close to Gando's room, the wet-diaper scent was stronger than before.

"I'm not real sure if Gando knows what's going on or understands me," Tawny said, "but when we get into his room, just follow my lead."

A knob-turn later, Phillip got his first glimpse at Tawny's catatonic, grey-faced friend, who could have easily passed as her father.

"Gando, baby," she murmured, kissing him on the forehead. "I'm here to clean you up. Doctor Pilday is here too."

Phillip couldn't tell if Gando comprehended what was going on, but he respected Tawny more than before.

"I'm going to change your sheets and give you a sponge bath," she said. "The doctor will stand on the other side of the bed to make sure you don't fall out of bed."

With their gloves in place, Tawny motioned for Phillip to roll Gando's upper body while she attended to his hips and legs.

Gando was heavier than Phillip expected, and there wasn't an easy way to grab ahold of the man. Nonetheless, Phillip bear-hugged the patient and rolled him to his side. Then Tawny added a final push and Gando oozed onto his side as expected.

Phillip marveled at Tawny's knowledge and compassion. He'd never seen anybody change sheets like that.

"Everything is going just right, isn't it doctor?"

Phillip took the cue and focused on the patient. "Why yes, you're doing it perfectly."

While Phillip stood next to Gando, Tawny unhooked the nasty sheets at the corners of the mattress and tucked them against her patient's back. Then she wrapped the replacement sheets around the mattress.

Within mere minutes, half the bed had clean sheets. "Okay, Doctor," she said, "this is going to be the tough part. We have to roll our patient over the sheets behind him and back into his original position."

"Of course," Phillip said. "Just like we always do."

"Alright then," Tawny said, "I'll stay on this side and push while you stay on the other side and pull."

Remembering the earlier experience, Phillip knew how difficult it was to roll Gando from his back to his side. Now they had to roll the man the other way and over an additional hump of smelly sheets that were clinging at his back. He'd have to grip harder and better than before. "I got it," he said to Tawny.

Tawny counted to three and Phillip pulled too hard. Gando instantly rolled to the edge of the bed. "Oh crap," the faux doctor said, "he's slipping."

Suddenly, Gando banged onto the floor with a groan. Tawny hustled around the bed.

"I don't think he's hurt," Phillip said, "but we shouldn't move him anymore. The same thing might happen again."

"Agreed," Tawny said, "I'll call 911."

While they waited for an ambulance and somebody to help get Gando back into bed, Tawny kissed her false husband on the forehead and gently grabbed his hand.

Shortly thereafter, a paramedic found a knot on the side of Gando's forehead. "We're going to have to take him in, as a precaution," the expert said. Tawny nodded.

Outside, the paramedics wheeled the gurney toward the ambulance. A neighbor asked Tawny what had happened. "He fell out of bed while we were changing his sheets. We probably shouldn't have been drinking—"

The neighbor covered her mouth and glared at Phillip. "Oh, my goodness."

"It was an accident," Phillip said. "Could have happened to anybody."

Phillip and Tawny followed the ambulance to the hospital and were eventually advised that the doctors wanted to keep Gando overnight for observation.

There wasn't anything else Phillip or Tawny could do for Gando, so they returned to her place.

"You know something, Tawny?" he said along the way. "I

always knew that you had your act together, but this evening proves it. You were in control the whole time."

"Well thank you, Phillip. Now you know why I regularly drop by Wilson's place – to get away from it all for a change."

When they returned to Tawny's back porch, Phillip opted for some more wine and thought about Miranda. If she hadn't authorized him to fill lonely hours with the company of other women, he never would have met Tawny.

20

AFTER THE TAWNY EXPERIENCE, Phillip and his partners spent the next morning working on his app, but he still had to work at Wilson's in the latter part of the day.

Several hours into his shift, one of his familiar customers came in for a visit.

This time Jerrie Jean wore tight jeans, a sleeveless tank top and more makeup than usual. She took the corner booth, and Phillip promptly trotted her way.

"Hi, there," he said. "You're looking very nice today. Are you alone?"

She nodded. "What's wrong with me, Phillip?"

"Uh-oh. Before we get into that, why don't I buy you a drink? Perhaps a beer or a margarita?"

"There. See!"

"See what?"

"The last time I was here, I told you that Russell wanted me to buy beer because it's cheaper but I bought a margarita. You remembered all of that because you connect with people, but Russell ain't like that. He only thinks of himself."

"Well, I'm sure he has some other redeeming qualities. For now, I gotta get your drink."

After a short trip to the bar and back, Phillip slid a

free margarita in front of his customer. "I'm sorry about Russell," he said. "He doesn't seem to appreciate you."

Jerrie Jean sipped her drink. "Not only that. If it wasn't for my kids, I'd be alone all the time."

Phillip smiled. "I can relate to that. That's why I got this job. To make new friends - like you."

"Russell hardly ever comes around and when he does, he wants something. You'd think he'd take us all for ice-cream or to a movie. But no. I practically have to beg to get any support. He doesn't even thank me for taking care of our kids. I need to feel validated once in a while."

Just then, two cars full of customers pulled into the outer lot. While the group made their way toward the entrance, Phillip addressed Jerrie Jean.

"I'm sorry, but I'll have to seat them over here."

"I understand, but I still want to talk with you. Would you be willing to come to my place tomorrow morning? The kids will be at their grandma's house and we can talk in private. I need to ask you something."

The next day, Phillip waited 'til mid-morning to ring Jerrie Jean's doorbell. As before, a hint of cleavage hid behind a gold chain. Her arms shot around him.

"Come in."

The last time he'd done something like that, he ended up changing the urine-soaked sheets of a frail man and taking that man to the hospital. This was much better.

"It smells great in here," he said.

"Thank you. I'm making brownies." She pointed toward a large sofa with high arms on either end. "Let's sit right there for a bit."

Phillip took the left end of the couch and expected Jerrie Jean to take the chair across from him, but she plopped right next to him.

"I ordinarily use this time for chores," she said. "That's what happens to moms. It takes a lot of work to take care of kids."

"Yeah. I've seen my sister's kids."

"When my kids visit with their grandparents, I don't get a break. Instead, I have to work on other things like grocery shopping and cleaning the bathrooms and doing the laundry. It would be a lot easier if Russell would help, but Grandma sees the kids more than he does."

"My grandma is like that too. By the way, your cologne is awesome. What do you call it?"

"It's called Bleu de Chanel. I'm glad you like it."

"Now that we're settled in, what did you want to talk about?"

"Well, as you know, Russell and I are not getting along, so I've been thinking about looking for somebody else. But I've heard that most men don't want to take on another woman's kids. You know a lot of people, so I was wondering what you think I should do."

"I don't have a lot of experience in that kind of thing, but most of the moms I know have older kids or relatives who can help out while they take care of everything else."

"That's what I've been doing but the grandparents can't keep up and they have lives of their own."

"It's a dilemma, all right. Maybe you could find somebody else in the same boat and take turns with the kids. Aside from that I don't know what to tell you. Is that what you wanted to talk about, because I have to get to work in a little while."

"You can't go now. Those brownies aren't done. And I still want to show you my house. I decorated the place all by myself."

"Okay, but I don't have a lot of time today. It's going to be busy at the bar. They're gonna need me."

"Please stay, Phillip. I need you, too. You're the only man that's nice to me."

"Really? That's hard to believe."

She rose and took his hand. "The least you can do is check out my new bedspread. I bought it just for you."

Phillip grinned. "If you're suggesting what I think you're suggesting, what about Russell? What if he comes around?"

She tapped the end of his nose. "I told you before. He only comes over when he doesn't owe child support. It's my turn to play around for a change. Besides, I haven't told you my secret yet. You want to hear my secret, don't you?"

"I don't know. I'd say that's up to you."

She smiled mischievously, slipped her fingertips inside the waistline of his jeans and whispered.

"Other than Russell, I ain't kissed another man in seven years."

He looked her in the eyes. "Are you sure you want to do this?"

She wiggled her fingers behind his belt. "I invited you over, didn't I?"

He grabbed his phone. "I'll see if I can get somebody to trade shifts with me."

"Good idea, but I ain't talking about no quickie."

A little later in Jerrie Jean's spotless bedroom, soft music played and she pulled him down onto the white-tasseled, deep-red bedspread. "How do you like it?" she asked.

The first few gentle kisses grew into genuine passion, until Phillip pulled back slightly and looked into her eyes. "You're really turning me on."

"You, too," she whispered. "I need you, right now."

By that time, Phillip genuinely liked Jerrie Jean. Among other things, she was straightforward, incredibly responsive and insatiable.

21

AFTER SEVERAL MORE VISITS WITH JERRIE JEAN, Phillip found himself exhausted on her bed.

She kicked the remainder of the sheets aside and eased her arm over Phillip's pounding chest. "Is there anything else you'd like me to do?" she asked. "Just say so. I'll do it. That's what lovers do."

"I like your enthusiasm," he said, sucking at the air, "but I need a breather."

She finger-brushed his disheveled hair. "You said that you love me, right?"

Phillip dreaded that question. Throughout his relationship with Jerrie Jean and his other hook-ups, he'd made it clear that he was waiting for Miranda. Yet Jerrie Jean ignored that message.

"I'm sorry if I misled you," Phillip said, "but Miranda gets released in a couple weeks. I'm not looking for a new life partner."

"Maybe not, but you have affection for me. I can tell, right?"

Not wanting to hurt her feelings, he hoped for a soft landing. "Affection? Sure, but it's more like a friendship thing than a girlfriend thing."

"And affection is a degree of love, don't you think?"

He emptied his lungs again. "I guess you could say that, but I've decided not to get serious with anybody new."

"That's not good enough. I want to be the best lover you've ever had. Has your wife ever offered to do that?"

"I don't think we should talk about her."

"Why not? If you love me on any level, we should be able to tell each other the truth. Right?"

"I guess so. What is the question again?"

"I asked you if Miranda ever offered to be the best lover you ever had."

"Not in so many words, but minimum-security prisons aren't very private, so we've been restricted."

"Then I've been better for you in a few weeks than she has been in five years. Right?"

"I guess you could twist it like that," he said while sitting up. "These questions are a whole new side of you."

Jerrie Jean grinned. "I know, but you said you like variety and I wanted to please you. That's what lovers do."

Phillip's throat was dry. Until that moment, he had exercised Miranda's authorization to sleep with other women without regret, but Jerrie Jean didn't get it. Clearly, she was driven by something other than having fun, and Phillip needed to straighten her out.

"You misunderstand, Jerrie Jean. When I told you that I liked variety, I should have said that I liked a variety of women so that nobody got serious."

"Other than Miranda, who is your favorite?"

"Really? A favorite? I don't want to pick anybody."

"I told you I'm different. Now, answer my question. Who did you like the most?"

Phillip shrugged. "Well, if I had to pick one, I guess I'd pick Tawny."

Jerrie Jean rolled her eyes, "Really? That old grandma? Why?"

"Well, she knows what she's doing and she's likeable. I can't say that about everybody."

"Okay then, tomorrow is Saturday. She'll probably be at Wilson's. When she comes in, you call me, and I'll meet you at the bar."

"Why do you want to do that?"

"Easy. I want to see my competition."

"This isn't a contest."

"Sure it is. If I'm your best lover, you won't need anybody else. It's either that or the other thing."

"What other thing?"

"I think you should tell Miranda that she is no longer needed."

"What? I'm not going to do that."

"You don't get it, do you? Miranda doesn't love you like I do. She just clings to you because you can set her up once she's out. But when you ain't looking, she's gonna dump you like a wet diaper."

"That's what my grandmother thinks, but you're both wrong. Even if you are correct, I couldn't leave Miranda until she is released and meets her son. That's critical to her and I promised."

"Alright then, how long is it going to take you to do that?"

"I don't know. She gets released at the end of next week. When that's over, I'll know more, but I won't change my mind."

"That's a deal. And I'll guarantee that Miranda is just playing you along."

* * *

The following evening, a quarter-moon escorted Phillip, Jerrie Jean and Tawny, one at a time, to Wilson's bar.

Tawny hadn't even tasted her first drink when Jerrie Jean calmly approached the older woman. After whispering something in Tawny's ear, Jerrie Jean strutted right out the door.

Naturally, Phillip wondered what Jerrie Jean had said,

but Tawny remained unfazed, which was one of the reasons Phillip liked her.

The next day, Mr. Wilson took Phillip aside. "I just got a call from Tawny's brother."

"Yeah? So?"

"Apparently, that Jerrie Jean woman said that you proposed to her, and she wanted Tawny to back off - or else."

"That's crazy. I'm already married - to Miranda."

"I know that, but trust me, Tawny's brother has got acquaintances that you don't want to meet, and I don't want my place torn up. You'd better tell your little bed-buddy to mind her own business before somebody gets hurt."

Phillip paused, then shook his head. "Okay. I get it. I'll let her know."

Shortly thereafter, while waiting tables, Phillip understood why Russell never wanted to tie the knot with Jerrie Jean. The woman was a full-blown basket case. Affectionate and loving one minute, a reckless coocoo bird the next. That was precisely the kind of drama he wanted to avoid when he began playing with women.

In the hours that followed, Phillip was on high alert in case Tawny's mysterious brother might show up.

Then around nine o'clock he took a call from one of the women he'd met some weeks back. "Hi, Valerie," he said to the charming Australian. "It's good to hear from you."

"I'm sorry to bother you, Phillip," she said in a somber voice, *"but I've got some bad news. As you know, Levi nearly busted us in bed."*

"Yeah, he was coming home early from a hunting trip. I couldn't forget that."

"Well, a little while ago our neighbor told Levi that he saw you sneak out of the house. Levi got pissed and wanted to know who I was with. I held out for a while but then he started screaming and slapping me. Now I've got a horrible split lip and one eye is swollen. I had to tell him where you work."

"Oh, my God. When did all this happen?"

"Okay, thanks," Phillip said. He turned around just as a two-fisted monster smashed into his face like a wrecking ball. His nose cracked. His hands shot to his face. The pain was excruciating. A gusher of blood sprayed his mouth, his chin and the floor.

"Next time, I'll kill ya," the bad boy said before walking out.

Having seen the entire ordeal, Mr. Wilson brought Phillip a wet towel. "We gotta get you to the hospital, Stud."

Three hours and one broken nose later Phillip had had enough of his girlfriends.

Fortunately, Miranda wouldn't see the injuries because he had a couple weeks to heal before he was scheduled to pick her up once and for all.

22

FINALLY! AFTER FIFTEEN YEARS OF WAITING for my release date, it finally arrived. I awoke before the sun came up. If everything were to go as planned, I'd be freed around noon.

My only reservations had to do with Phillip. He hadn't visited me for two weeks. He did call, however, and said that he was busy at work and that the short-term celibacy would make our reunion more exciting.

After breakfast, my peers held a going-away ceremony to commemorate the event. They made cupcakes and passed around a *Happy Freedom* card and sang *"Happy Release Day to You."*

We all agreed to keep in touch, but generally, when inmates get released, they don't want anything to do with the former house of bars.

Thankfully, Phillip rolled into the outer parking lot a little early. His sister was with him.

The guards allowed some last hugs and we eventually got to the final minutes.

Outside and just beyond the bullet-proof doors, Phillip held a huge bouquet of sunshine-yellow roses. Both he and Ellen wore smiles as big as my own.

Nearly all of my fellow inmates floated into the main lobby while we watched the clock dispose of the last few seconds.

Then at precisely noon, guard Janet Dean stood beside me. My peers began to clap in unison. At the double glass doors, the buzzer rang, authorizing my exit.

I purposely paused in the area between the inner and outer sets of doors. Behind me, the Lighthouse represented my past, a time and place where I'd been confined to the indoors and waited and waited and waited like a driver stuck in rush-hour traffic.

But, in front of me, an imaginary green light invited me to take a two-hour drive to Phillip's home where I would retake my life.

Finally, and with the applause still reverberating in my head, I opened the door and placed the toe of one foot over the last threshold like a swimmer testing the water temperature. Naturally, it felt wonderful.

A final crescendo of support indicated that it was time for me to take the ultimate leap. I grinned and hopped past the door frame and rushed to Phillip's arms. My precious husband passed the roses to his sister and we bolted for each other's arms. As we embraced, tears of joy filled my eyes and the valediction was complete - and a new reality was born.

The three of us quickly shuffled to Phillip's car. Before getting in, I tried to do a somersault on the lawn, but I wasn't coordinated enough. I laughed out loud before standing up. Then I held my hands high in the air before I yelled a heartfelt "thank you" to God almighty.

In the car, I shared the front seat with Phillip. Ellen sat in the back.

"So how does it feel to be out of the cage?" Ellen asked.

I nodded. "Cage is correct. I'm very, very happy, but also numb and scared."

"Scared? About what?"

"All sorts of things. I'm extremely wary of every police officer on the planet and the legal system. If they think you've done anything wrong, they can ruin your entire life before you know what hit you."

"I see what you mean," she said. "That could be scary."

"Another thing; when you're behind bars, other people make your decisions for you. If anything goes wrong, it's their fault, but out here, in the free world, I'll have to make my own decisions. What if I get them wrong?"

"I'm sure you'll do just fine after you build up some confidence."

"That's one reason I'm so thankful for your brother," I said while tapping Phillip on his arm. "He's been my rock for the past five years. He's visited me a lot, comforted me a lot and kept a positive attitude."

"And made love to you a lot," Phillip said, from behind the wheel, "but you don't have to thank me for that."

"That too," I said to him. "I can never repay you, especially for making the arrangements for me to meet Trevor. There were years and years when I thought that it would never happen. Now, that special day is just weeks away."

"It wasn't easy to coordinate," Phillip said to Ellen. "Trevor is going to London right after we meet with him. There's no telling what will happen after that."

Ellen tapped me on my shoulder. "I'm very happy for you, Miranda. I know how much a mother loves her children."

"Speaking of happier things," Phillip said, while turning into a mall, "let's go shed the past and get you some new clothes."

The idea was both quirky and logical. "I don't know what I'd do without you guys. I can't wait to get a job so I can pay you back."

"You keep saying that, but you don't have to pay me back. You're my wife. I want you to have nice things."

"I know you do," I said while Phillip pulled into a spot near the Victoria's Secret store, "but your generosity makes me cry with joy."

A moment later, while walking toward the main entrance, I wiped away a perpetual stream of happy tears.

"It's been fifteen years since my last visit to a shopping mall."

Ellen nodded. "Amazon has changed everything, but when you want something 'right now,' nothing beats the malls."

Just inside the entrance, I got another one of those first-time-in-fifteen-years reminders. "Oh my gosh, I smell restaurant food."

Ellen grinned. "That's Lucero's Mexican restaurant. They have great sopapillas. We can eat there if you'd like."

"I'd love that, but I already ate too many cupcakes. Can we come back another day?"

"Besides," Phillip said, "we're here to get Miranda a bunch of clothes."

"Okay, brother. We've got our marching orders. Let's do it."

After we'd purchased a mound of new clothes and accessories, we needed a sit-down break. "Next stop is Victoria's Secret," Phillip said. "I'm sure my lovely wife wants to look sexy."

"Oh b.s., brother, you don't fool us. You're the one who wants her to look hot."

"Well, after five years of restrictions, I think we're both ready for something more interesting, huh, Miranda?"

"You know something?" I said, "Prior to my prison days, I would have been uncomfortable talking about that kind of thing, but some of those prison ladies are raunchy, and it rubs off, so let's just say, I'm going with the flow and asking questions later."

"Good enough," Phillip said before turning to Ellen. "And how 'bout you, sis? Do you give Gregory lap dances?"

Ellen laughed out loud and glanced at me. "Let's just say I have three kids for a reason."

By that time, I'd only been away from the Lighthouse a couple of hours and I already felt like a completely rejuvenated person.

23

AFTER BUYING SOME CLOTHES, a hairdryer, some cologne and other toiletries we returned to Phillip's car and literally packed the trunk and the area behind the driver's seat. I couldn't stop smiling because it had been years since I'd done anything whimsical like that.

While we pulled away, I asked Phillip something that was on my mind.

"I'm very grateful for all these things, but would there be any chance we could get a small dog sometime? They are such loyal friends."

"You've asked me that before, but we're living in Juju's rental home and she doesn't like the idea."

That was definitely a huge disappointment, but I was also accustomed to other people making the policies.

"I understand," I said. "It's Juju's home so she makes the rules."

"Juju can be stubborn," Ellen said from behind me, "but when she gets to know you better, she could change her mind. We'll certainly put in a good word for you."

"Thank you. I'm not going to lie, I'm disappointed, but I want to stay positive. For instance, I can't get over how well you guys and Breanne have treated me. Without you I probably would have died in prison. Now, I'm here with a new and special family."

"That's a great attitude," Ellen said.

"Why not? I might have thirty additional years of freedom, and I get to meet my son. That's a lot."

Eventually, we reached a residential area where Ellen tapped me on the shoulder.

"This is my stop and my kids will be home from school pretty soon. If you don't mind, I'll wait to introduce you to them at the party. Enjoy all your goodies."

As Phillip and I watched his sister move toward her front door, we were all alone for the first time since I was sent to the Lighthouse. He spoke first.

"I'm sorry I didn't visit you more lately, but you're a wonderful woman and I knew you didn't belong in there. It made me sad."

I patted his forearm.

"That kind of thing happens to lots of prisoners and their spouses. Some get through it, some don't. I'm one of the lucky ones. I have a new sister-in-law plus a brother-in-law and I'm an aunt. That's all I care about."

"That's good. I just wanted you to know that I wanted to make our visits exciting, but it was the same old routine for both of us. I felt like I'd failed you."

"I'm sorry you got dragged into my shithole life, honey. I wouldn't have blamed you if you had moved on."

"I wouldn't do that. I love you."

"You don't know how much that means to me. I'm looking forward to building a new life with you, starting when we unload all these packages."

"I don't know about you," he said, turning his head toward me, "but I can't wait to hug you and kiss you and make love to you without wondering who's outside the door or how much time we have."

"Maybe we could just stay in bed for 24 hours. That would be romantic."

"I'm glad you think like that, because I do have a surprise for you."

I smiled and recalled the days when we first met. We'd been riding his trike for a couple weeks when we found ourselves in a fancy airb&b. He was so gentlemanly that I had to make the first move, so I walked in on him while he was in the shower. That worked perfectly.

"A surprise, huh?" I said, "I think you've done enough for me already."

Ultimately, Phillip pulled in front of Juju's rental home. "It's just a typical stucco home," he said, "but Juju and Gramps lived here for a long time. Now, she lives in my parents' home and gives me a good deal on the rent."

"Well, it's a priceless change of pace to me. I can hardly wait to wash the windows – not because they're dirty, but because there are no bars on them."

Phillip smiled and escorted me to the front door. After releasing the lock, he unexpectedly bent down, cradled me in his arms and carried me over the threshold and into a non-pretentious living room.

"We never got to do this when we got married," he said. Then he kissed me and set me on my feet. I actually got a love-chill up my back.

"If you don't have any objections," he said, while locking the door, "I've got something naughty we can do right now."

At that moment, I could've just climbed under the sheets of a simple bed and melted in his arms, but I didn't want to ruin his surprise.

In the back bedroom, he had laid out three semi-skimpy female costumes, each with a little netting or lace or ribbons attached.

"Put one on," he said. "I'll wait for you in the hall." I nearly laughed in his face. He'd seen me naked so many times that there was nothing left to the imagination.

On the other hand, I had almost forgotten how to play

much of anything. Plus, I owed him a lot more than that, so I scanned the options.

I had my choice of a naughty schoolgirl with pin-on pigtails, a fluffy bunny rabbit, complete with headphone-like ears, or Supergirl with a cheap red nylon cape.

For no particular reason, I picked the bunny rabbit outfit and tucked my 50-year-old body into place. I opened the door and "hopped" into the hall, where Phillip was wearing a leather jacket, his motorcycle helmet and a grossly undersized jock strap. I had to chuckle.

"Where did you get these costumes?" I asked.

He looked me up and down and then spun me around.

"Amazon. How do you like them?"

"Well, we said we wanted to liven things up. I just didn't expect it the very first time."

"Why not? We've been restraining ourselves for five years. It's time to let loose. He took my hand and tugged gently. I smiled and hopped around a little bit just to be a good sport.

24

After a full night of complete privacy, Phillip took me for a late breakfast and then to his parents' home, where Juju lived.

I'd only met her once. That was way back in my first days at the Lighthouse, when Phillip and I got married. Her dyed red hair, bee-hive hairdo and a fine dress had made a formal impression. She disliked me right from the beginning.

For one thing, I was thirteen years older than her grandson, so she automatically assumed I was using Phillip to access wealth that I couldn't get otherwise.

Another thing that bothered Juju had to do with Trevor. When I became pregnant, I didn't know who the daddy was. It had to be one of two identical twins. Don and I had just split up, but I also held some affection for Mac who was kind and lent me comfort for a short while. In Juju's mind, that behavior automatically qualified me as immoral.

"If a woman has more than a few intimate relationships in her lifetime," she had said to Phillip, "it amounts to promiscuity."

Phillip had made numerous attempts to explain it to Juju, but it was a fool's errand because she'd already made up her mind.

Anyway, the haughty matriarch met us at the door.

"Come on in. Sit down," she said, more like a movie usher than a loving grandmother.

Phillip and I shared her plush sofa while she sat in a matching chair.

"So, you're out of jail," Juju said, belaboring the obvious. "Was this your second time, or third, or what?"

Fortunately, Phillip had prepared me for her nastiness so I wasn't going to let her get under my skin.

"I know that you don't believe me, Juju, but I never should have been convicted in the first place."

"That isn't what I asked you. My not-so-bright grandson married a jailbird and could have done a lot better. It's as simple as that, or am I wrong again?"

"All I can tell you is we love each other and make each other happy."

"Love? What would a fifty-year-old jailbird and a Boy Scout know about love? I heard that you met in a truckstop while you were scavenging through the trash. Is that true?"

Man, this woman was tough. Most of her information was accurate, but she knew how to couch it in the most demeaning way.

"Yes, but I was very hungry and vulnerable."

"And along came a naive numb-nuts on a tricycle, with a tiny little dog, no less. That must have been a fairytale to you."

Phillip shook his head.

"That bike was no toy, Juju. It weighed a lot, especially with all the gear in the trailer."

Juju stayed focused on me.

"You must have been disappointed to find out my grandson wasn't carrying any drugs."

"To tell you the truth, I liked him because he was kind to his dog and smart and non-threatening."

"That's a bunch of hooey. We all know that my grandson was nothing more to you than a naïve little boy with a ticket out of town."

Phillip leaned forward.

"You're wrong, Juju. I've been visiting Miranda once or twice a week for five years. If she was devious, I'd know it by now."

"I'll tell you what I think, buddy boy. I see a young man with a lot of potential who makes bad decisions. You didn't know love from lust when you met this woman."

Just then, Phillip got a text message.

"Uh-oh," he said. "I'm sorry, Juju, but we've got to go. My partners are having a problem with our app. We have to fix it right away."

"Alright, buddy boy," she said. "I know how much that computer stuff means to you. We can regroup later. Gimme a hug."

"I'd like that, but I want you to know that Miranda and I really do love each other and none of your poisonous words can change that."

She nodded as if she liked his backbone. Then, she turned to me. "I'm sorry if I'm too harsh for you, but I don't know any criminals. I'm going to give you the benefit of the doubt, but to tell you truth, I'm very skeptical about you."

"Well, thank you. I guess that's all I can ask for now."

In the car, I spoke with Phillip, "Thanks for taking my side, honey. Some people aren't very tolerant of former prisoners. I can't blame them. Now you've got problems with your app. I'm so sorry all of this drama is piling on your shoulders."

He smiled at me. "Don't you get it? I got a message alright, but it was somebody else. I just wanted to get you out of there before she chewed your head off."

Surprised, I chuckled. Then, "That was smart of you. I didn't want to be disrespectful—"

"I get it; she was barking like a mad dog. You didn't deserve that."

"Hopefully, I can change her mind someday."

"I wouldn't worry about it. She couldn't do much damage even if she wanted to, unless she revokes her trust and gives the money to a charity or somebody else. I just don't think she'd do that."

When back at home, Phillip and I returned to the bedroom and put the rest of my new clothes and toiletries away.

In the bathroom, I pulled out the cluttered cabinet drawer and noted a few over-the-counter meds. I began cleaning them out and found a tube of lipstick. Since Phillip didn't have any roommates, I assumed the tube belonged to Juju from the days when she had lived there.

Curious, I removed the lid and expected to see some old, dried-up product, but instead, a creamy dark-red formula appeared to be brand new.

Stunned, I wanted to believe that the tube belonged to Juju, but I looked in the mirror, and that person slowly shook her head, suggesting that some other woman had visited my husband.

I threw the tube into the trash.

25

THE LIPSTICK ISSUE WAS A GLOOMY wake-up call for me. Even though I had authorized Phillip to interact with women until my release, I also said I didn't want to know any of the details.

That kind of thing could stir up disappointment or anger or thoughts of revenge. In my case, I felt a bit of jealousy and would have liked to discuss it with Phillip, but that would drag out regrets and negative thoughts. I'd already had enough of those. Instead, I swallowed my pride.

The next morning Phillip served me french toast and bacon in bed. That was something positive and just what I needed.

"You know something," I said. "After years of sleeping on a cot-sized mattress, you make me feel like I am your queen."

"You are right about that, Your Highness."

"Can I ask another favor? My son's birthday party is just a couple weeks away—"

"I'm way ahead of you. I've already made arrangements to call Trevor's folks today to confirm that we're still coming. They'll be glad to verify that you really did get released."

I crossed my fingers.

"I'd like to talk with them too."

A short while later, Phillip got Trevor's mom, Bertie Montgomery, on the line and put the call on FaceTime.

"We'll be there the day before Trevor's birthday," Phillip said to her, "just like you wanted."

"*Good,*" she said, "*I'm glad you can come at that time because right after that, Trevor is going to London as part of a student exchange program. I don't know exactly where he's going to be or when we'll have his new contact information after that.*"

"Is there anything else you need from us?" I asked.

"*Not really, Miranda. Just remember that we've always kept Trevor's adoption a secret and we want to keep it that way. Since he doesn't know you, you can use your own name; just tell him that you're one of my classmates from high school. That will be easier on everybody.*"

I didn't particularly agree with her logic, but due to the adoption rules, she and her husband, Chester, didn't have to let me see him at all. Nonetheless, I knew from Phillip's past contacts with them that they felt obligated to let me meet Trevor because I'd donated a big hunk of my liver to him and saved his life.

"I understand," I said, "but I was hoping you'd change your minds and let me call him more often."

"*We don't even know where he's going to live yet, but I doubt it. We're very grateful for what you did, but if it comes out that he's adopted, then our other two children will put it all together. Many adopted children get shook up when they learn things like that. We'd rather have stability.*"

My son's adoptive mother reminded me of a nervous bird, but I didn't want to ruffle her feathers. "Okay, I understand."

"*Alright then, we'll see you next month.*"

"Yes, of course. We'll see you then, for sure. Bye now."

After we disconnected, I spoke to Phillip. "Something's not right. Bertie cut the call off and sounded apprehensive."

"I wouldn't worry about it," Phillip said. "She's just afraid that you'll blow her cover."

Just then, Phillip's phone caught another call. He glanced at the screen and frowned, as if he were irritated.

"I gotta get this," he said before slipping out the back door and into the yard.

While I waited for my husband to return, I looked out the picture window in the living room and tried to understand Bertie's philosophy regarding Trevor's adoption. It seemed overly protective to me because I'd always believed that people who adopted vulnerable children deserved a badge of honor.

More impressively, Bertie and Chester had repeated the procedure three times. That surely warranted a front-row seat on a jet to heaven.

26

FOR QUITE A WHILE, Phillip was supposed to deal with his loneliness via simple, meaningless physical encounters, not overnighters or affairs of the heart. But he'd simply gone too far with women such as Tawny Jones, Jerrie Jean Bedford and Valerie Mitchel. He was also getting unwanted calls.

Thus far, he had managed to disguise those calls from Miranda by saying they were from his partners and other business associates, but the rope was getting shorter, and he might have to level with Miranda, even though the truth could upset her.

On one occasion, Phillip got one of those nefarious calls and had to slip into the bathroom.

"What do you want, Jerrie Jean? I already told you that you and I are done. I don't like all these calls from you."

"*You don't really mean that,*" she replied. "*I've got some new sheets and want you to help me break them in.*"

"How many times do I have to tell you, I can't do that anymore?"

"*I know, but you also said that I was your best lover and that you'd leave your wife as soon as she got out of jail.*"

"That's not what I said, Jerrie Jean, and you know it."

"*That was the gist of it. Why don't you tell that saggy old woman that you've got work to do and come see me? I'll make it worth your while."*

"No. No. No. If you don't stop pestering me, I'll be forced to get a restraining order, and I don't want to do that because you have enough troubles."

"You wouldn't do that to the mother of your baby, would you?"

He paused. "What the hell are you talking about? You told me that you can't have any more children."

"I never said that. You must have misunderstood me."

"Alright then. We can settle the matter by getting a DNA test. I'll pay for the test. I'll support you if I'm the daddy."

After a brief pause, Jerrie Jean continued.

"Okay, you caught me, but what are you going to say when I tell you I've got pictures of us in bed? I can send you a picture right now."

"Oh bullshit, Jerrie Jean. We both know that you're bluffing again."

Just then the picture arrived. Phillip didn't know when she managed to take pictures of their encounters, but she probably did it via time-delay on her cell phone.

"You got it, right?" she quizzed.

"Yeah, Jerrie Jean, I got it. So what?"

"I bet your wife would be very disappointed in you if she knew what we'd been doing."

"I don't want you to hurt her, Jerrie Jean. She's been through enough."

"Well then, why don't we work something out?"

"What the hell do you mean by that?"

"Simple. You've got other things I could use, and I have what you want. We can make a trade?"

"You're crazy, I don't have anything of yours."

"But you do have a lot of money, compared to me, and don't deny it. You told me all about your trust and that app of yours."

"But I don't get that money until the app sells and I don't have any legit buyers right now. It could take months or years."

"Okay, but I know you've got a big trust too. There must be at least twenty-five thousand dollars in there that you don't need as much as I do – to raise my kids."

Phillip had had enough. "That's it, you went too far. I won't submit to extortion so this time I'm the one who has been recording this call and I'm definitely going to the cops. That ought to put an end to your little con games."

She went dead-silent for a few seconds.

"Why don't we compromise?" she said. "If you'll give me twenty-thousand dollars, I'll delete all of the pictures of you and me. That should be fair."

"Forget about it, Jerrie Jean. Your goose is cooked. I'm hanging up now."

"No. No. No. Don't do that," she said with a more desperate tone. "Just give me ten thousand dollars. I need it for my children, and I'll leave you alone."

"Nope. I'm filing charges. I hope you enjoy prison, Jerrie Jean, because Miranda sure as hell didn't."

AFTER PHILLIP AND I CONFIRMED the bulk of the details regarding Trevor's upcoming birthday party, we made arrangements to visit his sister's home for dinner and to meet her three children - two boys and a girl.

Since my only sibling was severely disabled when he was a toddler, I had no nieces or nephews of my own. That's why I couldn't stop smiling when six-year-old Theresa wanted to show "Aunt Miranda" her Barbie dolls.

After the kids were sent to bed, Phillip and I hung around for a while, then went to a dark nightclub, where we drank wine and danced 'til midnight. I was a little rusty but that wasn't important because we were falling in love all over again, in spite of the foreign lipstick I'd discovered in the back of a drawer in our bathroom.

The next morning, Phillip insisted on getting me a driver's license.

"But to do that," he said, "you'll need a birth certificate. I assume that you don't have your original one. Is that correct?"

"You're right. I forfeited all my belongings when…well, you know."

"That's what I thought, but it's not a problem. We can get you a replacement birth certificate. Those same people can get you a passport so we might as well take care of both things while we're at it."

I remember shaking my head.

"This is too much. I don't need a passport."

"I know, but you could need it later and we'll already be in the building where they handle that stuff."

"I'm taking up too much of your time and money, honey. Don't you have to work or something?"

"Yeah, but all I gotta do is check with my partners in case they need anything and I've already done that. If we have some extra time, we can look into renting a car for you until we can get something permanent."

"I don't need my own car, honey. That's way too much to ask of you."

"Sure, you do. You don't want to rely on me whenever you have to go anywhere. This way we can split chores. You can get some of the things you need and look for a job - if you still want to do that."

I wrapped my arms around him.

"I've always known that you're a special man."

Just then, his cell phone interrupted us. He glanced at the screen. Then he said, "That idiot won't give up." He quickly turned his phone off.

"What was that all about?" I asked.

"Not much. Some lady got wind that I've got an app coming out. She claims that she had the same idea, so she keeps threatening me, but I flipped the tables on her, said I was going to the cops for extortion."

"That sounds scary."

"Don't worry. I'm not really going to turn her in. I just want her to back off."

Something told me that there was more to the matter, but I didn't want to rain on the moment. "Just be careful, okay, Phillip?"

"No prob. This kind of thing happens a lot when you're getting close to bringing your product to market."

With that topic put to bed, Phillip and I were back on track. I got my license and was added to Phillip's auto insurance. After that, we went to a nearby parking lot so that I could practice driving. I felt like a shaky high schooler in a Driver's Ed class.

While driving around the lot, Phillip introduced me to a few of the controls that had become popular on modern cars while I was incarcerated.

"Okay, then," he eventually said. "I need to go to meet with my partners. This will be a good time for you to drive in the streets and get the hang of things again."

I nervously wiggled us out of the parking lot and headed to his office.

"I'm a dummy when it comes to technology," I said, while looking in my rearview mirror. "When do you expect to sell your app?"

"There are people checking it out right now. We could make a deal with them and let them finish it up, but we'll get more money by waiting."

"I know how long and hard you've been working on that app. What's to prevent your partners from backing out and starting over without you?"

"No problem. I had Breanne handle everything. She had them sign a 'no-competition' clause. The papers are air-tight."

"I'm not surprised. She was fantastic when she handled my case. I'm looking forward to seeing her at the party."

"You know what else is great?" he asked. "For somebody who hasn't been behind the wheel for fifteen years, you're doing everything perfectly."

"I'm still a bit nervous, but it's definitely coming back to me."

After Phillip's meeting with his partners, we went to Wilson's so that he could formally resign as a waiter.

"So, this is where you worked when you got bored, huh?"

"Yep. Now that you've got an ID, we can have a couple drinks."

"But I'm a bazillion years old. They won't check me for an ID, will they?"

"Now that you mention it, probably not. I just wanted you to feel like a normal person."

"I appreciate the sentiment," I said as I parked his car. "I might get tipsy, and you'll have to drive home."

Inside, we slipped into a booth near the windows. Almost instantly a semi-sexy brunette about Phillip's age came for our drink order.

"Hi Francie," Phillip said while nodding toward me. "You've heard me speak of Miranda."

"I sure have. Nice to meet you, Miranda. I'll bet you're happy."

"Thanks, I'm trying to get reacclimated, and get a job. Do you like waiting tables?"

"It pays the bills," she said before turning to Phillip. "How's your nose?"

"My nose? Oh, yeah. That sucked."

"I don't doubt it," Francie said and turned to me. "A bad guy's fist 'bumped' into your husband's face. Poor baby bled all over the place."

That was the first time I'd heard anything about a fight, so I looked at Phillip for confirmation.

"She's right; some guy found out that his wife came in here a few times. He thought I was dating her. Didn't ask any questions, cold-cocked me when I wasn't looking."

At that moment, I thought I saw Francie wink at Phillip, as if there was more to Phillip's story.

28

AFTER PHILLIP TURNED THE TABLES regarding Jerrie Jean's threat, she panicked and left several frantic messages for the only person she could turn to.

As the father of her children, Russell Blackstone was the impulsive type and would know how to deal with Phillip's threat. For one thing, Russell wouldn't allow anybody to screw his common-law wife or mess with their kids.

When Russell arrived, Jerrie Jean's red eyes begged for sympathy. She told him about her trysts with Phillip, then said, "I'm really, really sorry, honey. I did it for all of us. Honest."

"What the hell are you saying, Jerrie Jean? That you fucked some nerd as a favor for the kids and me? How the hell do you explain that?"

She shook her head and wiped more tears.

"I know it sounds stupid, but he's got a lot of money and he's getting more. I thought if I could get some of it, me and you wouldn't have so many financial troubles."

"Just what did you do anyway?"

"Do you mean in bed, because—"

"No, you idiot. You already admitted that much. We'll deal with that later. For now, I want to know how much money he has and how you were going to get it."

"I took secret pictures of him and me in bed, and I threatened to tell his wife unless he paid me twenty thousand dollars."

"What made you pick that amount?"

She sniffled. "He's getting more than that from his grandmother. I was hoping I'd get enough that you wouldn't have to pay child support no more."

"I guess some of that makes sense."

"I know, but he recorded my call and said he was going to turn me in for extortion. He has all the proof he needs. I can't bear the thought of going to jail and losing the kids. You have to get me out of this, Russell, then I'll do whatever you want forever. I won't make you pay child support no more, whatever you want."

"I get that."

"Thank you, thank you, thank you, Russell. I'll make it up to you. You'll see."

"I haven't agreed to do anything so far. Are you sure you want to end the problem, because there's only one way to guarantee that he'll keep his mouth shut."

She squinted at him. "You don't mean kill him, do you?"

"What else is there? It's the fucking he gets for the fucking he got."

"Oh, my God, Russell. Can't we just threaten him or beat him up or something?"

"Sure, but that would just piss him off even more. It's all or nothing. You either take your chances and let him run to the cops whenever he gets a wild hair, or you 'guarantee' he won't separate you from the kids."

"Oh shit. How long would I have to go to jail?"

"Well, blackmail is a heavy-duty crime, especially since we're talking about so much money; and you already have a record for assault when you got pissed off and threw half the knives in the kitchen at me. They'll definitely charge you with a felony. There will be a bond until the trial."

Jerrie Jean drew a shaky breath.

"Yeah, but how long?"

"'Course, you could go for a plea deal. I'd guess you're looking at two to five years. Something like that."

"I can't do that, Russell. I can't afford to be away from our babies that long."

"You don't got to worry about that. If you are sent to prison, the kids will have visitation rights."

She shook her head. "No. I don't want my babies to see me in jail. Maybe I can call Phillip and change his mind."

"How the fuck you gonna pull that off? He ain't gonna believe anything you say cause you've already taught him that you can't be trusted. Besides, after what you did, he probably thinks that the kids would be better off with a foster family, beginning right now. He could turn you in, whenever he wants to."

"I don't want that either."

"Then you've made your decision. We gotta take that asshole out."

"Okay, Russell. I hope you know what you're doing."

"Desperate situations call for desperate measures. We're going to need Brady."

"Your goofball brother? We haven't seen him for a while. What's he got to do with this?"

"First off, he's a half-brother, and second, he's a minister. I've told you that before."

"I thought you said that was all a gag."

"It started out that way when he and a couple half-drunk buddies found out they could get a minister's license virtually overnight just by filling out an application and sending in a few bucks."

She swatted a tear. "How does that help us?"

"The dude may be a pothead and a drunk and a goofball, but he's performed some weddings for a few hundred bucks and a keg of beer."

"What does that have to do with anything?"

"Simple. If we're going to take out Phillip, we need an alibi. The beauty of it is, Brady and me have different last names. If he is willing to say that me and you were getting married at his place at the exact same time that your boyfriend died, it would be impossible to pin the hit on us."

"Oh, my God, Russell, do you think he'd do that?"

"There's another thing. The cops can't make married people testify against each other, so all we gotta do is get married, and stick to our story - and that, my dear, is what you call a 'kick-ass' alibi."

"Alright, Russell. That sounds like it will work."

"Okay, then. All we gotta do now is pick the time and place to take out that asshole."

"Well, he has an office with his business partners," Jerrie Jean said. "If it happened around there, it might look like they were the ones who did it."

"Okay. That'll do."

"Thank you, Russell. Thank you. I can't thank you enough. Thank you, thank you."

"And now, I want you to take your fucking clothes off and apologize to me, like never before."

"Okay, Russell. Anything you want. We can break in my new sheets."

29

When I initially moved in with Phillip it was glaringly obvious that his housekeeping skills were a notch or two beneath mine, which afforded me an opportunity to contribute something of my own to our little team.

For several consecutive days, he went to his office to see his partners and check on the progress of his app. Meanwhile, I happily took care of other chores.

My very favorite project was washing the windows. The lack of ugly bars gave me a very warm feeling.

Every few days I called Phillip's mother, Anita, and sister to have friendly chats.

Throughout those days, Phillip exhibited numerous romantic gestures. One night, we drove an hour to the beach, just to see the sunset.

Another time, I cooked one of my favorite casseroles for him. Right away he had an idea.

"There's a big moon tonight. Let's take your dinner to the park and eat at a picnic table."

We ended up taking a bottle of wine too.

My only regret involved loneliness. When Phillip wasn't around, I was on my own and wished I had a dog to keep me company.

In spite of these wonderful activities, there had to be a

first quarrel. Up to that point, Phillip and I had not been together long enough to get under each other's skin, but now we were in the midst of a 24/7 relationship and spawned some minor disagreements.

Naturally, the first spat revolved around Juju. Back in the big-girl prison, I'd seen a number of women with personalities similar to hers. Generally, they liked to be in charge.

In this case, I thought it would be nice to paint the front door of Juju's home, so I asked Phillip to tell her I'd do all the work. "Nothing says 'welcome' like a clean white door and a new mat," I commented.

You'd think that she'd be grateful for such a gesture, but instead she flexed her muscles, and Phillip instantly took her side. "What's her problem?" I asked.

"She says it doesn't need painted."

"Go look at it yourself. The old paint has faded. I can fix that for her. I'm a good painter."

"I told her that, but she doesn't want to paint it, and it's her house, so let's just drop it and keep the peace."

Just then I realized something. "I see what you're doing," I said. "You stick up for whoever isn't present."

"What's so wrong with that? It's the opposite of back-stabbing somebody."

"True, but nobody knows your real position. That's timid."

"Timid? I'm not afraid of her. I simply don't want to fight over a stupid door."

And that was the end of it.

Later I got to thinking about the interesting places he'd taken me back when I was on the run. Not many people could make a con feel special, but he overlooked all of my failings and got me out of prison and brought me back to a normal life. I still wanted to repay him so I decided to brighten up our bedroom instead.

For one thing, the closets looked as if they had survived a

war, so I waited until I was alone to straighten them up and prepare the carpet for a good cleaning.

The next day after he left for work, I assumed he hadn't vacuumed or cleaned under the beds for a long time so I got on my knees to see it there was anything under there, like files or a leaf to the kitchen table. Right in the middle there appeared to be a silky cloth napkin.

I fetched the kitchen broom and ran the broom-handle under the bed to claw back the napkin, but I got an awful slap in the face.

Unfortunately, the "napkin" proved to be a pair of sexy panties, which confirmed my earlier suspicions involving the lipstick in one of the drawers.

Once again, I regretted authorizing him to play around with other women. It was supposed to be subdued and akin to a meeting with a hooker - do the deed, and quietly move on.

But another woman's underwear underneath the very bed that he and I shared was cavalier and hurtful.

Completely disappointed, I trashed it.

30

I suppose that every marriage has its ups and downs, but I didn't expect Phillip's rollercoaster ride to include lost panties and wild over-nighters.

While I was trying to figure out if I should confront Phillip or not, he caught me off-guard. It had to do with the end of a prison sentence.

Eighty-one thousand women got released from state-run penitentiaries every year and a lot of them celebrated with a party. For some reason, Phillip liked that idea and planned a lawn party for me.

I should have been flattered by his sentiment and efforts, but all of the party-goers were Phillip's friends and business partners, and therefore were bound to know my background.

Actually, I would have preferred to cancel the party and keep my past a secret, but this party was more important to Phillip than me and I just went along with it.

The festivities were to begin at 1:00 and Phillip had advised everybody there would be an introduction at 1:30 so that we didn't have to tell my story over and over again. I definitely liked that idea.

Phillip had rented a few picnic tables for the occasion and his delightful sister, Ellen, brought paper plates and plastic forks plus a large cake that had a nice icing-message: "Today, the World is a Better Place."

I wondered how many of the attendees would actually share that sentiment. Phillip's grandmother probably wouldn't.

Anyway, it was an "adults only" party to protect children from the big-bad convict.

Ultimately, I donned some of the classy clothes and jewelry that Phillip had bought for me.

Phillip's parents came from out of state for the occasion. Early on, Frederick wandered into the house in search of hors d'oeuvres while Anita and Breanne invited me to sit with them at one of the picnic tables.

I'd met Anita a few times while I lived at the Lighthouse and Breanne was the angel attorney who had erased a huge chunk of my original sentence. Naturally, I hugged them both.

After a short while, a few neighbors and Phillip's partners, Craig and Allen, along with their wives, took up another table.

As newcomers trickled in, most of them scanned the attendees, doubtless to get their first glimpse of the lady con.

It didn't take long for people to loosen up, in part because a keg of beer found one of the tables, and an eclectic blend of micro-brewed beers filled a large cooler.

That was about the time that decked-out Juju made her entrance, along with a gray-haired neighbor-lady whom she knew. I once hoped that Juju would become the mother I never had, but that idea blew away.

Given her disdain for me, I expected her to skip the party entirely, but she and her neighbor came right up to Breanne and Anita and me.

"There's my favorite attorney and my precious daughter-in-law," she said, before making eye contact with me, but neither of us said anything.

Anita hugged her mother-in-law. "Your son is in the house."

"We haven't met," the neighbor said to me. I'm Colette. I live up the block. How do you like Juju's home?"

"It's lovely," I said. "I owe a lot to Phillip and Juju and Breanne. I'm very grateful to their whole family."

"What's the best thing about your renewed freedom?"

"Well, aside from being with you guys, one of the best parts of the day is the ten minutes after I wake up and realize that I get to set my own schedule and there are pleasant things to look forward to."

Breanne nodded in my direction, "You've always wanted to meet your boy. Any progress in that regard?"

"Oh, yeah. Phillip has all of that worked out. We'll be visiting them pretty soon."

"Where'd you say he lives?"

"Cincinnati. We're going there for his sixteenth birthday. Since I was forced to put him up for adoption, this will be the first time I get to see him. I'm hoping that I can have regular scheduled conversations with him after that, but his parents don't want him to know that he's adopted, so they're being sorta difficult."

"Any other plans?" Colette asked.

"For one thing I can't imagine being a full-time homemaker, so I'd like to look for a job."

"I'm a homemaker. What do you have against that?"

"I'm sorry if I offended you, Colette. I don't have anything against anybody, it's just that I've always worked outside the home for a living."

She turned her head just as Phillip stood on a small stepstool to get the crowd's attention.

Before he began, Juju leaned toward me and whispered in my ear. "You need to get to a beauty parlor. All that gray hair is unflattering."

31

WHILE I TRIED TO FIGURE OUT if Juju was insulting me or if she genuinely wanted to give me some constructive advice, Phillip gained everybody else's attention.

"Hello, everybody," he said. "My name is Phillip and I want to introduce you all to our guest of honor. Her name is Miranda Pilday. She is my wife and I'd like her to stand up so everybody can meet her."

While I would have preferred to avoid the attention, good manners urged me to accommodate my husband's request, which also prompted a smattering of applause.

"You may know that Miranda has been living 'elsewhere' lately," he said with air quotes and catching a few giggles, "but I thought we'd go over her backstory one time so that we don't have to repeat the same old saga over and over. For starters, contrary to what you might have heard, Miranda is a very honest and law-abiding person."

My husband went on to explain that I had been arrested fifteen years earlier for something that I didn't do. He also explained that I had shared some of my liver with my son, which saved his life and led to my escape from a hospital.

"Unfortunately," he added, "the Department of Corrections doesn't like it when people escape, even if the original charges were dropped. Nonetheless, there was no violence, so the original charges were exchanged for a five-year stay at a more benign facility in Glendale."

By that time a few people were glancing my way with sympathetic eyes. Phillip pointed to me. "I love her with all my heart. I hope you'll give her a fair chance. That's all she wants." Then, he turned my way again. "Is there anything else you'd like to add?"

I scanned my audience briefly. "Just one thing," I said, standing. "I can understand why a lay person would doubt that a woman such as myself would serve hard time if I were not actually guilty of any serious crimes. All I can say is, think of it the other way around. Would a court cut my sentence at all if I were truly guilty of killing three people as they originally claimed?"

"That's a very good point," Frederick said from off to the side.

"I believe her too," Ellen added while a few other heads bobbed up and down in my favor.

Breanne rose too. "I'm Miranda's attorney. She was definitely exonerated of the most serious crimes for which she was wrongly charged, but, unfortunately, she had to commit some minor crimes to prove her innocence regarding the more serious ones. I can tell you she certainly deserves your respect and love just like anybody else does."

"Her past is over now," Phillip tagged. "She and I are having a lot of fun just catching up, if you know what I mean."

I'm not sure if my face reddened from embarrassment or not, but once again Phillip earned some smiles. He paused another moment, then walked slowly toward me. "Seriously now, I want everybody to know that my exquisite and beloved wife deserves all of our best love. Now let's have a toast."

He looked right at me, lifted his beer in the air and softened his tone. "To Miranda Pilday, an extraordinary woman if there ever was one. These are the people who love you." Then he kissed me.

Applause broke out, drinks were raised, and tears sought

the corners of my eyes. All I could do was hug my man and receive pats on my back from all my new friends.

Moments later, and with my history out of the way, a tall dude with a cowboy hat wandered over to our table, removed his hat and ran his fingers through his balding wavy hair. "I'm Henry, a business associate of Phillip's. Sounds like your life has been one bad rodeo after the other."

"You've got that right, Henry, but hopefully it's all over now."

"I'll be pulling for you. I'm curious about that app that your husband and his friends have been working on. Are there any big problems with it that you know of?"

Colette bobbed her head. "I'm curious about that app, too. What is it, exactly?"

Just then Phillip showed up with a big grin. "I can answer that question, Henry. It's called B-LostNoMor. My poor partners have heard my marketing pitch about a thousand times, but if they don't mind hearing it once more, I can recite it for you. It should explain everything."

"Go for it," Craig said from the partner's table.

Phillip nodded. "Alright, here goes:

"When you were lost in an unfamiliar airport or a park or anyplace else, you needed B-LostNoMor. B-LostNoMor is a micro-version of the typical GPS programs that you use in your car or phone. It can lead you to any square inch of your choice. For instance, if you're in a courthouse, or an amusement park or a subway or mall, it'll direct you right to the spot you want to go. At a sporting event or a concert, it'll lead you to the closest restroom and refreshment stand and direct you back to your seat. Then it'll lead you back to your car. When you're at a large building like a hospital or office complex, B-LostNoMor will be your very own receptionist. In a grocery store, it can take you right to any item in the store, or, if you have a grocery list, it will show you the shortest route in the store and lead you to each item on your list. To

top it off, the app will get the user a picture of the precise item he or she is seeking. In conclusion, my dear friends, from now on, you won't B-LostNoMor."

After hearing Phillip's pitch, several of us applauded and complimented him.

Right after that, Colette, Ellen and Breanne wanted to mingle with the others. That left Juju and me at the table, where she leaned toward me. I hoped that she was ready to bury the proverbial hatchet, but I instinctively knew better.

32

While I was alone with Juju, she stared at me for a moment, then said, "You keep saying that you're deeply indebted to our family. Do you really believe that, or is that just prison chatter?"

"Of course I do, Juju. I wouldn't be living in this fine home if it weren't for you guys. That's for sure."

"Well then, how are you going to pay your debt?"

"I don't have any money at the moment, if that's what you mean, but I intend to get a job."

Juju shook her head. "I'm not just talking about money. You've literally screwed up my grandson's entire life and you should fix that."

"I'm afraid I don't know what you mean."

"Don't play coy with me. You are way too old for him; hell, you're old enough to be a grandmother and then some."

"That's true."

"Darn right it is. My grandson and I have been at odds ever since the first day he met you and I don't like it. He and the others believe that you were wrongly convicted, but you don't fool me. Your reduced sentence was simply the result of a legal technicality."

"Like I've said before, I'm sorry you feel that way, Juju, but if you can't believe Breanne, I wouldn't be able to prove it to you. All I can say is Phillip and I definitely love each other."

"Hogwash. He needs to be with somebody who can give him some babies before I croak."

"If it makes you feel any better, he and I have talked about that a lot of times. He says that he's happy with things just like they are, and so am I."

"That's another one of your fairytales. I've encouraged him to hook up with ladies his own age. His sister knows some too. One or two of them have caught his eye."

Juju's snide comment was disappointing, but it wasn't a surprise. "If you're insinuating that Phillip has been involved with some other women while I lived at the Lighthouse, I actually authorized it."

She tilted her head to the side. "Then you're a damn fool - but fortunately for you, I've got a proposition for you."

"A proposition? What kind of proposition?"

"I'm prepared to slip you a thousand dollars cash if you'll get out of our sight, forever."

"What? You know something, Juju? I've put up with a lot from you, but this is totally crazy. Whether you like it or not, Phillip and I are going to stay together."

"Oh, I get it. You need more than that. Let's make it five thousand dollars. You can get clear to the other coast with that kind of money. All you have to do is get a divorce and stay away forever. That's a lot of money and the best I'm going to offer you." She gently tapped her finger to her lips. "This will be our special little secret."

I wanted to scream. "Listen to me, Juju. I admit that Phillip and I have to overcome a problem or two, but we love each other and are good for each other, so you can keep your money."

Suddenly, from across the yard, Phillip was on his stepstool again. "Listen up, everybody. I'd like you all to follow me to the front yard. I've got a surprise for my sweet wife."

I didn't know what Phillip had in mind, but I was pleased

120

to get away from Juju. I turned my back to her and joined the parade.

In the front yard, our guests could see their vehicles lined bumper to bumper on either side of the street. My husband wrapped his arm around my waist. "See that white Chevy Camaro across the street?" he asked.

"Yeah. What of it?"

He dangled a key chain in front of me. "It's all yours. It's three years old and has all the papers, so it should be reliable for a long time."

My jaw dropped while oohs and ahhs swirled around. I almost asked him if he was serious, but the jack-o-lantern grin on his face was all the answer I needed.

No doubt about it, he made me feel loved. I threw my arms around his neck. "You are the kindest and most generous man I've ever known."

"Not only that, I have arrangements for a three-day mini-honeymoon. You'll never guess where we're going."

"What? Back up a bit. Did you say a honeymoon?"

"Yeah. When we got married you were already staying in the Lighthouse and we never had a honeymoon. All women want honeymoons. This one is just for three days cause I'm real busy right now, but we'll go to Rome or Paris in a few months. That was why I wanted you to get a new passport. Now guess where the mini-honeymoon is."

"Gosh, Phillip, this is all happening too fast."

"That's why we've got to catch up. Here's a hint. The name is very familiar to you."

"I don't know. Could it be Las Vegas? Maybe a tour of Silicon Valley?"

"Nope. We're going to Miranda, California. It's a little town in the middle of giant redwood trees, just a few hours north of San Francisco. You won't believe this next part, but the Miranda Motel just happens to be two miles north of Phillipsville."

I grinned. "Are you kidding me?"

"Nope. Miranda, California and Phillipsville, California are stuck together, just like you and me."

"I gotta admit, that is too priceless to ignore."

"I know, but I can look it up for you if you don't believe me."

"I trust you, but I might look it up anyway, just to learn more about the area."

"When I read about the place, I knew it was perfect for a three-day weekend. I got us a cute cabin all to ourselves."

"Wow. I don't know what to say."

"Just say that you're glad that we're leaving tomorrow."

I nodded my head enthusiastically. "I love you."

33

I was stunned when Phillip said we were going on a mini-honeymoon, but two days later, I was in the driver's seat some twenty miles from home with a big smile on my face.

"How do you like your car?" Phillip asked.

"I love it. It's very responsive, but I'm not sure I want to drive it through the tunnels in the redwood trees. What if we get stuck in there or break the mirrors?"

Phillip put his hand on my leg and smiled. "It's up to you. Some people just walk through the tunnel."

"You know something, Phillip? This trip is the most exciting thing I've done in quite a while."

"What about when we first met? We were like Bonnie and Clyde."

"Except I was scared to death the whole time. Now, I'm going on a legitimate honeymoon, and when that's over we're off to see Trevor. This is the best week of my entire life."

"And don't forget, we might be able to tour Europe in six months or so." He reached under the seat and grasped a small package. "Everybody has their own cellphones these days, so I got you an iPhone."

I actually felt butterflies in my stomach; not about accumulating material things, but that he genuinely wanted to please me. I wasn't accustomed to that. "You never cease to amaze me."

"You're welcome. I just wish Juju would give you a fair chance."

"Me too, but for now we have a lot of positive things we can focus on."

Just then, Phillip's phone chimed. He checked the read-out. "I'm sorry," he said to me, "but I gotta take this one."

"Go ahead. I'm enjoying the drive."

Minutes later my husband was embroiled in a heated conversation with one of his partners. While they did that, my mind drifted to an enigma that bothered me.

On the plus side, Phillip could be the sweetest man in the world, but the lipstick and underwear that I'd found in his bedroom indicated that he was out of control.

I kept wondering how many non-prostitutes shared the very same bed that he and I had been using. Just thinking about it irritated me, but I decided to wait until the honeymoon was over and then confront him about the matter. For starters, I wanted a brand-new mattress and an appropriate apology.

Suddenly, another call came in. Phillip glanced in my direction. "I'm sorry," he said. "I know that this is supposed to be a honeymoon, but when you work for yourself, you can't ignore your clients, or they'll go elsewhere."

That was the other part of my enigma. Up to that point, I hadn't realized how many calls and text messages Phillip got every day. I marveled at his ability to juggle so many people and projects at once. "I understand," I said. "Do whatever you have to do."

A short time later we pulled into a rest area and both headed for the restrooms.

* * *

When alone in the restroom, Phillip scanned his phone and found several dozen messages from Jerrie Jean.

The last time he'd spoken with her, she'd tried to blackmail him, but he still had the recording of her threats and intended to report her to the police, after the honeymoon.

Among Jerrie Jean's current messages, there were both rambling lovey-dovey comments and threats to screw up Phillip's relationship with Miranda.

He assumed that he could obtain a restraining order against her, but she was so looney, she might ignore the document and make everything worse.

The underlying fact remained: His life would be a whole-lot simpler if Jerrie Jean and Miranda never crossed paths.

The best option, he thought, was to remind Jerrie Jean that he was serious about turning her in, especially if she continued to harass him. That way she might tuck her tail between her legs and leave him alone.

A call would be better than a text message because she would be able to hear the seriousness of his tone.

As hoped, she answered his call, but sounded angry. *"Are you recording me again?"* she demanded.

"Have to, Jerrie Jean. You can't threaten people and get away with it."

"You're the one who should watch his back."

"There you go again - making threats. Actually, I think you're mentally disturbed."

"It's too bad for you, asshole, because I gave you everything. You even said I was your best lover, but you've lost that now, and a whole lot more."

"You're not listening to me, Jerrie Jean. I'm meeting with detectives in a few days to press charges against you for extortion and stalking me. You got that?"

"Yeah, I got it, but if you really want me to go away, why don't you slip me some money, let's say ten thousand dollars? Then I'll go away."

"You keep digging a deeper hole, Jerrie Jean. I'm hanging up now before you get yourself in more trouble."

34

After our potty break, Phillip and I were back on the road. "I heard you arguing with that Jerry fellow," I said. "Is everything okay?"

Phillip shook his head. "It's not a guy. It's a woman. Her name is Jerrie Jean. I met her and her husband at the bar. They are having financial troubles and want me to loan them some money so they won't lose their house. I barely know them, but they won't give up."

Phillip's comment was plausible, but he hadn't mentioned anybody by that name. I wondered why he would keep something like that from me.

Naturally, I didn't like the secretive stuff, but I didn't want to put him on the defensive over something that could be totally innocent. Once again, I elected to enjoy the honeymoon for now.

A while later, our headlights shone on a forest of gargantuan trees, with trunks as big around as a 7-Eleven.

We cruised through the not-booming metropolis of Phillipsville and coasted the last two miles to our one-horse getaway in Miranda, California.

After we parked, we entered the office of an eight-cabin motel and a pint-sized store. "Good evening," Phillip said to the grandmotherly woman behind the counter. "I'm Phillip Pilday. My wife is Miranda. We have a reservation."

The woman grinned. "Call me Katherine. We've had guys named Phillip stay here before and we've had a few Mirandas stay here, but this is the first time we had 'em both at the same time."

It was also the first time I'd shown my new ID to anybody. We finished the paperwork and Katherine handed us a brochure with a few of the nearby sights. "The diner's got good home-cooked food," she said, "but we don't get a TV signal because the trees block it out and we don't get cable. However, we have a bunch of movies on DVD that you can borrow; that includes adult movies if you're interested in those."

"We won't need that," I said.

Later, we dined on homemade pot-roast and mashed potatoes, both of which deserved a blue ribbon. After that we went for a short walk and gawked constantly skyward. "This could kink our necks," Phillip said.

"I know what you mean. It's as if we're in a blackened canyon of a big city."

"Only this place smells a lot better," hubby noted.

As we strolled along, we tried to see stars and the moon, but they were hiding above an extra-thick blanket of majestic dark trees.

We gave up and sat in a swing on the porch of our cabin for a while. We held hands and recalled the day that a con-on-the-run met a somewhat naïve, yet romantic, explorer on a three-wheeled motorcycle.

Eventually, we slipped into the bedroom, fluffed up the pillows, opened a window and listened to the soothing wind rustle through branches hundreds of feet over our heads. "Do you want to know something," I said, "you have a knack for finding romantic places."

Even though we hadn't cleared the air of a few potential problems, I genuinely loved Phillip.

35

THE NEXT MORNING, my head was in the proverbial clouds. In addition to enjoying the redwoods with my husband, there were only two days separating me from meeting Trevor. After cleaning up and eating a typical breakfast in the diner, Phillip snagged the brochure that Katherine had provided us and we embarked on our own sight-seeing tour.

Just down the road, a massive tree known as The Chandelier mesmerized a small parade of people who actually drove their vehicles through a tunnel that somebody had bored through its trunk.

At another stop, a monstrous tree had fallen over, revealing 2,500 tightly-packed rings, each one representing a year of that tree's former life. Astute nature-lovers labeled some rings that were there when Jesus roamed Jerusalem on the other side of the earth. It was truly spectacular.

Still in awe, we visited the Avenue of the Giants in Humboldt Park. Those monsters made the two-hundred footers look like saplings.

Still later, my favorite fave of all the faves was two albino redwoods; they were not as massive as all the others, but there were only four hundred of them in the entire world. My new phone captured a lot of great pictures.

If the day had ended right then, it would have been a

perfect dream. Unfortunately, my life didn't usually function that smoothly. When back at my car, I slid the key into the ignition only to get dead silence.

"Uh-oh," Phillip said. "I don't know a lot about cars."

Neither did I. We opened the hood and wiggled some wires, but that didn't do any good. A Hispanic family offered to take us for gas. "Thanks," Phillip said, grabbing his cell phone, "but we've got plenty of gas. I'll call a tow truck and have it taken somewhere."

Two hours later, the sun was resting on the horizon when our tow truck pulled into a neighborhood auto repair shop and unhooked our car. The manager could have gone home by then, but he had waited for us. He pulled my car into his shop and hooked up a series of cables before sharing his diagnosis. "Your computer is zonked."

"Crap," Phillip said, "I don't suppose you can fix it?"

"Not tonight. The best I can do is have one delivered tomorrow. It should get here in the afternoon. You might be back on the road about this time tomorrow."

"How much will all this cost?" I asked.

"Don't know exactly. Computers are usually over a thousand dollars, then add four hundred dollars for taxes, labor and shop supplies."

"Alright," Phillip said. "I guess we can get an uber to take us back to our cabin. Then we'll stay in touch."

All of that sounded reasonable to me, but it presented another unwanted problem. "But what about Trevor and his folks?" I asked Phillip.

"What about them?"

"We told Chester and Bertie that we were going to fly to Cincinnati the day after tomorrow to meet them and Trevor, but this might screw that up."

Phillip patted me on the shoulder. "Relax, Miranda. We can call them and explain what happened. I'm sure they'll understand and allow us to arrive a half-day later. Then all we gotta do is get a different flight."

"That's cutting it awfully close. Those people are jittery enough."

"Okay. Let me chase down an uber driver. After that we can call Trevor's folks."

I blew out a deep breath. "I wish I was as level-headed as you are in situations like this."

Since I didn't have Bertie's number on my phone, Phillip made the call. When Bertie answered, Phillip handed me his phone. "We'll still be there," I said to Bertie, "but we have to catch a different flight and change rental cars. We know we're imposing on you, but we're hoping you can work with us."

I could tell that Bertie was uneasy about the new schedule. After more reassurances, she agreed to our proposal and that meant I'd see Trevor the night before his trip out of the country.

36

The next afternoon, Miranda's car was repaired as expected, so she and Phillip gathered their things and began the drive home.

With a mishmash of thoughts concerning Phillip and her son, she still wanted to clear the air regarding Phillip's interactions with other women while she was pinned down in the Lighthouse.

When the redwoods were way behind them, Phillip reached for Miranda's hand. "You know something," he said, "this peace and quiet is just what I needed."

"I'm glad for you, but after fifteen years of incarceration, I'm extremely anxious to see Trevor. I also have something else on my mind. Can I ask you a couple questions?"

"Sure. Of course. What is it?"

"Well, we've always said that we wouldn't keep secrets from each other, right?"

"Yeah."

"Good. Then, I'd like to discuss the arrangement we made when I was initially confined to the Lighthouse."

Suddenly, Phillip's hand tensed. "I thought you never wanted to talk about that."

"I didn't, but this is an exception. I know that I told you it was okay to go to bed with somebody once in a while, but that was supposed to be rare and discreet and devoid of affection. Correct?"

"That's right. What are you getting at?"

"When you and I went to Wilson's I got some strange vibes."

"Really? Like what?"

"When Francie told me that a man punched you in the face, I saw the two of you trade glances, as if the story was deeper than that. I don't know if the two of you have a relationship or not, but I do know that lots of ladies go to bars to meet guys and vice versa."

Phillip smiled. "If that's what you mean, Francie and I were strictly co-workers. There was no hanky-panky going on."

"Maybe not, but you both implied that the bad guy thought you were messing around with his wife."

"I can explain that."

"I'm sure you can, but you've also been getting suspicious phone calls from various women, including somebody called Tawny."

"Don't worry, it's just a coincidence."

"Not good enough, Phillip. You've been sneaking off to talk to several ladies. That's very disturbing."

"Not really. Most of those calls were from my partners."

"Oh really? Are you telling me that all of those mysterious calls were 'rare'?"

"Yeah. Pretty much."

"Then how do you account for lipstick in your bathroom and sexy white panties that I found under our bed when I was cleaning up?"

Phillip went silent. Then he mumbled, "I'm afraid you've caught me off-guard. I don't know what to say."

"That's like cheating on me, Phillip. You've abused your privileges and I'm pissed off and disappointed. I'm having doubts about our entire marriage."

Phillip lowered his head a moment. "Okay, I admit it. I haven't been perfect. I'm sorry."

"Sorry? That's not even close to good enough. I've been dealing with sadness and waiting to confront you, and all you can say is you're 'sorry.' That's what somebody says when they belch. This is threating our very relationship."

After another pause, Phillip nodded gently. "I don't want to lose you, Miranda. What can I do to show you how much I love you and how badly I feel?"

"Well, for starters, one of us should stay in a hotel for a couple days. Then we can both decide if we really want to be in this relationship."

"I'm alright with that, but I already know the answer. I want to spend the rest of my life with you."

"I'm glad that this is easy for you, Phillip, but it's not like that for me. I've already wasted a big chunk of my life behind bars and I don't want to waste more time living with somebody I can't trust."

"Okay, I get your drift. I'll do whatever is necessary to keep you. If it's okay with you, I'll drop you off at the house and I'll check in at a hotel."

* * *

For the next two days my emotions were a non-stop rollercoaster. I couldn't eat or sleep. Part of me knew that Phillip had betrayed me and I didn't want more drama in my life. On the other hand, I'd played a role in Phillip's downfall by allowing him to interact with other women.

Finally, my cellphone rang. By the gentle tone of Phillip's voice, I could tell that he was deeply saddened. He apologized again. *"I want you to know that I will do anything to save our relationship,"* he said. *"I'm serious and totally committed to our relationship."*

"You hurt me, Phillip. I don't know if I can ever get over it."

"I know that, but if you don't mind, I'd like us to take a walk on the beach without any interruptions and talk. We'll have a nice

dinner and a couple drinks and watch the sun set. It shouldn't take very long to get there."

I always admired the romantic side of Phillip. He was clearly trying to resolve the matter so he deserved a chance to speak his peace in his own way. "Okay," I said, "that sounds nice."

"Alright then. Can you get to Finnegan's Grill by the beach at five o'clock?"

37

T HE FOLLOWING DAY Phillip rehearsed some of the things he wanted to say to Miranda. When it was time to go to Finnegan's Grill, he observed a beautiful horizon, on which a faint orange glow rested like a florescent blanket.

He reached for his cellphone to text a message to Miranda indicating that he was well on his way, but he quickly discovered that his pocket was empty. He instinctively glanced across the seat to see if he had laid his cellphone there by mistake.

In that brief moment of hesitation, a large pick-up pulled alongside him and intentionally forced him to swerve to his right.

Pissed off, Phillip turned his head toward the driver.

Then he saw a gun.

38

I ARRIVED AT THE PARKING LOT OF FINNEGAN'S on time but Phillip wasn't there. I lowered my window and admired the beautiful sunset. While I waited, I thought about meeting Trevor the very next afternoon, thanks to Phillip. In fact, given all that Phillip had done for me over the past five years, I was fairly certain that I was going to pardon his sexual dalliances and put it all behind us.

Meanwhile, minutes faded away with no sign of my hubby. "Don't worry," I said to myself. "He's just lost track of time."

I seized the phone that he bought me and tapped another text message.

After additional empty minutes, I supposed that I had misunderstood the appointment time. If that were the case, Phillip could be a half-hour away or more. I needed something to do to kill time, so I elected to go for a walk on the beach. After putting a note on my windshield, I followed a trail down to the beach where I removed my sandals and walked in the sand for roughly twenty minutes before returning to my car. The note remained untouched.

More worrying was accompanied by a half-moon that pushed its way into the equation. I considered calling Juju, but the woman was always difficult and would surely find some way to make this into my fault.

Rather than quarrel with the matriarch of the family, I elected to drive up the beach a couple miles just in case Phillip parked somewhere else, or his car broke down or he was in a completely different restaurant.

As I pulled away from the curb, all sorts of ugly possibilities pushed their way into my fragile mind. I hoped Phillip wasn't in a hospital or jail or kidnapped for his app.

I glided slowly along the Coast Highway and kept wishing that he'd turn on his phone and check in. But none of that happened.

As the sky darkened, my hopes faded. I hurried home to see if Phillip was there – perhaps passed out on the floor or something similar.

All along, I kept calling his cellphone, while I prayed that I'd soon be laughing with him over our misunderstanding.

When back at the house, there was no sign of Phillip or his vehicle or his cellphone. I took several deep breaths before calling Juju.

"Hi Juju, it's me, Miranda. I'm sorry to interrupt you, but do you know where Phillip is?"

"No. Why would I?"

"We were supposed to meet for dinner, but he didn't come. He's not at home either and he's not answering his phone."

"Has it occurred to you that he might not want to go home for some reason? I wouldn't blame him if he's in a bar."

The only bar I knew of was Wilson's, so I gave them a call, but neither Mr. Wilson nor Francie had seen Phillip.

For the time being, I was out of ideas, so I called the police station to make a Missing Person's Report, but they said that the absent person had to be missing for 48 hours before they'd begin a file.

All I could do was sit and watch the clock.

39

Whenever there was a deadly shooting on a California highway, the authorities wondered if it was a one-of-a- kind event or if a nefarious serial killer was nearby and poised to pop off additional drivers.

Such was the case on an off-ramp in Los Angeles, where an SUV ended up on its side, driver's side up.

For the public's safety, the authorities wanted to clear the area as quickly as possible without sending everybody into panic mode.

While a half-dozen traffic cops scooted rubber-necking drivers away from the show, they knew that a sniper could take them out on a whim.

Two pairs of wary detectives worked their way up the road's shoulder where they observed the deceased driver dangling in mid-air from his seatbelt.

The lead detective, a slim, middle-aged man with thinning hair and wire-rimmed glasses, hustled toward the officer in charge, trailed by his pudgy Chinese subordinate.

The younger detective scanned the area for any assassins who might be intending to make somebody else dead. His thin-nosed leader flashed his badge to the original officer. "Hello, Sergeant. I'm Lieutenant Scooter Nagley. What do we have here?"

"Sir, when we arrived, the driver was hanging in the air, dead and alone. He's been shot twice or more. It's very bloody in there."

"Well, the multiple shots imply that it was personal or road rage, so we might get away with just one death."

"Let's hope so. Thus far, none of our people have reported seeing any additional suspects. Maybe I'll get to see my kid's basketball game tomorrow night after all."

"I'm with you, Sergeant. Did you check the victim's ID?"

"No. We left him how we found him so you guys could evaluate for yourselves."

"Good job."

"Yes sir," the sergeant said, reaching into his shirt pocket. "There's something else. When we got here, there was a woman in a red Explorer pulled over along with her two kids. She told us that a big-wheeled truck pushed our victim's car off the road before spraying him with four or five shots. We sent the mom and kids away so they wouldn't get hurt, but here's her contact information for you."

"Good. I'll send somebody to talk with her. You got anything else?"

"Not for now, but I'll contact you if anything new pops up."

Even though it was looking more and more like a one-person killing, the lieutenant called in two additional detectives to get the license plates of the damaged vehicle and to see if they could find an ID on the victim without disconnecting the seatbelt until the forensic team could do their thing.

At the SUV, Sergeant Reba Bramwell, a lanky African-American in her late thirties, squatted and shone a flashlight into the car, where she noticed a large puddle of blood beneath the dangling body. "There's at least two wounds," she said to her partner.

"At least he didn't suffer," Detective Chico Roybal said.

Minutes later, Bramwell managed to extract the victim's wallet from his back pocket and handed it to Detective

Roybal. He flipped it open. "Looks like our guy is Phillip Pilday. His address is a few miles from here, but his license expired a while back."

"Alright then, I'll ask the lieutenant if he'd like us to check it out."

40

WHILE JUJU AND ELLEN were putting away the dinner dishes, somebody knocked on Juju's door. "Probably Mormons," Juju said.

Seconds later, the taller of two gentlemen held up a badge. "I'm Lieutenant Scooter Nagley, ma'am. There's been an accident up the road and we'd like to talk with you."

Juju opened the door and the visitors stepped inside. "What's this all about?" she asked.

"Like I said, I'm Lieutenant Nagley. My partner is Detective Yang. Does Phillip Pilday live here?"

"He used to live here but he moved to my rental home about a year ago."

"If you don't mind my asking, ma'am, who are you?"

"I'm Phillip's grandmother. I live here with my daughter and her husband, but they travel a lot, so they are not here right now. This is Ellen. She's Phillip's sister. Now, what can I do for you?"

"Well, ma'am, a couple hours ago there was a shooting on a highway off-ramp north of here. Our people collected the victim's wallet. I'm very sorry, ma'am, but the ID indicates that the victim is Phillip Pilday."

Juju's face went colorless while Ellen's hands flew to her

own mouth. Juju glared at the lieutenant. "That can't be. I just talked with him a few hours ago. There must be a mistake."

Lieutenant Nagley nodded to Detective Yang, who pulled the wallet from his pocket. "Is this his billfold?" the young detective asked.

Dumbfounded, Juju and Ellen dropped to the sofa where they collapsed together and wept.

"We're so sorry for your loss," Yang said.

A minute later and tear-soaked, Juju raised her head. "How? Why?" Ellen continued to sob beside her.

"Not certain just yet, but it appears he was shot at least twice. That implies that it was somebody he knew. We'll get an autopsy. All I can tell you is we want to catch the perpetrator ASAP, but we need to clear the people closest to the victim before we look elsewhere. I need to ask you a few uncomfortable questions. Would that be okay? It'll just take a few minutes."

Juju sniffled and slowly nodded her head.

"Thank you, ma'am. You said you talked to your grandson earlier in the day. Was he here when you had that conversation?"

"No. I was alone at the time."

"Did Phillip seem under stress?"

She shook her head and sniffled. "Not particularly. We have words from time to time, but it doesn't get dangerous."

"She's right," Ellen said through slow whimpers of her own. "We all love each other."

The detective looked at Juju again. "What was the argument about?"

"Mostly his marriage. He's too good for that woman."

"I see. What does he do for a living?"

"Self-employed," Juju said as Ellen handed Juju a box of tissues. "He's working on a technology product with a couple of his friends."

"Tell me a little about that."

"He designed one of those apps that everybody talks about.

It was his idea but he needed some people to help with the software so Craig and Allen work for him."

"We have some evidence that the owner of a truck with big tires might be involved. Any idea who that might be?"

Red-eyed, both Ellen and Juju slowly shook their heads.

"Can you think of anybody who would have a grudge against him or anything along those lines?"

"No. Everybody loves our Phillip."

"You said he moved out of this home. Where does he reside now?"

"In my rental house. I bet that damn jailbird is behind this."

The detectives traded glances. "What do you mean by that?"

Nearly hysterical, Juju wiped her nose on a tissue, then said, "Phillip is a sweet boy, but he married a murderer when she was on the run."

"Are you saying that his wife is an escaped convict?"

"Not anymore. She was released. A family attorney got the murder charges dropped. I knew something like this was going to happen. Now, that inmate killed my sweet grandson."

"We'll look into it," Nagley said. "Can you give us her name and contact information?"

Ellen dabbed her tear-soaked cheeks. "I want to say something about the other side of the coin, if that's okay."

"Yes, ma'am. Go ahead."

"Just recently Miranda was discharged from a minimum-security facility. Juju has never liked Miranda. But the rest of us, including the family attorney, believe in her."

"Noted," Nagley said, standing. "Anything else?"

"Oh, my God," Ellen whispered. "I gotta notify Mama and Daddy. Mama will fall apart without her baby boy."

41

Still waiting for Phillip, I opened the living room curtains and paced back and forth while making countless and fruitless calls to his cellphone.

Then, two things happened simultaneously: I got a text message from Ellen and an unfamiliar car with two official male adults pulled up. I cupped my hands to my mouth and raced to the door. "Is this about my husband?" I asked.

"Yes, ma'am," the elder one said while showing his badge. "I am Lieutenant Nagley and this is Detective Yang. May we come in?"

I looked at the younger one. "Is Phillip okay?"

He shook his head slightly while the lieutenant spoke. "I'm afraid that Mr. Pilday was shot while in his vehicle. He didn't survive."

It was as if my internal electricity shut off and a dam was about to break. "I knew something went horribly wrong," I whimpered, "but—"

"Naturally, we want to catch whoever did this," the lieutenant added, "but time is of the essence. We'd like to ask you a few questions. Can you handle that?"

"I'll try," I mumbled between sobs.

"Thank you. For starters, do you know anybody who drives a green truck with over-sized tires?"

"No. Is that who did it?"

"We don't know. Most crimes like this are carried out by people close to the victim. We'd like to eliminate you as a suspect. Where were you from four o'clock to seven o'clock?"

Sobbing, I blew my nose, then tried to communicate. "Phillip and I were supposed to meet at a restaurant at the beach, but he didn't show up, so I went for a walk. Then I drove around to see if I could find his car."

"I see. Is there anybody who can corroborate any of that?"

I sniffled again, then, "No, I didn't talk to anybody until I called his grandmother. She hadn't seen him either. When I got home, Phillip wasn't here."

"Yes, ma'am. We've already spoken with her."

"In that case, I bet she thinks that I did it."

The lieutenant glanced at his understudy, then returned to me. "That's correct. She told us of your imprisonment. If you don't mind my asking, why were you incarcerated in the first place?"

I dabbed my eyes, then dispensed a two-sentence crash course about being absolved of killing three people and that I had to break out of a hospital to prove my innocence.

"We'll have to run a background check and get a copy of your records for verification."

"I don't care right now. I've just lost my husband. Can't we do this later?"

"Just a few more questions, ma'am."

Suddenly, I had another awful thought. "What about Phillip's parents? Has anybody notified Frederick and Anita?"

"Yes, ma'am," Yang said. "Phillip's sister said she was going to call them."

"Oh, my God. those people will never be the same."

"Moving on," Nagley said, "do you know where we can find Mr. Pilday's phone?"

"No. I've been calling him all day, but he hasn't answered. He might have lost it or turned it off."

"Okay then, we're going to need permission to look at your phone records. Phillip's too."

"Alright, but I'll have to ask my attorney first. It'll probably be okay, but she has advised me to call her whenever I get into legal matters."

Nagley glared at me. "What about another woman? Mr. Pilday could have been living it up while you were in the cage. Anybody, including yourself, might have become jealous and lost control."

"No. No. No. We had an agreement."

"Agreement? What kind of agreement?"

"Men get horny when their wives or girlfriends are in jail. If they can't get what they need from their spouses, they look for somebody else. So, I said it was okay for Philip to go out once in a while so that he didn't feel like he had to sneak around."

"B.S.," Detective Yang said, "No woman wants her man to bounce around in strange beds."

"Think whatever you want, but I need to call Ellen now."

"We're almost done. If you had to guess who killed your husband, who would you pick?"

"Well, I guess it could be Phillip's business partners."

"Partners in what?"

"A software development company. Those guys want to sell the rights to the program because it's a lot of work for them and they need money, but Phillip wanted to wait another year before selling it. Now, would you two please leave me alone?"

"One last question, ma'am. Are there any guns in this home?"

"Not that I know of, now go away."

"Yes, ma'am. You've been very helpful. Thank you. We'll get in touch if we have any additional questions."

Yang nodded. "Sorry for your loss."

When the suits walked away, I was deeply saddened and all alone. I even missed my friends back at the Lighthouse. At least those ladies could console me. Instead, I called Juju and Ellen.

42

Lieutenant Scooter Nagley and Detective Danny Yang went to the office building in which Phillip's partners worked. They flashed their badges at a security guard and made their way to the fourth floor. In a conference room of one of the suites, the detectives paid close attention to Craig and Allen when they were advised that Phillip had been murdered.

After the shock subsided, the detectives had a few questions.

"We were told that you guys are working on a software program with Mr. Pilday," Yang said to Allen. "Is that correct?"

Both partners nodded.

"We also heard that you've had bitter words with Phillip. Can you explain that?"

"Certainly. Craig and I do most of the technical work while Phillip focused on legal matters and marketing. It irritates us a little because we do most of the grunt work, but it never gets ugly."

"Are you sure?" Yang asked. "Our sources tell us that you two wanted a bigger piece of the pie. Is that true?"

"Pretty much. We thought everybody should get an equal share."

"And Mr. Pilday wanted to wait another year before selling

it. That could have made for some big-time friction between you guys."

"I already told you that we do all the tedious work. It's easy to get bitter in a situation like that, but if you think we had anything to do with the murder, you're wrong."

"Craig is correct," Allen said. "We even went to Phillip's party when his wife got out of jail."

"Alright. We'll look into that. Where were you fellows at the time of the accident?"

"I can answer that one," Craig said. "We were at a seminar about taxes, and then we went to a cocktail party."

"Both of you?"

"Yes, and I can tell you that the cocktail party was a lot better than the seminar."

"Can anybody verify your attendance?"

"Sure. There were about twenty of us who listened to some dude with a Captain Hook beard and a bow tie until late afternoon. From there, a bunch of us met at The Three Finger Bar for a few cocktails."

"When did you leave the bar?"

"We hung round 'til seven-thirty or so. I can give you a list of names."

While Nagley proceeded with the questions, Yang took a list of names into the hall to see if he could verify the partners' whereabouts at the time of the murder.

"Now that Phillip is dead," Nagley asked, "what happens with the app?"

"There's no change in ownership of the app, but we got some life insurance to keep the project going."

"That's a common motive in many murders, you know."

"Maybe, but it's just one hundred thousand dollars. That's chicken-feed compared to selling the app."

"Let me see if I've got this right. You two get to split the insurance money and you each get twenty-four percent of the proceeds. Phillip's wife would get the rest, if and when the app sells. Is that the deal?"

"Yeah, that's the gist of it, but now we can hold out longer, thanks to that insurance money."

"Changing topics, does Mr. Pilday have any other associates or competitors who might benefit from his demise?"

"It's hard to say. People come around but most of it is friendly interest."

"Along those lines, has anybody tried to blackmail any of you for some reason?"

"Not that I know of, or Phillip would have said something."

"What about secret lovers? Perhaps Mr. Pilday had an affair that got ugly. Anything like that?"

"Well, he was married to Miranda, but he said he got some additional action on the side."

"Oh, really? Did you doubt him?"

"Why would we?" Craig asked. "He was a lucky stiff in more ways than one, if you get my drift."

"Cute. Miranda tells us that she and Phillip had some special arrangement, such as an open marriage. Do you know anything about that?"

"Yeah," Allen said. "As we heard it, she was the one who suggested he date other ladies."

"Did he do that?"

"Not in the beginning, but eventually he landed a part-time job at a bar not far from here. He got it on with some of those chicks."

"You got any of their names?"

"He never brought anybody around, but the place is called Wilson's. It's a few miles from here. You could probably get some names there."

"I'm back," Detective Yang said, returning to the room.

"Any luck?" Nagley asked.

"Yeah. I got a picture of the sign-in sheet regarding their seminar. Then I called several folks who verified these gentlemen's stories. They check out."

"Well, that answers a few questions," Nagley said to

Craig. "By the way, we've got people looking for a light-green truck with large tires. Do you know anybody who has a vehicle like that?"

"Not me," Craig said, while Allen shook his head.

"Okay, gentlemen. That's enough for now. We're very sorry for your loss and good luck with your app."

43

AFTER A VISIT WITH PHILLIP'S BUSINESS PARTNERS, Lieutenant Scooter Nagley and Danny Yang drove to Wilson's bar. Once inside, they presented their badges to a waitress and asked to speak with the owner.

When Mr. Wilson arrived at their table, he pulled out a chair, spun it around and saddled it. "What can I do for you fine officers?" he asked.

Nagley began, "We're homicide detectives. As you may know, one of your former employees was killed recently—"

Wilson's brow wrinkled. "Really? I hadn't heard anything like that. Who was it?"

"Phillip Pilday."

His brow tightened. "Really? Damn, I'm sorry to hear that. We all liked Phillip. What happened?"

"He caught a pair of deadly bullets while driving."

"That's a genuine bummer. He was a nice guy."

"I'm sure. Naturally, we're looking for the perpetrator."

"Of course. How can I help?"

"We heard that he worked here. How did you meet him?"

A small smile found Wilson's lips. "I'll never forget him. He was a bit of a loner. Used to come here as a customer to meet some ladies. Then I had to fire a bartender, and Phillip wanted the job. He was the only person I ever knew who offered to work for free. As it turned out, he wasn't after money; he just wanted to meet a few ladies."

"Exactly what did he do?"

"He was non-threatening so I let him wait tables, paid him minimum wage and tips. It only took him a few shifts to get the hang of things. By then, the customers liked him, so it was a good fit all the way around."

"Did you know that he was married to a prisoner?"

"Oh, yeah. He was an open book about that. That was one reason I hired him. Everybody knew about her. I think her name was Samantha or something like that."

"Actually, her name is Miranda. Phillip's partners told us that he indeed hooked up with some of your customers."

"You could say that. We have a lot of customers, both male and female, so it's easy to meet people. He always told the ladies about his wife and that he was simply looking to have fun. A fair number of them were of the same mind."

"He sounds like a model citizen. Was there anybody who didn't like him?"

Wilson grinned. "This is a bar, gentlemen. Sometimes people drink too much, get loud or obnoxious. Dust-ups are inevitable."

"Did he get involved in any scuffles?"

"He once got punched out by the husband of an Australian woman named Valerie. The dude broke Phillip's nose. I had to take him to the hospital to stop the bleeding."

"Interesting. Do you know how to find Valerie?"

"No, but I think Phillip hooked up with her a few times. That's how I know her name."

"Well, if she shows up again, call us, asap. We'll run on over or talk with her via phone. Anybody else?"

"A few of them. After he was here for a while, he got the hang of things and interacted with a number of the customers. He wasn't the boisterous type, so people liked him."

"Can you give us some names of those ladies?"

"Several of them. For instance, a 50ish regular named

Tawny. She drifts in on most Saturdays. Phillip dated her a few times. Her brother got pissed when he thought Phillip mistreated his sister. I don't think anything came of it, though."

"Alright, anybody else?"

"Now that you mention it, I can think of one green-eyed-monster."

Danny Yang scrunched his forehead. "What's that?"

"Jealous woman," Wilson said. "I don't remember her name, but she's come by several times, usually with her other boyfriend. They were here the other day, paid with a credit card. I can get a copy of the receipt. That'll have her name on it."

"Good. Can we look through your other receipts? You might think of somebody else."

"Sure. We can go to my office. I'll have Francie bring your burgers back there. Would you like a beer, on the house, while we're at it?"

"Maybe some other day," Nagley said.

As hoped, Wilson's records proved fruitful. The cops came across the name Jerrie Jean Bedford, along with two additional women that Phillip had dated.

Suddenly, Wilson perked up. "Now that I think of it, a year or so back, Phillip said that he rented one of those three-wheeled motorcycles and went for a ride that turned into an over-nighter. I don't know her name, but you might be able to chase her down by finding the rental place and then finding out where they went."

"Alright, Mr. Wilson," Scooter Nagley said. "Thanks for your help. We'll check everybody out. We're leaving a couple business cards in case you think of anybody else. Just give us a call."

"Sure will. And you fellows come back when you can remove your leashes."

44

When Phillip was taken from me, I sank to a bereavement level that I'd not experienced since my twin brother passed on.

The only other people I knew were Phillip's partners and family - but none of them knew me very well and Juju didn't like me.

Alone and distraught, I slumped around the house while I cried and feared what my future would be like without Phillip.

Adding to my woes, Phillip and I were supposed to be visiting Trevor in Cincinnati, but that journey was aborted well before it began.

Finally, after a very long stint of lonely tears, I elected to call Phillip's family. They had known him a whole lot longer than I had, and not just an hour at a time, so they had to be suffering as much as I was.

Aside from the misery-loves-company factor, I wanted to assure them that I didn't have anything to do with Phillip's death, so I grabbed my phone.

"I know that," a very sad Ellen said, *"but Juju is having fits. She keeps saying it's your fault and I keep reminding her that Breanne insists that there is no evidence proving that you have ever been dangerous. Obviously, Phillip understood that too."*

"I'm glad you comprehend me, Ellen. That means a lot to me. Thank you for that."

"No problem, but if you don't mind, I've got to hang up now. Phillip is supposed to be moved to a mortuary today and Juju wants to work out the burial details."

Huh? "Isn't that supposed to be my responsibility?"

After a brief pause, *"Now that you mention it,"* she said, *"I don't really know who's legally in charge of that. Juju just took over, like she always does."*

"I realize that I haven't known Phillip for as long as you guys, but I'm his legal wife. I ought to have a voice in the matter."

"Seems reasonable to me, but if Juju has to pay for everything, she'll probably be pretty bossy."

"Well, I don't really mind if she wants to take care of it, but I'm on Phillip's checking account, so I can pay some of it, if that will help."

"I'll pass that along to Juju and let you know what she thinks."

A few hours later, Ellen called me back. *"Juju is willing to pay for everything and it's okay for you to attend the services but she thinks it would be better if you sit well behind the real family and Phillip's long-time friends, who watched him grow up."*

"But I'm his wife. That's 'real family,' too."

"Not in Juju's eyes."

The last thing I wanted was a war with anybody, especially Juju, so I implemented a plan of my own. "If I let you guys handle everything, would you make sure to keep me in the loop?"

"That's reasonable," Ellen said. *"I'll meet you there if you want some company."*

Not long thereafter, Ellen gave me the address of the mortuary and told me when to go there without risk of bumping into Juju.

As it worked out, I appreciated my chance to have Phillip all to myself. I cried like a baby and thanked him for all the trust and love that he had afforded me during the five years we were married.

That afternoon, the medical examiner confirmed that

Phillip had died from gunshot wounds and was not drunk or at fault in any way.

Two long and miserable days later, we had the services.

I waited until the last minute to enter the large hall. In spite of Juju's rule, I walked right to the very first row and sat next to Phillip's mother. We held hands the whole time.

When the services were over, there was a get-together in the basement of a nearby church. I assumed that Phillip's parents felt more pain than everybody else, so I spent most of my time commiserating with Frederick and Anita.

When I got home, I felt tired, puffy-eyed and empty. Then it occurred to me that I had other problems. Trevor and his other parents must have already celebrated his birthday. I shook my head because I should have been there for one of the best days of my life, but instead some jerk-wad with a gun killed my husband and that flipped my life over like a burnt pancake.

45

AFTER THE SERVICES AND A LONG AFTERNOON OF MISERY, I would have liked to call Bertie and Chester to explain why I wasn't able to get to our son's party. Trouble was, I didn't get my own phone until after I was released, so Phillip had always handled the communications, and his cell phone was missing.

Nevertheless, in a last-ditch effort to get the Montgomerys' number, I thought I'd check with Juju just in case Phillip had left the number there for some reason. Naturally she was sobbing when she answered.

"I'm sorry for your pain, Juju," I said gently. "I feel awful too. I wanted you to know that Phillip always thought the world of you."

"Thank you," she said softly, *"I noticed that you crowded into the front row. You weren't supposed to do that."*

"I went along with all your other decisions, but I'm Phillip's wife and deserved to be up front with the family. Other than that, I want to thank you for supervising the funeral arrangements. I would have done it myself or helped you, but Ellen thought you wanted to handle everything. So, thanks for that too."

She sniffled. *"I heard that you offered to pay some of the expenses. How could you afford that?"*

"I don't have any of my own money yet, but Phillip put me on his checking account."

"In other words, you were willing to spend somebody else's money."

"I know it sounds like that, Juju, but it's all I've got until I can get a job."

"Oh, really? Exactly who is hiring convicts these days?"

Her cruelty made me want to scream, but there was enough tension around there, so I simply answered her question. "I've got experience working in restaurants and beauty salons and painting houses. I ought to be able to find something. In fact, Phillip said I could be an Uber driver because I've already got a nice car and I like moving around."

"Oh, yeah, I almost forgot that my grandson bought you a car. That had to be fortuitous for you."

"I know that you're dealing with your saddened heart, Juju, but I need to ask you something else. It's off-topic, but it is important to me."

She sighed and sniffled. *"What now?"*

"Do you have the number of my son's adoptive parents? My own phone is new, so I haven't loaded it with their number yet. But when Phillip and I called them, we always used his cell phone. But nobody knows where it is."

"I can't help you. As far as I am concerned, you are a tactless woman who doesn't know her priorities. You should be focused on Ellen, and Frederick and Anita, not strangers."

"Listen, I know that all of you guys are deeply bereaved, Juju – I am too - but Trevor's other parents expected Phillip and me to go there. I need to explain what happened."

"Regardless, you are only worried about yourself. I want you to move out of my rental home and go far away."

I felt as if I were her personal punching bag. "I can't do that right now, Juju. I have no place to go and very little money."

"Tough toenails. My house, my rules," she said before hanging up.

I wasn't sure if she could force me out of her home that

easily, but I knew for certain that I needed a roof over my head; otherwise, I could be picked up as a vagrant, and that could cause a landslide of additional, unwanted chaos.

If Juju were to press the matter, I could get some money from my joint account with Phillip, and then stay in a cheap motel, but that too would be temporary and I'd be right back in the same predicament. I immediately called Breanne.

"Uh-oh!" Breanne said after hearing the problem. *"I'm afraid I can't help you this time, Miranda. It would be a conflict of interest for me to represent either you or Juju against the other."*

"Then can you recommend somebody cheap?"

"All I can say is it would be a good idea to get a lawyer who specializes in tenant/landlord matters."

"But experts cost a lot, and I don't have much money."

"In that case, there are pro bono attorneys who do volunteer work. If nothing else, you might call a big church. They usually have attorneys among their flocks."

That made sense so I did a little research and found several hotlines for tenant/landlord matters. I cried and sniffled while I left several messages.

Late that afternoon, a lawyer named Jasmine Schwartz returned my call. I explained Juju's threat and asked if Juju could force me out.

"Is there a lease?" Jasmine asked. *"If there isn't a lease, there's a standard process that the landlord has to follow to retake possession. It usually takes a month or longer to make somebody move out."*

"Okay. That gives me some time if I need it. While I've got you, who has the rights to my husband's things?"

"I'm sorry, but this line is strictly for tenant/landlord matters, but if I were you, I'd look for a will. If your husband has a will, that should govern who gets what, but if there is no will, it gets trickier. Either way, if you need me in that capacity you can retain me. It shouldn't cost very much."

"Thank you. You've been very, very helpful."

46

IN THE VAST MAJORITY OF MURDER CASES, the perpetrator was somebody close to the victim, such as a spouse or a co-worker with a grudge of some sort. When Plan A failed to reveal the perp, there was a high likelihood that the victim knew the killer in some other capacity.

When Lieutenant Nagley and Detective Yang searched for Phillip Pilday's killer, they followed the same basic protocol.

In very short order, Phillip's partners and entire family, sans Miranda, were cleared.

Miranda was still a person of interest so her interview was a mixed bag. For instance, she would inherit most of Phillip's belongings, so she definitely had a monetary motive to be rid of him.

Moreover, the former inmate couldn't verify her whereabouts at the time of the crime.

Also damning, Phillip's grandmother had openly pointed a suspicious finger right at Miranda's nose.

Further, the investigators couldn't put Mrs. Pilday at the crime scene.

Lastly, it didn't appear that she had access to a gun, nor the marksman-like skills it would take to wipe out a victim while rolling down the road. Of course, convicts met streams of nefarious people while incarcerated and any one of those folks could have helped Miranda eliminate her husband.

Bottom line, if Miranda wasn't Phillip's perpetrator, somebody else was, and Phillip knew a lot of people from Wilson's bar. Phillip could have had a dust-up with any of them.

Compounding the detectives' problem, a shit-ton of those people had learned that Phillip had a valuable app. He might as well have dared them to make trouble.

"What now?" Detective Yang asked his superior, while they drove to their office. "If we're going to interview all those customers, we might as well bring them in by the busload."

"And we don't have time to waste," the Lieutenant added. "Our perp could already be a hundred miles away. That's why I requested two additional people to assist us with the case. They're waiting for us right now."

"Great. Two groups of two. Who'd you get?"

"Sergeant Reba Bramwell and Detective Chico Roybal."

Yang nodded approvingly. "One African-American and one Hispanic. Good people, even though the Sergeant is taller than me."

"That she is," the boss smiled, "but I asked for her because of her hobby. She's won a little money playing poker in Vegas."

"Good for her, because I never win any money out there."

"She's supposed to be an expert at reading people."

"Good. Maybe she can teach me a few tricks."

A short while later, the four detectives gathered in a conference room. Bramwell extended one of her long, thin arms into her tote and grabbed her iPhone to take notes.

"We've already identified a handful of ladies who Mr. Pilday has been with," the lieutenant said to his newly formed team. "Any one of them could have wanted his money."

"A few of them have other boyfriends," Yang added, "and those boys might not want competitors."

"Who we gonna interview first, Lieutenant?" Roybal asked.

"We're going to start with the low-hanging fruit. I'd like you two to get back to that bar and have a chat with the employees – particularly the ones who interreact with the public. That means servers and bartenders as opposed to cooks and dishwashers. I want to know about anybody who has a grudge against Mr. Pilday."

"Alright. We can handle that."

"While you guys are doing that, Detective Yang and I will do a background check on Mrs. Pilday. That includes her criminal record and any other bad people she may have contacted lately, plus her former employer."

"Employer," Roybal asked, "What kind of work did she do?"

"According to Mr. Pilday's grandmother, Miranda was considered a low-risk inmate and allowed to don an ankle bracelet once a week and go off campus to work at a dog shelter.

"Well as far as I'm concerned," Bramwell said, "Anybody who loves dogs can't be all bad."

"Speaking of bad," Yang injected, "can you teach me to play poker?"

47

IN ADDITION TO MY MISERY CONCERNING PHILLIP, I had other concerns that needed attention. For instance, I had learned that landlords couldn't throw tenants out without reasonable notice, even if the landlord was Juju and I was the tenant.

At the same time, I certainly didn't want a war with any of Phillip's relatives, so I called Juju again to see if we could work something out. I began by advising her that I had called Breanne for advice.

"And what did Breanne have to say?"

"She said she couldn't represent either one of us against the other, so I ended up calling a different lawyer who specializes in things like this."

"How the hell can you afford an attorney?"

"I can't afford it, Juju. That is my point. Jasmine is helping me pro bono. She said it would take over a month to force me out, but I don't want this to be adversarial and I believe that Phillip would want you to cut me a little slack. I just want a little time to get a steady job."

Juju paused for a moment. Then, *"Well, it looks like you outsmarted me, inmate. I bet you're proud of yourself."*

"No Juju. I don't look at it like that. I know this is your home and I know when I have to be out. After that, I will stay in a cheap motel if I have to. I also plan to pay you back the same amount that any other tenant would have to pay to rent your house. Or, if it's helpful, I can work off some of my debt to you by painting some of the rooms. Phillip must have told you that I used to run a painting crew."

"You don't fool me, inmate. You're hanging around to see if you can find anything of value, such as his savings account or his coin collection. He's been working on that collection since he was in kindergarten, but you'd pawn it off in a flash."

"He told me about those coins. If I see them, I'll gladly give them to you. Honest."

"Maybe you would. Maybe you wouldn't. Regardless, I'm betting you're going to steal anything you can sell. I still want you out of my house. You're not welcome here. Do you understand me?"

Frustrated, I hung up and shook my already-tired head. Saddened, I snooped around the house for any sign of Phillip's coins so that I could return them to Juju in good faith.

I didn't find the coins, but I did stumble upon an interesting carboard box in a back closet. Inside, a row of folders was stacked behind a thinner file labeled, "Burt and Ernie."

I immediately smiled because I'd heard Phillip refer to Trevor's parents by those names.

I peeked inside the folder where Phillip had written a phone number that appeared to belong to Bertie and Chester. If they still had that number, I might be able to reach them and explain why I couldn't attend Trevor's party.

Excited for the first time in a while, I thanked God and Phillip for their respective roles in the matter and located my own cellphone. I instantly tapped out the number on the file - but the call went unanswered.

Unwilling to give up, I tried again and again and again, always with the same dead-end. Ultimately, it occurred to me that Bertie and Chester had blocked me because they were tired of making concessions for an ex-con who was flakier than a box of cereal.

If they truly were of that mind, Trevor would never hear about me.

Meanwhile, I hadn't heard anything from the police regarding Phillip's murder. That too was concerning because I knew that the investigators probably suspected me.

I couldn't do anything to prove my innocence so I told myself that I couldn't mope forever. That would be like another prison sentence.

I considered hiring a PI in Cincinnati to locate the Montgomerys and/or Trevor. Trouble was, I certainly couldn't afford a PI.

With no aces up my sleeves, I forced myself to perform my morning chores, and then to get out and face the world. After observing a few normal people and some playful squirrels, the melancholy subsided slightly.

While I was gassing up my car, Ellen called me with some news of her own. *"I heard what Juju said to you about moving out of her home,"* she said. *"I don't agree with her and told her so."*

"Thank you, friend. I don't want to be a bother, but there is a lot on my plate."

"If it would make you feel better you and I could go to lunch and talk things over. I might get Juju to change her mind about chasing you off. Do you like Chinese food?"

"You know something, Ellen? You remind me of Phillip. You are both uplifting people. I would love to go to lunch together."

Late the next morning, I found myself in a quiet booth swatting tears with my husband's sister. "Does Juju know about our meeting?" I asked.

"Definitely. I don't hide anything. That makes people suspicious. So, how are you feeling?"

"My heart still aches and I cry a lot," I said, "but I'm regaining some of my senses."

"Yeah. Us too."

"How about Frederick and Anita? It must be very agonizing to lose a child, no matter the age."

"That's true. It's been very painful for them, especially my mom, but they've decided they have to return home sooner or later. They're going to stay a few more days and then take their sorrows with them."

48

When Juju heard that Ellen had invited Miranda to lunch, Juju drove to her rental house, where the next-door neighbor was watering his flowers.

She pulled into the driveway, which prompted the neighbor to put down his hose. "I heard about Phillip," the man said. "I'm so sorry. How are you doing?"

"To tell you the truth, Blake, I'm deeply wounded and so angry I could growl."

"Sorry to hear that. You people have always been good neighbors."

"Thank you. My grandson's wife is making everything harder."

"I met her at the party, but didn't get to talk with her much."

"I think she could be behind Phillip's death, and I told the police as much. I just hope they arrest her before she gets away."

"If you're looking for her, she's not here right now. I saw her drive off a half-hour ago."

"That's good. I'm here to protect the family belongs before she steals us blind. I think she's already pawned off Phillip's coin collection."

"Oh, yeah, I saw that collection a long time ago. If you don't mind my saying so, your tenant is going to be disappointed. It's the kind of collection that has sentimental value, but there wasn't much numismatic value."

"Oh, really? That's news to me, but I'm still going inside to save anything of value before that awful woman drives off with all of our memories and valuables. I could use your help if you have a few minutes."

"I guess I could do that," he said, just as a cargo van turned onto the block, causing Juju to wave for the driver's attention. An elderly male driver pulled to the curb. The sign on the side of the truck indicated that he was from Jackson's Locksmith Services.

"I'm having the locks changed," Juju said to her neighbor.

"Sounds like a good idea."

"Damn right. That inmate doesn't scare me. I'll fight her all the way to hell if I have to."

A half-hour later, the locks had been changed and Juju had managed to fill her trunk with anything that Phillip's wife might try to pawn, including the vacuum cleaner, the kitchen knife set, and two cardboard boxes full of the family pictures that had adorned the walls for many years.

Satisfied that she saved everything she could, she thanked Blake for keeping an eye out. "That prison lady doesn't know who she's fooling with," Juju said. "I hope she gets a new wardrobe consisting of nothing more than orange jumpsuits. Hell, I'd even pay for it."

49

I WAS GRATEFUL THAT ELLEN had invited me to lunch. She knew a lot more about Phillip and his family than I did. For instance, I knew that he'd been home schooled, and that he'd read three books per week for years. But I didn't know he'd been beaten up by a neighborhood bully just because he was nice to the bully's girlfriend.

At another point, Ellen said that Phillip's trust came from Juju and her husband, but now that Phillip had passed, Ellen's kids became the next beneficiaries.

I also discovered that the furniture and knickknacks in the rental house belonged to Juju, but I was entitled to anything that actually belonged to Phillip. In other words, Juju owned the bed, but I inherited Phillip's clothes and books – things like that.

"I appreciate all of this information," I said while Ellen and I were finishing lunch. "Phillip never explained it."

She smiled and put her hand on my forearm. "Well, that is why we girls got to stick together."

After lunch, I stopped at a grocery store. Food didn't sound good, but I had to eat something. I wheeled a cart around aimlessly and gathered a dozen odds and ends before arriving at the self-service registers, which were new to me considering where I'd been living the past decade-and-a-half.

After fumbling with the scanner, a well-tattooed clerk, half my age, swooped over and examine my driver's license and address, all of which gave me an idea. "Do you guys have any job openings?" I asked.

"We're always looking for good steady people. Do you have any experience?"

I could have mentioned the endless chain of prison chores that I'd endured, but I thought the better of it. "My first husband and I had our own restaurant," I said, "I did everything from running the register to washing dishes to managing the help and bussing tables - but that was over fifteen years ago."

"That still counts and most of these jobs are fairly simple. I'm sure you could figure it out."

I smiled at him and posed my most germane question. "Would a police record be an issue?"

Slightly surprised, he feigned a smile. "Really? You?"

"It's a long story."

Intrigued, he led me away from the registers to the backroom of the bakery department where he introduced me to the store manager.

"This lady here is interested in a position at the store," he said. "She's got experience but she was wondering if a criminal record could hold her back."

"Well, to answer your question," said the manager, "we have been known to hire people with a police record. It depends on the crime; if you were convicted of a money-crime, you can't run a cash register or work the customer service desk for obvious reasons."

I shook my head. "It wasn't anything like that."

"Well, what was it then? We'll have to know sooner or later."

"To tell you the truth, I was wrongly convicted of three murders, but they eventually figured out I was innocent so I was exonerated."

He looked me in the eye, presumably to see if I was kidding, but I held steady.

"Wow. I don't know how the bigshots look at that. I can call them and get back to you."

I gave him my contact information, thanked him, and returned home, where I waved to my neighbor on his porch. I was feeling optimistic about getting a job of some kind. If I could pull that off, I could pay Juju some rent and she might go a little easier on me for a while.

I parked in my driveway and toted a couple bags of groceries to the front door, where my key didn't work. I may not have been a scholar, but I was smart enough to know who was behind the mischief.

I marched next door and quizzed my neighbor. "Did you see anybody messing around with my doors?"

He nodded. "Your landlord had the locks changed."

I immediately called Jasmine Schwartz, the attorney who worked pro bono for struggling tenants.

She confirmed that Juju didn't have the legal right to do that. "Okay then," I said, "What should I do, now?"

After some basic instructions I called Juju.

I'd barely informed her that she couldn't lock out her tenants without first going to court before she cut me off.

"The hell I can't," she said. "That's my damn property and we all know it."

"I know it's your property, Juju, but you don't have the right to lock me out, so you were actually trespassing when you changed those locks."

"Don't you lecture me, Madam Convict. You are the trespasser. Not me. I'll be damned before I'll let you run things."

"I don't want to run anything, Juju. I just want to get on my feet. Then I can pay rent, either here or elsewhere."

"Don't you get it? You are not welcome in my home."

"Have you spoken with Ellen, because she agrees with me."

"Hell, no. She's a spineless mediator, not a warrior and I don't want a convict in my home. You got that?" Then she hung up.

I stood there dumbfounded for a bit, then sighed. Since Jasmine's plan had failed, I turned to Plan B.

A short time later, a different locksmith showed up and the doors got their third set of locks in one day.

When I finally entered my temporary home, I had another rude awakening. Juju had removed all the pictures from the walls and a number of other items, such as the vacuum cleaner plus the file box from the closet in which I'd recently discovered a possible number for Trevor's adoptive parents.

I called Juju again, this time to advise her that I'd also had the locks changed and I would gladly give her a key whenever she wanted.

Predictably, she didn't answer her phone, so I simply left a message.

50

Predictably Phillip's death haunted me. Among other things, I wasn't sleeping well. One night I heard a faint squeak down the hall and sprang awake to find out I was still all alone, which was the exact opposite of prison life, where there were lots of people for support.

Anyway, that moment intensified my urge to get both a dog for companionship and some meds for my depression.

Meanwhile, Bertie and Chester Montgomery were still ignoring my messages, and I couldn't blame them. Sadly, any thoughts of meeting Trevor had essentially vanished.

In-between the tears and self-pity, I had to provide for myself and I couldn't dillydally because my resources were scarce and Juju's wick was short.

The next morning, while I was wondering whether I wanted to stay in California, I heard the slam of a couple car doors. Then, Lieutenant Nagley and Detective Yang made their way to my porch. "How are you doing?" the boss asked flatly.

The tone in his voice sounded more like he was obligated to ask the question than that of a genuinely sympathetic person. Nonetheless, I couldn't ignore him. "Well, I waited five years to be united with my husband," I said, "but he's been taken away in less than a month. How would you feel if that happened to you?"

"Point taken. May we come in?"

In the living room, we formed a three-cornered circle and the Lieutenant jumped right in. "As you know, we want to find the perpetrator of your husband's death, so we've been checking with quite a few people and we're getting some information that you left out when we last spoke. We'd like you to clarify some of these things."

"I'm not surprised. My life has been turned inside out and I'm not thinking clearly."

"We'd like to go over your case again. Where were you from three o'clock to six o'clock on the afternoon of your husband's passing?"

Due to my background, I knew that law enforcement people and convicts didn't particularly trust each other, so I had to be on guard. "You must think I'm stupid," I said.

"What do you mean by that?"

"You're going to ask me the same questions you asked before."

"Again, what's wrong with that?"

"I've been incarcerated for fifteen years. I've met thousands of inmates. A person learns things from those people."

"Meaning?"

"Meaning a liar can't usually remember the details of the lies they've told, but a person who knows the truth will usually have the same basic story."

He raised his head and nodded. "You still haven't answered my question."

"I told you already. Phillip and I agreed to meet at Finnegan's Grill by the beach. But he was late, so I went for a walk while I waited, but that didn't work so I took a drive to see if I could find his car."

"Then what?"

"I knew that something was wrong. I felt sick to my stomach, so I went home and worried and waited and cried until you guys showed up. When you asked if I could corroborate my activities, my answer was no and still is."

"Alright. Was there any particular reason that you were going to meet at that particular place at that particular time?"

"It was Phillip's idea, but I had a hunch that he was going to admit that he'd been romantically involved with another woman or two."

"Why did you think that?"

"I've told you before, we didn't see each other very much, but people need somebody to hold and talk to. I thought it would release a lot of stress if he could have a sleepover every once in a while, but I could tell he had real feelings for somebody, and that dinner was his opportunity to clean the slate. I only gave him permission to have some casual flings."

"While we're on the topic, when was the last time you 'squeezed' somebody other than Phillip?"

"If you must know, it's been a long time."

"When? Who?"

"Seven or eight years ago, when I was wrongly convicted, and sent to the big prison. The nights were lonely. Occasionally, my cellmate or I needed validation so we cuddled once in a while, but that was years ago and I don't know where she is now."

"Alright, my partner has some additional questions for you."

Yang nodded. "If our information is correct, Ms. Pilday, you had an off-site job for the year preceding your release at the Lighthouse. Is that right?"

"Yes. At a dog shelter. So what?"

"So, you were unsupervised and could have been messing around with somebody under the radar, and that person could have taken out your husband for you."

"Oh. You're wrong again. Phillip and I had a lot of things planned out. I wouldn't have put any of that in jeopardy."

"That's what you say now, but I think it was easy for you to deal with Phillip whenever he came by for a couple hours at a time; but when you were released, it became a 24/7 relationship. Phillip was running the show and that could have pissed you off."

"I know that you guys have to shake the trees, but I loved Phillip. I wouldn't have done anything to hurt him."

"Alright," Nagley interrupted. "We asked Phillip's friends and family what they thought about you. Do you have any reason to suspect any of them?"

"I already told you about Phillip's business associates…"

"All right, we're just about done here. We are expecting to get your husband's phone records along with his credit card records and his checking account to see who he's been associating with. Does that worry you?"

"Sort of."

"Really. Why?"

"Because you guys can keep that information to yourselves, then lie about it to trip me up. I've been wrongly accused before."

"Maybe so, but if you put up obstacles, we'll go to a judge and get the documents anyway."

"Okay. Okay. You can get those documents."

"That's better, and we'd like you to stay in the state until we get to the bottom of this."

51

After quizzing Miranda a second time, the detectives returned to Wilson's to locate other prospects who may have played a role in Mr. Pilday's passing.

As before, it was immediately obvious that Francie Baker knew more about the clientele than anybody else. As the head server, she was especially aware of the regulars and the heavy tippers.

Francie said she didn't have any information about the accident itself, but when Detective Danny Yang asked her what she thought of Phillip's app, she had praise. "Very impressed," she said. "I've blabbed about it to everybody."

"What about you?" Yang asked, "Have you ever been 'tight' with Phillip?"

Francie scoffed, "Hell, no. My five-year-old stays with my mother-in-law while I'm at work. I don't want to overload her, so I don't have time for hanky or panky, if you get my drift."

Yang grinned. "Exactly where were you when the killing took place?"

Francie smile, then rose and marched to the back room. Less than a minute later, she returned with a printout indicating that she was in mid-shift when Phillip was taken out.

Danny Yang took a glance at the paper. Then, "Good enough. What do you know about Mrs. Pilday?"

"Miranda? I know that she spent a lot of years in a cage, if that's what you mean."

"Have you interacted with her in any way?"

"Phillip brought her in one time to introduce her, but she was apprehensive."

"Apprehensive? About what?"

"Maybe because she hadn't been in public for a long time. She probably needed to improve her people skills."

"Could it be because she suspected you and Phillip had something going on?"

"If she thought that, she was mistaken. Besides, Phillip is not my type. I like the athletes and rugged guys."

Detective Yang slid Francie a business card. "Okay. Thanks for your help. If you think of anybody else who might have useful information, give us a call."

Back in the car and on their way to the next stop, Nagley and Yang updated their notes. "It looks like our next stop is going to be with Valerie Mitchell," Yang said.

"Okay. What's her story?"

"According to Wilson, Valerie's husband went on a three-day hunting trip without consulting her. Apparently, that pissed her off, so she went to Wilson's, met Phillip and invited him to spend the night with her."

"Guns and revenge. That can't be good."

"True. Evidently, hubby came home early, forcing Pilday to sneak out of a window. But a neighbor saw Pilday's escape and shared that information with Valerie's husband. In a fit, our hunter went to the bar and broke our victim's nose."

"Maybe Mitchell wasn't done," the lieutenant said, "only the next time, he had a projectile with Pilday's name on it. Just in case, we don't want to spook a guy with guns in his house, so we'll introduce ourselves and tell him we're investigating some other case. When we can see his hands and determine that he's unarmed, we'll change the topic, and see what he has to say about his wife playing house with Pilday."

Yang nodded. "Sounds good to me."

A short time later they reached the Mitchell home and hoped that there wouldn't be any violence. Just in case, they readied their weapons and moved to the side of the door frame before ringing the bell.

Right away, they could hear movement inside the home but no one came to the door. Sensing a problem, Nagley urged the occupant to come to the door. A few minutes later, the occupant pulled at the door and revealed a very scared 30ish blonde woman with an ugly collection of fresh facial bruises. "This time I want to press charges," she said.

Detective Yang brushed aside some of the women's hair. "Yes ma'am, we know how to make that happen. The Lieutenant will stay here with you while I call for some assistance."

In short order, a black-and-white wheeled to the curb of Valerie Mitchell's home. Detective Yang explained the situation to the officer, who promptly whisked Ms. Mitchell to a safer setting.

Clearly, Mr. Mitchell was the violent type. For the moment, he would remain in the Pilday suspects' pool.

52

THE NEXT AFTERNOON Phillip's cellphone records came in, allowing the detectives to chase down anybody who had been in touch with him just before the murder.

Among those records, Roybal and Bramwell observed a bunch of calls between Phillip and a business identified as M.R.E.

Curious, the sergeant placed a call and quickly learned that it was a small real estate firm known as the Christine Mighty Real Estate Company. Neither Bramwell nor Roybal had heard of the company, so they made arrangements to drop by.

In a smallish office at the back of a shopping center, a middle-aged broker with a bob hairdo, a classy pink silk blouse and dark blue slacks rose from behind a conference table. "Hi there," she said, "I'm Christine Mighty. Judging by the badge on your belt, I'm guessing you're not here to buy a home."

Detective Roybal nodded. "We're investigating the death of Phillip Pilday and your name is on a list of people who may have known him."

Her eyes widened. "Phillip? Dead? Really? I'm sorry to hear that. No wonder he quit taking my calls. What happened?"

"Gunned down while in his vehicle."

"That's really sad. He was a nice guy."

"Like we said, we have information indicating you may have been in touch with him recently. Is that the case?"

Ms. Mighty pursed her lips, but didn't quickly reply.

Bramwell sighed. "Let me make this simpler for you. You don't want to get caught lying to us or withholding information. That is considered a 'lie by omission,' and we'll have even more questions for you. So, I ask you again. What was your relationship with Mr. Pilday?" she asked.

"Alright, I was trying to make him into a client, so I slept with him once or twice," she said matter-of-factly.

"But you are wearing a wedding ring. Did your husband know about Mr. Pilday?"

Mighty looked back and forth between Bramwell and Roybal. "If you don't know, there is a ton of competition between real estate brokers."

"Keep going."

"Phillip was a potential buyer, but buyers don't have to be loyal to any particular broker unless they sign an exclusive arrangement."

"So, you are competing for a commission. How much money are we talking about?"

"Total commissions can be thirty thousand dollars or more, per house. The buyer's agent and seller's agent usually split the pot in some way."

Roybal whistled. "I'm in the wrong business."

Mighty nodded. "What I'm about to say doesn't apply to everybody, but in the right circumstances certain brokers get attached to their clients and they are more than willing to get extra-friendly with those clients if it locks down a buyer's signature and leads to one of those hefty commissions. Think about it. A lot of folks will roll around in the rack for a couple hours if they can net thousands of dollars and have fun doing it. I know brokers who have been doing that very thing for years. Other brokers might throw in some illegal drugs or a trip to Las Vegas, just to lock down the exclusive rights to that commission."

Bramwell scrunched her nose. "You don't hump your clients in the homes that you're trying to sell, do you?"

"I can't speak for everybody, but I only do it if the home is vacant or the owners are out of the way. Whatever it takes." She smiled proudly.

"So, what does your husband think of your arrangement with those clients?"

"Are you kidding? He loves it. Where else can we make two hundred thousand dollars per year?"

"Where is he now?"

"He's home, cleaning the bathroom."

"Alright then, give me his number. I'm going to call him right now and have him come down here. If he confirms all this, I think we can remove your name from our list."

"No problem."

While they all waited for Jalen Mighty to arrive and confirm Christine's story, the detectives had a few remaining questions.

"What do you know about Mr. Pilday's wife?" Bramwell probed.

"Not a lot. Phillip said she was getting out of jail, and he was considering getting a different home for the two of them. That's how I met him. Now I lose a big commission and I gotta find some other buyer. Do you guys mind if I make some calls while we wait?"

"Just don't call your husband. I don't want you passing information back and forth."

A few phone calls later, Ms. Mighty was removed from the detectives' list.

"That was strange," Roybal said to his boss, as they returned to their car.

Bramwell shrugged. "Regardless, her husband confirmed her story, and I couldn't detect any signals to indicate either was lying."

"Besides that," Roybal said, "they wouldn't kill a man who is worth thousands to them alive and worth nothing if he is dead."

Sergeant Bramwell smiled. "That too."

"What's next?"

"Good question. According to Francie Baker, a customer by the name of Marjorie Daniels had invited Phillip over one Sunday evening. She may have knowledge about Phillip's attacker, or she may have been involved."

A short drive later, a thin and visibly nervous smoker invited Bramwell and Roybal to come in.

Once inside, it appeared as if Marjorie was so distraught that she may have been harboring a huge secret that she wanted to get off her chest. After a few basic questions, the source of her stress was revealed to have come from a different matter.

She advised the detectives that just before meeting Phillip Pilday, her boyfriend had dumped her and moved away in the middle of the night with another lover.

Marjorie said that she had wandered into Wilson's and almost invited Phillip to spend the night, but Phillip seemed to read her and suggested they get together some other time. Thus, they never got out of the starting box, let alone make it to the finish line.

In the end, "almost having sex" with a decent man under those conditions was not illegal, nor did it constitute a motive for murder. Hence, Bramwell and Roybal scratched Marjorie off their list.

53

After reviewing Pilday's phone records and comparing names to numbers, Lieutenant Nagley and his bag-man, Detective Yang, created a new list of folks who might have information regarding Phillip's death.

Eventually, Nagley said to Yang, "I still think that Ms. Pilday is our most likely perp, but according to both Francie Baker and Mr. Wilson, there's a woman named Tawny Jones who comes into their bar regularly. It's believed that she and Phillip shared pillows more than once. Let's go check her out."

At their destination, an average-looking, 45ish brunette with red eyes opened the door. "You must be the police," she said.

"Yes, ma'am," Nagley said. "And you must be Tawny Jones. May we come in?"

Inside, the detectives sat on a large, plush sofa. After being advised that they were there to discuss Phillip's death, the woman appeared to be genuinely saddened.

Nagley said, "We have received copies of Phillip's phone records and your number came up multiple times. Anybody on our list could have played a role in Mr. Pilday's passing and that includes you. So, we want to eliminate you as a possible perpetrator and to determine if you know anybody else whom we should check out."

"This is very sad, but go ahead."

"For starters, how did you find out about Mr. Pilday's accident?"

"I got a call from Mr. Wilson yesterday. He said that Phillip was shot while in his car and that you guys are investigating. As I said, I'm deeply saddened."

"Yes, ma'am. It appears he was a nice man, but somebody had a grudge against him."

"So, what do you want to know?"

"Thank you. We have reason to believe that Mr. Pilday's demise could have been due to an intimate relationship of some sort. Just how close were you?"

"Not real close. I met him at the bar when he was hired as a waiter. He was a sweet man, younger than me."

"Were the two of you involved romantically?"

"That's awfully personal, isn't it?"

"Sorry ma'am, but 'jealousy' is a very common motive for murder."

"Okay, I get it. We had a few rendezvous—twice at his place and once here."

"Did you know he was married?"

"Yes. I knew that his wife was in prison and about to get out. Both Phillip and I had symbiotic relationships with somebody else so we were kindred spirits in a way."

"What's that?" Detective Yang asked.

"We were both temporarily trapped by our spouse's circumstances, so we filled each other's voids."

"How so?"

"Well, his wife is a wise woman. As I heard it, she knew that it would be difficult to keep him in line if she tried to control him from inside prison, so she backed off and let him play around a little bit. It worked too."

"What about you?" Yang went on. "You said you were also trapped. What's that all about?"

"Easy. I don't have much of a life because my husband isn't really a husband."

"Clarify that."

"Gando is a very nice man who I met after his wife died. He didn't want his daughters to lose their sense of family, so he hired me to be their surrogate mother. To enhance the arrangement, Gando and I referred to ourselves as husband and wife, even though he was a lot older than me and more like a big brother."

"That's interesting."

"His daughters knew the truth but we all played along. It worked well for four years, until Gando had a stroke - several others followed. Then, I became his full-time caregiver because the daughters deserved lives of their own.

"All of that made it difficult for me to have any kind of normal life, but a girl doesn't want to wilt like a dead flower. So, Phillip and I were playmates with no aspirations of getting serious."

"Alright. Where is Gando now?"

"Upstairs, in his room. That's why it smells bad in here."

"Oh really?" The Lieutenant said. "As you might expect, Ms. Jones, it's our job to verify these things. Can Gando corroborate your statements?"

"Not possible. He's comatose. Can't carry on a conversation."

"Then, you wouldn't mind introducing us to him. Right?"

"Suit yourselves."

Minutes later and in Gando's room, it was obvious that the man couldn't function. However, Nagel noticed a box of large bandages on a tray near the head of the bed and scooted closer. He pointed at a long, red scar on Gando's temple. "What happened here?"

"The bruise on his face?" Tawny asked while gently patting Gando's forehead. "A couple weeks ago, Phillip was helping me change the sheets and accidently dropped my sweet friend down the side of the bed, which scraped his face. The scar won't go away."

"That must have been one heck of a wound."

"We had to take him to the hospital. It looks better now."

"I'm not surprised and I can tell that you love this man in some way."

"I owed it to him. Like I said, he was very nice to me when I needed him most."

Nagley motioned to his subordinate. "Get a couple pictures of this."

Back in the living room, Nagley's investigation continued. "What would happen if Gando were to die suddenly?"

"What do you mean?"

"Well, who would get the home?"

"I don't know, but not me."

"It makes me think of other cases involving wounded seniors. Sometimes people are not fit for that type of care. In other cases, the caregivers end up stealing everything of value that the patient owns. You wouldn't be doing that, would you?"

"That's ridiculous. Ask anybody."

"I plan to do that. Like I said, we want to eliminate you as our perpetrator, so we are going to speak with the doctors who last worked on your friend. I want to see if this wound was just a one-time thing or if there is something nefarious going on. I've got a hunch that you'll be cleared. I just want another opinion."

Tawny's jaw sank and the color went out of her cheeks. "Go ahead. I wouldn't hurt my Gando. Honest."

54

After Lieutenant Nagley rounded up a number of leads from Phillip's phone records, credit cards and word of mouth, he gave Sergeant Bramwell and Detective Roybal some leads to chase down.

While walking to their car, Bramwell spoke to her partner. "Both Wilson and Francie Baker said we should check out Jerrie Jean Bedford. She lives twenty minutes from here and she is waiting for us to drop by."

On the correct block, Roybal pointed to the home. "Two cars in the driveway. Looks like Ms. Bedford is not alone."

Bramwell nodded. "Get a picture of the license plates, just in case."

At the door, Jerrie Jean said, "I hope you guys don't mind but my husband wanted to be here."

Suddenly a nondescript fellow wiggled himself into the door frame. "Hi. I'm Russell. Come on in."

Inside, when everybody was seated, Russell addressed the sergeant. "A black detective, eh? How long you been in law enforcement?"

"Long enough, but I'm not here to talk about me." She turned to Jerrie Jean. "As I said on the phone, we're trying to find Mr. Pilday's killer and your name is on a list of people who might know what happened."

"Sure. The three of us had a couple beers at the bar, but I sure as hell don't know why my name would be on any killer list."

"Me neither," Russell added.

"I didn't say you are a suspect. I'm just trying to see if you have any information that might be helpful in our investigation. Do either of you know anybody who may have had a grudge with Mr. Pilday?"

Russell turned to Jerrie Jean. "What about his wife? He talked about her."

Jerrie Jean raised her eyebrows. "That's true. While she was in jail, Phillip plugged any woman that walked. He said that she couldn't do a damn thing about it. If you ask me, she had a huge motive to get rid of him."

"Anybody in particular?"

"The only person I can think of is another grandma-type who hangs out at that same bar. Her name is Tammy or something like that. According to Phillip, he rode that plow horse a bunch of times. He also said that she had an awful temper."

"Anybody else?"

"No. Not really."

"In that case, ma'am, how would you characterize your own relationship with Mr. Pilday?"

"Me? I ain't going to lie to ya. We were 'friendly' a few times."

Russell raised a finger. "That's why me and Jerrie Jean got married. Show them your ring, honey."

Jerrie Jean smiled and lifted her left hand, revealing a modest ring.

"Yeah, I saw that," Bramwell said.

"Me and Jerrie Jean have two kids," Russell offered, "but we never tied the knot. When that Phillip guy started hanging around my family, I pulled my head out of my ass and asked Jerrie Jean to marry me. Ain't that right, honey?"

"Yep. I finally trapped you." She faced the detectives. "We

wanted to do it right away, but we couldn't take the kids out of school, so we found a funky minister up the road aways. They had witnesses and everything."

"When was that?" Bramwell asked.

"Roughly ten days ago, on a Friday. Based on what you said when you called me for this meeting, I think it was the same day that Phillip died."

"Okay. I have one more question. Do you mind if we look around your home?"

"Why?"

"I want to see if you have any guns that match the caliber of the gun that killed Mr. Pilday."

"Nope. Don't got nothing like that. You can look, but don't take too long. The kids are going to be home soon and we don't want to freak them out by having scary strangers in here."

After having completed her search, Bramwell spoke to both Jerrie Jean and Russell. "It appears you've got yourselves a solid alibi, but we like to verify things. I need contact information for your minister, if you don't mind."

"Sure thing," Jerrie Jean said while whipping out a pen and a small notepad.

"Before we leave," the sergeant said, "let me ask you something else. Did either of you kill Phillip?"

Russell stiffened. "Why do you ask that? We already told you we were at our wedding when that accident happened."

"I was just double-checking. I think we have what we need for now. If you think of anybody else, let us know."

"We sure will," Russell said, walking toward the door.

"Thank you. We might have to visit you again sometime."

"You folks do that," Russell said "We ain't got nothing to hide."

Moments later out on the porch, Roybal heard Russell whisper something to Jerrie Jean behind the door.

55

Detective Roybal waited until he and his superior got out of Russell and Jerrie Jean's hearing range. "That guy was awfully arrogant. Did you get any poker-like tells out of them?"

Bramwell smiled. "I think so. Russell was so animated he was difficult to read, but Jerrie Jean had an interesting gesture."

"Really? What was it?"

"Oh, no, you don't. A good poker player doesn't reveal her secrets to just anybody. I'll let you know if it comes up again. In the meantime, there's no rest for the wicked, so it's back to work for us."

"Yes, ma'am," Roybal said. "What kind of magic do we have up our sleeves this time?"

"Earlier, something on Mr. Pilday's credit card statement caught my attention. If I'm correct, it's a one-time thing and we can eliminate another person from our list, but first we're going to have to make a few preliminary calls, then we can report to the Lieutenant."

As planned, they checked Phillip's credit card account again and placed a bunch of fruitless calls until the Sergeant finally had the answer to her question. She called Nagley with an update.

"What you got?" the Lieutenant asked.

"It looks like we can eliminate the hygienist."

"Details, please?"

"Yes, sir. Mr. Wilson suggested that Phillip took a two-day motorcycle ride with one of his customers. Since we didn't know the woman's name, we scanned Phillip's credit card records for the shop where Phillip rented a big trike and then the motel where Pilday and the hygienist stayed."

"Very well. Then what?"

"Chico and I called a slew of dental offices and asked if any of their employees had frequented that particular motel in recent months."

"And?"

"A Lydia Cornell answered the bell. She was fairly stoic when she heard about Pilday's demise, but we learned that she had not dated him after that first time. We also learned that she was at work when Phillip was killed."

"Did she have any dirt on Miranda Pilday?"

"No. She said she knew of Miranda, but Miranda didn't know about her."

"Okay. You're correct, we can remove our hygienist from our list and move on. Good job, Sergeant."

56

After a sad and lonely night, I elected to visit my husband's resting place, which was near the end of a row where the sod had recently been disturbed and there was a temporary wooden headstone.

"I try to be nice to her," I eventually said to Phillip's spirit, "but when Juju appropriated her belongings, she effectively thought me a thief.

"I wish I could convince her that her

paranoia is unfounded because I really do respect all of your family members in one way or another."

Before long, my mind wondered to Trevor and then back to Phillip, where I asked him questions and then answered those questions as he might do. Among other things, I thought that he would want me to exhibit patience with Juju. After all, he loved us both, so there had to be some common ground somewhere.

Eventually, I kissed my fingers and tapped the wooden headstone.

With some of my misery tucked away, I drove past a vacuum cleaner store where there was a Help Wanted sign, plus another sign that indicated that they had refurbished vacuums for sale. I would have preferred to spend my limited resources on more glamorous things, but twenty minutes later

I had a job application in hand and a refurbished vacuum to replace the one that Juju had confiscated.

A short time later, I observed a Help Wanted sign on the window of a McDonald's. All those signs indicated that there were plenty of entry-level jobs around, so I was certain I could find some decent work and begin to rebuild my life.

Back home, I called Juju again. This time she answered, so I followed some advice of my pro bono attorney.

I remained calm while I informed her that I'd been to the cemetery to see Phillip. "I think he would like us to patch up our differences," I said.

Juju clicked her tongue behind her teeth, but didn't reply.

"I promise I'll get out of your home as soon as I possibly can, Juju, but I have the legal right to stay here for a little longer.

"I've also started looking for a job. If you're still listening, I've spoken with an attorney. If Phillip doesn't have a will, a lot of the things that you took out of here belong to me now, but I know they mean more to you than they do to me, so you can have them all."

She remained silent.

"I can hear you breathing, Juju. Can't you say something?"

"Okay. Get out of my home!"

"I already told you I can't do that right now. Besides, If I were to move on, the police might suspect that I had something to do with Phillip's death and that I'm trying to get away. I couldn't withstand that extra stress."

"Everything is always about you, isn't it, inmate?"

"No, it isn't, Juju, but I have real feelings too. I've lost my husband, just like you have, and my heart aches just like yours does. Would you be more comfortable with me if I were to pay you some rent money right away?"

"Now, that is priceless. Unless I'm mistaken, the only money you have is in Phillip's checking account, but he gets his money from a trust that my husband and I gave him, so if you were to pay rent from his checking account, you'd simply be returning my own money to me."

"I understand your point, but I've already put in several job applications."

Then I heard the click. I sorta understood Juju's hostilities. For the better part of five years, she had been her grandson's cheerleader, but he was taken away from all of us.

Feeling empty, I thought again of finding a canine companion.

57

Several days had passed since Juju heard from the detectives so she looked through the storage box that she had confiscated from Phillip's closet.

Toward the middle of the box, she located a folder with two life insurance policies and some notes. She extracted the folder and scanned the policies.

There was a modest amount of technical mumbo-jumbo but she got the gist of the polices and liked something in particular. She quickly called Detective Yang and set an appointment for the next morning.

The following morning, Nagley and Yang arrived on time. After the niceties, Juju pointed to her dining room table. "The policies are over there, complete with Phillip's notes. One of those policies could be Ms. Miranda's motive to kill my grandson. I'm sure of it."

"Okay let's have a look."

"Both policies are for fifty thousand dollars," Juju said. "The first one is for Phillip's partners. His note says he had a contract with them to provide enough money to finish their software app if something were to happen to him."

"That kind of thing is common in businesses," Nagley offered.

"Yeah, but the other policy is for Miranda. I'm not an expert at any of this, but that sure seems like a motive to me."

Yang looked up. "You just might have something here."

"'Course I do; we all know that my grandson's wife has been around shady characters for years. She could easily hire one of those goons. All she'd have to do after that is pay the hit man and keep everything else for herself."

Yang raised his head again. "Looky here. The back pages have double-indemnity clauses."

"Yeah, I saw that," Juju said, "but I don't exactly know what that means."

"Simple, the insurance company doubles the payout if the death is due to an accident as opposed to natural causes."

Juju whistled. "Are you saying that our convict could get one hundred thousand dollars for killing my grandbaby?"

"It wouldn't be the first time. Of course, we'll have to verify everything with the company that wrote the policies."

"What about his partners?"

"What about them?"

"They have a monetary motive too. If Miranda didn't kill my Phillip, then maybe they did it for the money."

"Doubt it. We already cleared them."

"I guess you're right. Those guys already have a bright future, so they wouldn't need to do that, but Miranda is as poor as a cockroach. She needs money. In fact, Phillip's coin collection is already missing."

"Oh really? how valuable is it?"

"I don't know. He got most of them from his grandfather."

"Most circulated coins aren't very valuable," Nagley said.

"Well then, can I ask you guys something else?"

"Yes, ma'am."

"I want that woman out of my rental house and the sooner the better, but she found some hot-shot attorney who said she could stay for a month or longer. That isn't true, is it, cause it's certainly not fair."

"'Sorry, ma'am that's not our department, but I'd suggest you check with an attorney of your own before jumping to conclusions."

"That's why I grabbed the pictures from the walls along with some other things. This way Miranda can't steal them, or pawn everything off, and there's no telling what other things Phillip had in his house. That convict could be ready to run off with everything, and that proves that she killed my grandson."

"Not quite, ma'am, but you've posed some interesting questions."

"But don't forget; she has a very shady history. I've always said that your people shouldn't have pardoned her."

"Well, it wasn't actually a pardon; they waived the remainder of her sentence, but I get your drift."

Nagley nodded. "Detective Yang is correct, ma'am, but this insurance policy might be fruitful. We'll look into it right away and let you know what we discover."

59

When Bramwell and Roybal initially interviewed Jerrie Jean and her husband it was asserted that their wedding just happened to coincide with Phillip's passing, which was an excellent alibi.

Regardless, Bramwell was a body language reader and she suspected that some of Jerrie Jean's gestures didn't always match her words, so Nagley taxed the detectives to do some additional digging.

Thus, a two-hour drive brought Bramwell and Roybal right to the driveway of a medium-sized frame home away from the city. At the rear of the gravel driveway, a pick-up truck and an SUV were parked in front of a four-car garage with over-sized doors. Two of the four doors were wide open, revealing enough broken-down furniture and useless bric-a-brac to open a small junkyard.

Almost instantly, a tail-wagging German Shepherd announced their arrival, which brought out a 40ish man, complete with well-worn coveralls and a lump of chewing tobacco under his lower lip. "Can I help you folks?" the man asked.

"Yes, sir," Bramwell said, with her badge wedged into her palm so he could see it. "We're looking for a minister named Brady Sullivan."

"That's me, but you don't got to be so formal. Call me Brady."

Wanting to get into the garage, Bramwell floated a question. "Thank you, Brady. Is there somewhere else where we can talk?"

Like a good boy, the odd-ball minister pointed his thumb over his shoulder toward an open garage door. "Follow me."

A tap on an automatic door-opener revealed a poor man's version of a man-cave. A big screen TV dangled over a Formica counter, and a hodgepodge of worn-out furniture could have blended in nicely at the local dump. "You folks can sit at the bar if you'd like. Can I get you a drink?"

"No, thanks," Reba said while observing several empty coffee cans on the floor. "If you don't mind my saying so, you don't look like a minister."

He grabbed a rusty coffee can from the floor, pivoted slightly and spit out a mouthful of gooey brown baccy. "I can assure you that I am licensed, but it's no big deal. Nearly anybody can get one. Just pay the fee and sign some papers."

"Do you have a lot of customers?" Roybal asked.

"Look around here. If I had a lot of customers, me and my wife would have nicer things."

"How do you get your customers?"

Brady wiped his mouth with a shop towel. "Usually by word of mouth. Once in a while I get a call off the internet."

"How did Russell Blackstone locate you?"

"So that's what this is about. I don't remember how he got my name, but a while back he called out of the blue and wanted to tie the knot with his girlfriend. My wife and a few other people were here so they were witnesses. I charged the newlyweds my standard fee: two hundred dollars and a keg of beer."

"Do you keep written records?"

"Got to. It's the law."

Bramwell smiled at the man. "If you don't mind, can we look at your records?"

In less time than it took to tuck a pinch of freshly shredded tobacco inside one's lower lip, Brady plopped a large notebook on the counter for review.

They only had to thumb past a half-dozen pages before Russell and Jerrie Jean's wedding registration page - complete with the same time and date as Phillip's death, plus signatures of three witnesses – confirmed what Russell and Jerrie Jean had claimed all along. Namely, they were getting married when Phillip Pilday was taken out.

Back in their car, Roybal spoke of the minister. "That dude may be as peculiar as they come, but anybody who only charges two hundred bucks and a keg of beer to put a ceremony together can't be all bad."

"The man is gross," Bramwell said.

"Did you get one of those 'tells' of yours?"

"Not this time. His spit-habit helped him conceal any nervous feelings."

"Regardless," Roybal said, "we found out what we wanted to know: Russell and Jerrie Jean had a wedding at the same time Pilday was shot, so they aren't Mr. Pilday's killers."

"It sure appears that way. I'll buzz the Lieutenant and fill him in."

"Bottom line," she told Nagley, "as ministers go, the dude is one-of-a-kind, but he has the credentials and complete records of the wedding."

"*Okay then,*" Nagley replied. "*That confirms the newlyweds' alibi and we can move on. Along those lines, we've got some news about Pilday's insurance policies.*"

"Go ahead, boss," Reba said. "You're on speaker. What did you learn?"

"*As you know, we had our own folks review the policies. They confirmed that the face amounts were as suspected: 50K each and double indemnity. However, we didn't know if the policies were still in effect. Additionally, companies like that don't release confidential information without approval from their clients or a court order. Bottom line, we had to get a court order."*

"Nothing is ever easy, boss."

"Yeah. That's why they pay us. Anyway, it took a little while, but we found out that Mr. Pilday's contract with his business partners legally required him to take out such a policy and name them as the beneficiaries in the event of his passing."

"That's just as we expected."

"Correct, but at the same time, Pilday took out a similar policy in which Miranda Pilday was the beneficiary."

"Also expected."

"Not entirely. Our victim paid the premiums for the first policy, but he stopped making payments on his wife's policy for some reason, and that voids our suspect's policy."

"Why would Phillip do that?" Roybal asked.

"Like any other insurance, it happens all the time. Sometimes they get a better policy elsewhere or they need the money for other things or it just slips through the cracks."

"And poof," Roybal said. "There goes Ms. Pilday's motive to kill her hubby."

"Maybe so," Nagley replied, *"but based on our previous conversations with Miranda, she doesn't know that the policy is void and I don't intend to tell her, because we can continue holding the money motive over her head and if she really is our perp, which I think she is, the pressure will ultimately squeeze a confession out of her."*

"Chalk one up for the good guys."

"There's one other thing: The insurance companies usually won't pay out while there's an ongoing investigation."

Bramwell spoke next. "That's a bummer for Phillip's partners."

"Not so. Their policy is completely separate from Mrs. Pilday's policy, and it's paid-up and current, so they're going to get their money before long. Now, what about you guys? What are you up to next?"

"We've got a date at a biker's bar concerning Tawny Jones."

"*Alright. Keep me posted.*"

60

I HADN'T HEARD FROM THE DETECTIVES for a few days so I called Lieutenant Nagley to find out why they hadn't caught the killer.

"What a coincidence," he said to me. *"Detective Yang and I have something to discuss with you. We'd like to drop by your place in an hour or so, if that's okay."*

At my dining table, I asked Lieutenant Nagley the obvious question. "Who are you talking to besides me?"

"I'm not at liberty to reveal that information to you right now."

"But I'm clear, right?"

"Thus far, we've cleared a number of people, but we have not been able to eliminate you or several other people."

"Maybe you're talking to the wrong people."

"I can tell you one thing. Most women in your situation are more devastated than you appear to be."

"What? That's crazy. I care a lot, but I've been disappointed so many times I'm pretty jaded. Then there's the other reason."

"Oh really," he said, while looking at Yang and back to me. "What other reason?"

"I've said this before. I definitely loved Phillip, but we didn't have any kids or a long history. Our relationship has been a part-time endeavor and probably not as deep as other marriages."

"Nevertheless, we're running out of leads, which means you're moving to the head of the class. If you did it, things will get a lot easier for you if you admit what you did."

"No. No. No. No matter how many times you guys try to pin this on me, I'm going to tell you the same thing. I had nothing to do with my husband's death because I loved him. Period!"

"If you say so, but things are looking worse for you."

"I don't know how anything could get worse."

Nagley turned to Detective Yang. "Show her the policy." Yang removed a few papers from a file he was holding and turned them so that I could get a look. "Do you know what this is?"

"The headline says it's a life insurance policy."

"Not just any policy, Ms. Pilday. We got it from your husband's grandmother. Do you see the second paragraph? How much money are we talking about?"

"Wait a minute. I know what that is. In my early years at the Lighthouse, Phillip and I were sitting on the patio when he said that he bought a life insurance policy for me. I loved the sentiment but I thought it was unwarranted."

"Nonetheless, he didn't throw it away. How much money are we talking about?"

I looked more closely. Then, I said, "Fifty thousand dollars."

"That's correct. And a few lines later, it says something about a beneficiary. Do you know what a beneficiary is?"

"Yes, and you don't have to be so damn condescending."

"That's the least of your worries. Bottom line, Phillip bought the policy for you. Any junior detective can tell you that a policy like that can easily morph into a motive for murder."

"Good for them."

"We're not done yet. I want you to take a look at the bottom of page two, where it says 'double indemnity.'"

I flipped to the spot, "Okay. So what?"

"That means that your husband wanted you to have an extra fifty thousand dollars if he died in an accident, which he did. Are you going to tell us that you didn't know about that, either?"

"Well, I'd say it proves something else. Phillip was an unselfish man, and anybody who knew him was lucky."

"Or, it could mean that you have a hundred thousand reasons to want your husband dead."

"Say what you want, but I'd say, it's a hundred thousand reasons to love him."

"I wouldn't be so cocky if I were you, Ms. Pilday. The insurance company tells us they don't pay the money while there's an active investigation going on, therefore the only way for you to end the investigation is to confess. 'Course, they don't pay the killers of their clients either, so you're screwed either way."

"Not if we catch who really did it."

"We've already drilled that well, and it keeps coming up dry. I can't prove it right now, but it's just a matter of time. You could have hired somebody to kill your husband for this insurance money or because he cheated on you. Why don't you just admit it? You'll feel better when you get this off your chest."

"And sometimes you people are wrong. You can push me around all you want. That doesn't make me guilty. It just proves that you're a bully."

Nagley sat back for a short time, then sighed.

"Alright, then, I know how we can clear up a few things. I'd like you to come to our building tomorrow for a polygraph. We can straighten this out right then. How does ten o'clock sound?"

"I'd rather not."

"Why not? An innocent person doesn't have anything to hide."

"It's not that. Those machines are unreliable, and you guys can manipulate everything."

"Well, I've got news for you. If we can't clear you, we'll be on your tail forever."

"Like I said, I'd rather not."

"Yeah, but you've spent a lot of time behind bars. You've made friends and contacts. It would be very easy for a person like that to hire somebody else to do her dirty work. A poly could reveal whether you did that or not."

Frustrated, I glared at him. "Don't you get it? I don't trust you people and your crystal balls."

He shook his head, then laid his handcuffs on the table in front of me. "You're the one who doesn't get it, Ms. Pilday? A person who avoids a poly is extremely suspicious. In fact, Juju thinks we should arrest you right now and she has a point. You have motives, and the opportunity, and you don't have an alibi. The way we see it, you're at the edge of a cliff. Are you going to save your ass or jump?"

Unfortunately, I was backed into a corner. If I took the poly, they might trip me up so that I appeared guilty, or I might get real nervous, or the test results could be inconclusive. In their minds that would be just as good as guilty.

More damning, it appeared as if Juju was fully prepared to testify against me. That would rip me to shreds emotionally and a jury would probably believe her. Distraught, I went against my better judgement and made an exception. "Alright. Alright. I'll do it."

"That's better," Nagley said in a cocky tone. "We'll see you at ten o'clock tomorrow. Don't be late."

61

After I agreed to take Nagley's damn polygraph test, I knew I'd made a gigantic mistake.

Due to my prison days, I'd seen a slew of people who had horror stories to tell about those tests. After all, there was a reason that courts didn't allow any testimony that was gleaned from those tests – they simply weren't one-hundred percent reliable.

As fresh paranoia nibbled at me, I remembered OJ Simpson's case and other criminal cases in which crooked authorities planted evidence on somebody to get a successful conviction. I didn't want to be the next one.

In a worst-case scenario, Nagley and Yang could frame me somehow, and I'd get a one-way ticket to a big-girl's prison for the rest of my life. There would be no freedom, no sunsets, no Trevor – just jumpsuits, hopelessness and tears.

The more I thought about it, the more I regretted telling the Lieutenant that I would take the damn test. It would be a lot safer to get the hell out of there until the real killer was caught.

The detectives were expecting me at 10:00, so I had some time before they could figure out that I wasn't coming in. There was no telling what would happen after that, but I wanted to get as far away from the drama as possible.

I packed two large suitcases of clothes and some toiletries into the car that Phillip gave me. Then I grabbed my cell phone and realized that investigators frequently track such phones, so I left both the phone and my laptop on the kitchen table.

With such a small footprint, I could go virtually anywhere without Nagley or anybody else finding me. The question for the moment was, where should I go? One option was to chase down Trevor if possible, but I elected to do something else first.

Nearly three hours later I arrived at Dixie's Doggie Shelter, where I had worked part-time for the last year of my incarceration. I remembered a cute pug named Elmer and I hoped he was still there. When he saw me, his fast-wagging tail proved that he remembered me too.

A short time later I went into Dixie's office where we shared a mama bear-sized hug. "I'd like to adopt Elmer," I said. "That is, if he's not reserved for somebody else."

My friend's toothy grin revealed that I'd hit a happy nerve. "He's been waiting for you, Miranda."

After another happy hug and a little paperwork, I bought a used doggie carrier from Dixie and rushed for Elmer's outdoor cage. My cute little gangster-faced lap dog jumped into my arms.

Before leaving, Elmer and I slipped back into the office, where I borrowed Dixie's computer and checked out a few things that I'd been wondering about.

Having finished my self-assigned first step, I got in the front seat with Elmer. We had a great conversation while I drove across town, toward a used-car lot. "Their website said they buy 'Any Car For Cash,'" I said to my four-legged buddy.

While we followed the traffic, I knew this was a lot of paranoia for an innocent person, but I also knew a few things about police investigators. Some of them play dirty, and I sure didn't want to be dragged into an interrogation room where they might even declare that they'd found the gun that killed my husband under my bed and blame it on me.

"At a time like that," I said to Elmer, "they whisk you away and lock you in a cage. Neither of us need to be reminded how awful that is."

Out of self-preservation, I thought it wise to get away from those crazy people. Then they'd have to leave me alone and look for the real perp.

About that time, we arrived at Kosar's Fair Deal Car Lot, which I had located when I borrowed Dixie's computer. "It's a good thing that Phillip gave me all the car's papers," I thought, while opening the glove box.

I rolled down Elmer's window so he'd have plenty of air and I moved toward the front door. Almost instantly, Elmer whimpered. I knew how it felt to be deserted, so I marched back to the car and put him in his little travel case and we went for the office.

62

"It's better to get all cash," I said to the young salesman who met me at the entrance to Kosar's Used Cars.

At first, he thought I was there to trade my vehicle for something nicer, but when I said I was a seller, not a buyer, he called in the owner.

Back in the lot a pudgy man with black slacks and a white belt approached. "I'm Oliver Kosar," the new guy said while glancing at my car. A couple of tire kicks later, he observed my suitcases in the back seat. "You coming or going?" he asked.

Since I was trying to travel incognito, I told him a complete fib just in case somebody should come looking for me. "I'm going to Mesa, Arizona, to stay with my sister-in-law."

The man had no reason to doubt me, so he went into his office where he looked up the value of my car on his computer. A minute later, he spun the monitor my way. Come to find out my car was worth nineteen thousand dollars.

"Of course, that's the retail price," Kosar said. "I can't give you that much because we have to fix anything that's broken and guarantee the vehicle for 90 days - plus make a profit when we sell it."

"Okay. How much can you give me?"

He shrugged. "You said you wanted 'real cash;' is that

absolute, because I can give you a little more if you take a check."

"I still prefer cash."

"Okay, If you insist on getting cash, I guess we could give you around thirteen thousand dollars, but like I said, I can get you another thousand bucks if you take a voucher to our bank and get the money there. That way we don't have to deplete our cash."

I knew for certain that I didn't want to be on a bank's surveillance cameras. I also suspected that Oliver would jump over the moon for a five-thousand-dollar profit, so I offered to accept fifteen thousand dollars.

We bartered for a couple rounds and ended up agreeing to fourteen thousand dollars in real cash, plus a ride to a nearby shopping mall that I'd discovered earlier, thanks to Dixie's computer.

After signing a few papers, I stuffed the money in my purse, the young salesman drove Elmer and me and my bags to a modest nearby mall. Along the way, it occurred to me that any of the folks who worked at Oliver's dealership could call a shady friend of theirs and reveal where they could find a single woman with a purse full of cash.

A few nervous moments later, we pulled into the mall and located the beauty salon where I was allowed to bring my bags and dog carrier inside while I got my hair cut and dyed dark brown.

While the beautician did her thing, I noted that it was well past the ten o'clock poly appointment that I had with Nagley and Yang. Glad to be far away, I wondered what their next move might be, if anything.

After my hair was done, I looked ten years younger. I was allowed to leave my bags in the corner while I took Elmer with me to a bench in the center of the mall.

After extracting my little friend from his carrier, I scratched his head and marveled at my clever use of Dixie's computer to find both Kosar's Car lot and the beauty shop in the mall, but I wasn't finished.

My next goal was to find a completely different vehicle so that Nagley wouldn't know what to look for. Thanks to Craigslist I located a high school kid who wanted to sell his Jeep. That enabled me to drive to find the Montgomerys and learn whatever I could about my son.

Naturally, I could have taken a plane to Cincinnati and back, but that would've required me to show my ID, and could have blown my cover for Nagley and his friends. Plus, now I had a dog.

I patted my four-legged buddy on the head and included him in a conversation. "After we get some sleep, Elmer, you and I are going to Cincinnati to find out where Trevor is. This may be the only chance in my whole life to meet him. I can't ignore that.

"But first, I'm going to take you to the pet store over there and get you some real good food; then we can go get a hot dog for me."

63

When Miranda Pilday didn't show up for her poly, Lieutenant Nagley sent Detective Yang to her house, but neither Miranda nor her car were there.

The detectives elected to give her until sundown to make alternate arrangements, but when that came and went, it appeared that Miranda had run away. Naturally, the detectives' suspicions regarding her husband's mysterious death intensified.

As murder suspects go, Miranda had several strikes against her, but Nagley et al couldn't put the murder weapon in her hand nor put her at the scene of the crime. With that many holes in their case, the lie detector could have made a big difference.

Considering the circumstances, Yang called Phillip's grandmother and asked if they could come over to ask more questions of both Juju and Ellen.

By the time the detectives got there, Phillip's sister had arrived and completed the small group. "Did you arrest that convict yet?" Juju asked the detectives.

Ellen openly sighed. "I wish you'd quit calling her that, Juju. I've spoken with her several times and she's obviously not the killer."

"Regardless," Nagley said, "we go where the evidence

is and we have assembled some strong circumstantial evidence, but we need more. That's why we set Mrs. Pilday up with our polygrapher."

"I bet she flunked it."

"No ma'am. She didn't even show up as requested."

"Ah-ha! Did you hear that, Ellen? Why would that woman be hiding if she's innocent? As far as I am concerned that's more proof that she's the one who set up our beloved Phillip."

"It may be suspicious, Juju, but it doesn't prove anything. She could have forgotten about the appointment or changed her mind or had a medical emergency. I happen to know that she's been talking with attorneys lately. Maybe one of them is getting involved."

Yang smiled at Ellen. "How do you know so much?"

"Me? I watch crime shows on TV and I read a lot."

"Well, you're correct, but you forgot one thing. Sometimes friends or family members provide sanctuary for their troubled loved ones."

Juju sat forward. "What the hell are you talking about, Mister? If you're implying that we are hiding Miranda, that is an insult to our entire family."

"I don't doubt you, but your granddaughter is correct too. There are lots of rabbit holes in a case like this."

"That's right," Nagley said. "To be perfectly honest, Phillip has charmed quite a few ladies. Since romance and jealousy are common motives for murder, any one of those ladies could know what happened or have been involved in his passing. For now, we can tell you that the absence of your brother's wife is indeed suspicious."

"I have a question about lie-detectors," Ellen said. "Why are they still in use when they are inadmissible in court?"

"Good question," Yang said. "Think of them as an A-minus in school; they are very good, but not perfect, and crimes have to be proven 'beyond a reasonable doubt' to apply."

"Regardless," Nagley said. "If we don't find Mrs. Pilday pretty soon, we're going to officially elevate her status to a full-blown 'suspect.'"

"Good," Juju said, "And stop calling her 'Mrs. Pilday.' You can call her anything else but she is not a Pilday. None of us behave like that."

"I'll try to remember that, ma'am. Nonetheless, we already went by your rental house. There was no sign of her or her car. In the meantime, we need to know where she might have gone. Do either of you have any ideas along those lines?"

"I do," Ellen said. "Miranda has a son in Cincinnati, whom she has never met. His name is Trevor. She and Phillip were planning a trip to see the boy, but that's when Phillip was killed."

"Okay. Do you have any names or contact information?"

Suddenly, Juju perked up. "Now that you mention it, I think I know their names."

She went to the back bedroom and retrieved the box that had the life insurance file in it and removed the lid. "Yeah, here it is, right on the front of this folder. Looks like one of them is Bertie Montgomery. There's even a phone number."

The lieutenant grinned. "Now we're cooking."

64

Call it a hunch, or a woman's intuition, or a poker player's tells, but when Sergeant Bramwell was resting in her lounge chair at home, she had an epiphany. She had had second thoughts about the registration book that she and her partner had viewed in the garage of that off-beat minister.

The page concerning the marriage of Russell Blackstone and Jerrie Jean Bedford seemed in order, and was perfectly written. All the other pages in the book were as sloppy as a D student's handwritten book report. Why would that be?

The good sergeant considered calling Lieutenant Nagley to withdraw her previous statements regarding Jerrie Jean and Russell's alibi for the time of Phillip's death, but she had just stirred up new doubts about her other doubts.

While she thought it over, she grabbed a bottle of wine and watched some TV until she finally fell asleep.

The next morning, and with very little sleep, the talented sergeant called the boss. "I know this sounds like I'm a mixed-up teenager who can't make up her mind," she said to Nagley, "but I'd like to take Detective Roybal for another look at that wedding book."

"Isn't that place a couple hours away?"

"Yes, it is."

"*Couldn't you just call them and ask for a copy of the page in question?*"

"Not really. I don't want to give them a chance to mess with the evidence."

"*I get that, but it's a long shot and we have other people to interview. What about that other woman — that Tawny Jones and her hot-headed brother? She's also a potential suspect. Have you pinned them down?*"

"I haven't had a chance to check with the doctors, but I should be able to verify the brother's whereabouts at the time of Phillip's death."

"*How are you going to do that?*"

"According to Francie at Wilson's place, the brother hangs out at Bikes and Babes Bar. It's frequented by small motorcycle gangs, so they have good surveillance cameras."

"*I'd rather you chase down that lead and help me squeeze Miranda Pilday. She's much more likely to be our perp than those other people.*"

"In that case, I'd like to take one of my vacation days and check out that minister again on my own time. I know that it might be a wild goose chase, but I've got to follow my hunch."

"*Alright then, if you'd rather waste a vacation day than follow our basic agenda, that's up to you. I'm certain that the citizens of California will appreciate your generous donation of your time.*"

"Okay. What about Detective Roybal? Can I bring him along?"

"*Same deal. I don't care what you two do with your own time, but I don't want to chase long shots until we have to.*"

When Royal joined the Sergeant for their usual rounds, she told him, "I can't thank you enough for helping me, but before we hit the road, I want to drive by Jerrie Jean's home."

"Oh, yeah? What's over there?"

"Simple. If she and Russell are involved in Mr. Pilday's death, Jerrie Jean is the weaker link. I'm hoping Russell is off to work and we can catch her alone."

At Jerrie Jean's home, there was no sign of Russell's vehicle.

"Looks like you nailed it," Chico Roybal said. "What's the play?"

"I've been trying to get a read on this woman, but her husband has dominated the conversations."

"I get it. You want to see if she has any of those 'tells' that you speak about."

"Exactly. I'm going to blow smoke up her ass and see if that starts a fire."

"Sounds painful."

When Jerrie Jean answered the door, Bramwell stepped back. "Hi, Jerrie Jean. You remember us. I'm Sergeant Bramwell. This is Detective Roybal. We'd like to verify a couple things so that we can get you and Russell off our radar. May we come in?"

Jerrie Jean must have liked the tune of that song because she nodded, stepped aside and the three of them slid into the living room. "Before we begin," the Sergeant said, "I've been wondering if anybody has ever told you that you have a very lovely smile?"

"Huh. I guess so."

"Did you inherit it from one of your parents or did you have braces?"

"No braces. My dad has a nice smile."

"I'm jealous. I bet that smile has turned the heads of many men."

Jerrie Jean smiled. "You said something about removing Russell and me from your murder case?"

"That's true. The first thing we want to do is verify some simple things regarding your background."

"Okay."

"I understand that your birthday is February 29; is that accurate?"

"Yeah. I'm a leap-year baby. I'm thirty-four years old, but I've only had eight birthdays."

"That's interesting. Were you born in California?"

"Yes."

"It says here that you've lived in this home for more than five years; is that true?"

Jerrie Jean nodded.

"Lastly, we've got your children's names as Nickie and Johnny. Can you confirm that for me?"

"Yes, but why do you need that?"

"There's a new book in our industry. It predicts that stable people are less likely to commit major crimes. I think you would score above average, so I'd like to be thorough. Just give me a quick answer, then I'll get to the main point of our meeting today."

"What was the question again?"

"Are your kids named Johnny and Nickie?"

Jerrie Jean nodded.

"Okay, moving on, once before I asked you and Russell if you knew anything about Phillip's death and you said no. Do you remember that?"

"Yes."

"And I believe you. Oh, that reminds me, the last time we were here, when we left, Detective Roybal and I heard Russell and you giggling behind the door. People don't usually derive amusement from somebody's death."

"Well, Russell didn't like Phillip, so he was just being silly. He's always been like that."

"But you were giggling too."

"I know, but I was faking it – to keep the peace with Russell. After all, we haven't been married very long. I wanted him to know I'm on his team."

"If you were 'just faking it,' as you say, then you could have had feelings for Phillip and hidden those feelings from Russell. Is that what you're saying now?"

Jerrie Jean clenched her jaw. Then she said, "Not really."

"Which is it? Were you relieved because your secret lover died before Russell knew the full extent of your relationship or were you lying to Russell about your feelings for Phillip?"

"If you put it that way, I guess I was done with Phillip and looking forward to a family life with Russell and my kids."

"That's what I thought, and I don't have any additional questions. Thanks for your time."

65

"THAT WAS PRETTY IMPRESSIVE," Detective Roybal said when he and the sergeant were back in their car. "Now we know that Jerrie Jean's hot button is her kids."

"We learned more than that. She has a tiny tick in the corner of her mouth when she fibs. We may need to know that."

"Clever. What else?"

"That phony survey exposed that she has a short fuse and gets frustrated easily. She's definitely our weakest link. Now we're going to the minister's place again."

"Fine by me. For what purpose?"

"I advised the Lieutenant about the inconsistencies in the registration book, but there was something else that caught my attention since the last time we were there."

"Really? What?"

"I didn't say anything to Nagley because he was already in a negative mode, but can you think back to the last time we were in Minister Brady's garage?"

"Yeah, I remember it pretty well. It needed a good cleaning."

"Did you notice the resemblance between Minister Brady and Russell Blackstone?"

"No. I didn't notice anything like that, but it's probably just a coincidence. Everybody looks like somebody else."

"Perhaps, but they both have a prominent widow's peak and only a small percentage of the population has those."

"What the heck is a widow's peak?"

"A V-shaped hairline. You've probably seen them. If these two guys are related, neither of them wanted us to know about it."

"But they have different last names."

"They could be cousins or half-brothers with different dads."

"Well, it's a stretch, but it won't hurt to ask him about it."

"That's what I think, too. Another objective is to get the contact info of the wedding witnesses. I want to find out if they will confirm the wedding ceremony."

"In that case, it would probably be the least suspicious to take a picture of the entire registration page."

"Agreed. People in these outer neighborhoods have a strong sense of community. If they think their neighbors are in some sort of trouble, they just might sweep the secrets under the proverbial rug."

"I get that. Folks like to hang with people they can relate to."

"Right. In the meantime, I need you to shift your thoughts to one of our other potential suspects."

"Sure. I can do that. Who we talking about?"

"Tawny Jones. The Lieutenant wants to know what the doctors thought when Phillip and Ms. Jones brought her special friend to the hospital, after he fell out of bed. Nagley spoke with them once before, but they haven't called back."

"They're probably very busy."

"Too bad. We're busy, too. Remind them that we're talking about a homicide and senior abuse. We need to know if Jones and Pilday were pissed off at each other when they arrived at the hospital. If that is true, it could mean that she or her colorful brother wanted Pilday dead."

"Let me get that straight. You're thinking that the biker guy could have killed Phillip because he dropped that Gando dude and jacked up his head. That seems like a stretch to me."

"It is, but it was a large wound and Jones could have had some other motive. Either way, people have killed for a lot less."

"Okay, I got it."

"While you do that, I'm going to call Gando's daughters. I want to find out if they ever suspected this Tawny person had stolen anything from their father's home, or if there is a history of abuse."

From there, Bramwell and Roybal attended to their self-assigned duties and eventually arrived, unannounced, at Minister Brady's house. The same dog barked and came to check them out.

"You folks are back, I see," Brady said when he heard the commotion. "How can I help you this time?"

Within minutes they were all standing at the makeshift bar and Brady retrieved the wedding book and scooted it toward the sergeant. "If you don't mind my asking," he said, "why is this book so interesting to you folks?"

"I can answer that," Roybal said while his superior sought the page in question. "A few weeks back and a couple hours away, a man was shot and killed. We're trying to eliminate some people from the suspect pool."

"Oh. That's a good idea. What does my book have to do with anything?"

"We're trying to verify whether the Blackstones were here when the crime took place."

"That sounds important."

"Are you sure the wedding was on a Friday?" the sergeant asked, while running her fingers across the pages.

"Yep. Those people said they wanted to get married as soon as possible and we were able to do it on short notice."

"Would you mind if I took a picture of that page? We need it for the file."

"Be my guest."

"Thanks. Can I ask you something else? You wouldn't happen to be related to Russell Blackstone, would you?"

66

AFTER BEING ASKED IF HE WAS RELATED to Russell Blackstone, the minister grinned. "Me and the groom. Related? No. We ain't related. I come from the south. I don't know where he comes from."

"Okay. Thanks. Just curious."

"Glad to help."

As Bramwell and Roybal shuffled toward their car, the latter addressed his superior. "You know something? I can see why certain people would like this kind of wedding. It saves a lot of money and hassles."

"Not only that," said Bramwell, "some young ladies are of legal age but have strict parents who don't want them to get married. Rather than fight, those young ladies come to places like this and leave their folks out of it."

"Hadn't thought about that."

"Good job, back there. I got a good shot of the witness names. Let's move up the road a bit and Google them."

Three miles later, they rolled up to the driveway of an alleged witness at the wedding in question. A silver-haired woman opened the door. "Are you Doris Bell?" Bramwell asked, flashing her badge.

"Yes."

"We're investigating a murder quite aways from here and we think you might be able to help us. May we come in?"

"Me? That sounds important. Okay."

Inside, Doris's home was spotless. Bramwell verified that Doris had been a witness at the Blackstone wedding, then got to the main point. "Was that a Friday or Saturday?"

"Oh, that's easy," Doris said. "I always do my laundry on Fridays. No exceptions. I'm free the rest of the time. That wedding was definitely on a Saturday."

Bramwell's face lit up. "Don't take this the wrong way, ma'am, but on a scale of one to one hundred, how confident are you about that?"

"I'm tempted to say a thousand percent, but we all know that's impossible so my answer is, 'I'm one hundred percent certain that the wedding was on a Saturday.'"

"That's very interesting. Would you be willing to testify to that in court, if needed?"

"Certainly. I'm a good citizen. I'll do anything to help, unless it's Friday, of course. I do my laundry on Friday. No exceptions."

Riding on clouds, the investigators had a two-hour trek to get back to home base. En route, they got a call from one of the doctors who worked on Tawny Jones's special friend. "Sorry we didn't get back to you folks sooner," he said, "but I've talked to all the parties involved. We can't be totally certain, but it didn't appear as if there was any malevolence."

"Thanks, doctor. I think we can leave you alone for a while."

After ending the call, the sergeant turned to her partner. "It's been a productive day, but I've still got one loose end that I'd like to tie down."

"Oh, yeah? What's that?"

"The doctor wasn't very convincing, and that bed-ridden man was pretty banged up. I'm going to Bikers and Babes Bar because Tawny Jones's brother hangs out there. A badass like that could have killed Phillip Pilday for his sister. You can go home if you want to. And we'll catch up tomorrow."

"No way. I know that place. It's for bad boys and their rough gangs. Bottom line, we're partners. I'm going with you."

Inside the bar, a tall dude with lots of shaggy hair and a leather vest approached Bramwell. "I ain't never had no black chick," he said. "You up for some instant action?"

"No," she spewed. "I prefer guys who know how to bathe once in a while."

After a few more steps, a muscular guy at a table with a beefy woman tapped Roybal on the arm. "How would you like to arm-wrestle my old lady? Loser buys a round of beer."

Instead, the detectives scurried towards the well-tattooed bartender and asked if he knew Tawny's brother.

The bartender pointed at a pool table. "He's the one with the nose ring."

The detectives prompted the bar manager to let them scan the surveillance video for the night of the shooting. No doubt, the man with the nose ring was in that bar, shooting pool at the time of Phillip's death.

67

I DIDN'T ENJOY SIDE-STEPPING the detectives and their poly test, but I knew that guys like Nagley could be ruthless so I wanted to get far away from them and hope they'd find Phillip's attacker.

To do that I decided to go see the Montgomerys in person. I hoped that they'd understand why I didn't get to Trevor's party. Better yet, Trevor might still be around or I might persuade Bertie and Chester to give me his contact information.

Actually, if the Lieutenant and his subordinates were to saddle their ponies and look for me, they'd have no idea that I'd changed my hair and successfully swapped my Camaro for a Jeep at a mall. To top things off, I'd left my laptop and phone at home just in case they tried to trace me via those items.

Elmer and I checked into a motel that accepted pets. I used a bogus name, paid in cash and put down a hefty cash damage deposit in lieu of a credit card.

In our room, Elmer joined me on the bed, where he licked my face as if to thank me because he'd been sleeping on a cement slab for months.

After a long night of much-deserved sleep, a crack of sunlight began to crawl up the window frame. I rolled out of bed and looked forward to getting back on the road, but first, I took Elmer for a walk. The freedom was so foreign to him that he ran in cute little circles.

"It's going to be a long day, buddy," I said. "But if we stick with it, we should get to Trevor's house by dinner time tomorrow."

After breakfast, I got my deposit back and we headed east. Sometimes we listened to the radio. Other times, I chatted with my four-legged friend in a comforting tone, like a mom who reads to her kids at night.

The whole time, tears came and went while I regretted losing Phillip and missing Trevor's birthday party. I prayed that Trevor hadn't left for London yet. If he had, I might never meet him.

68

AFTER MIRANDA SKIPPED OUT on the polygraph test, Lieutenant Nagley and Detective Yang asked Juju and Ellen if they knew where Miranda might be. The best guess included chasing down the adoptive parents of her son, Trevor.

Armed with the Montgomerys' phone number from Juju, Nagley hoped to contact them and recommend they call the local police to watch for Miranda.

Unfortunately, the Montgomerys didn't answer the call. Not to be deterred, Nagley instructed Yang to call the Ohio State Police and have somebody go to their home. This time Yang got through. Officer Darcie Pettibone took Yang's call.

"Can do," she said, after learning the goal. "What's the perp's name and alleged crime?"

"Name's Miranda Pilday. AKA Miranda Munchak. No other aliases that we know of. For now, she's a suspect in the murder of her husband. He died from a gunshot, so she could be armed and dangerous."

"Got it. Any other identifiers?"

"Yes. She's fifty years old, medium height, light-brown hair with gray streaks. Drives a white Chevy Camaro with California plates. No known accomplices."

"Got it, detective. What do you want us to do with her if we find her?"

"Try to apprehend her and hold her until we can get there. Shouldn't take more than eight hours."

"Alright, Detective. We're on it. We'll keep you informed."

A short time later, the case of Miranda Pilday had been handed off to officers Farrell Harper and Amy Kudlow in Cincinnati.

At the Montgomerys' door, a curly-haired, fortyish woman eyed the officers. "Is something wrong?" she asked.

"Are you Mrs. Montgomery?"

"Yes. What's going on?"

"Ma'am, Do you know Miranda Pilday?"

"Her again? That woman is a walking disaster. What did she do this time?"

"We don't know the details but apparently her husband has been killed."

Bertie's hands went to her mouth. "Oh, my God. That explains why they didn't come to the party. But why are you telling me all this? Are we in any danger?"

"Nothing imminent that we know of, but Ms. Pilday has told others that she has a son who may live here. We think she may want to speak with him."

"Over my dead body. Besides, he's staying with my sister in Florida right now."

"We had London in our notes. Is that incorrect?"

"We told Phillip and Miranda that Trevor was going to London because we hoped they'd give up and leave all of us alone."

"But he's currently in Florida. Is that right?"

"Yes. He's been there about a week now. We don't like to lie to people but that woman is Trevor's biological mother. We adopted him and raised him. She's been a nuisance ever since she found out who we were."

"Okay, ma'am. We just wanted to advise you that we'll have some patrol officers driving around just in case you need us."

"Thank you for that."

"If you do see her, stay away from her. Give us a call. We'll take care of it."

"Oh, my God. Are you sure we're safe?"

"We'll be a heavy presence. Just stay alert and call us if you see something suspicious. She may be driving a white Camaro."

"Okay. I've seen her on FaceTime a couple times, so I ought to recognize her."

"Thank you, ma'am. You be careful now."

69

WHEN IT WAS DETERMINED that Miranda could be en route to Cincinnati, the local authorities printed some flyers with her picture on them and put out a BOLO for a white Chevy Camaro. At the same time, patrol cars began wandering past the Montgomerys' home on a regular basis.

At one point an elderly gentleman, wearing a Cincinnati Reds' baseball hat, waved down one of the police vehicles.

He said he was familiar with the Montgomerys and that the neighbors kept an eye out for one another.

"The important thing," the officer said, "is to give us a call if you see that white car."

"Will do."

70

IN THE MIDDLE OF THE COUNTRY Elmer and I loaded my luggage into the Jeep I got by selling my Camaro. "I don't know what the police are doing about my dodging their lie-detector test," I said to my little pal, "but as you know, I've been in jail a long time because of 'technicalities.' A person is wary of things like that, especially when the cops turn into biased bullies.

"This way," I continued, "they might interview other people who knew Phillip and catch the real killer. Then we can return to Juju's home until I can get a job and start over."

Just then, we reached Utah, where I initially met Phillip at a large truckstop just beyond the state line.

At that time, I was still recovering from donating part of my liver to Trevor. Phillip was the first person who believed in me. He was so kind that I said he was sent to me by God.

Deep into my memories, I pulled into that same truckstop, parked the car and cracked the windows so Elmer could get some fresh air while I was inside. But when I walked toward the building, I heard him whimper behind me. I wanted to run back and bring him with me, but most restaurants didn't accept animals other than service dogs.

Before we left, I bought a cool red, white and blue hoodie for Trevor just in case he was still at the Montgomerys' home.

71

Meanwhile, on a busy street, north of Los Angeles, a pair of traffic cops pulled over a young driver whose automobile matched a vehicle that had just come up on their BOLO list.

With guns at the ready, the officers carefully approached the vehicle from behind. "Hands on the wheel, where we can see them," the female officer said.

The driver did what he was told. "What did I do?" he said, while staring at the officer's weapon.

With one officer on either side of the back of the man's car, they cautiously moved forward. "Keep your hands where we can see them," the female said, scanning the back seat.

"Okay, anything you say."

"I want you to get out of the vehicle and lean against it."

"Yes, ma'am."

They patted the young man down and secured his ID. While the lady officer verified the vehicle's ID, her partner dropped back to contact their home base.

The lady cop asked the driver, "Where is Miranda Pilday?"

"Who? I don't know who that is."

"Then where did you get this car?"

"Kosar's Used Cars. Yesterday afternoon. For back and forth to work. We can go over there if you want to. It's not far. Mr. Kosar will recognize me."

They put the man in the back seat of their squad car and waited for two detectives, named Nagley and Yang, who slipped behind the first police vehicle.

Before long, everybody made it to Oliver Kosar's lot, where Kosar himself confirmed the young man's story. "That vehicle was real clean," he said to the officers. "It was a good deal for all of us."

Having cleared the man, the traffic cops returned the shaken driver to his car while the detectives stayed behind with Kosar.

"This was a sweet one," Oliver said on the way to his office. "Ms. Pilday had the title and that young man had the money he needed. While I'm on a hot streak, are either one of you guys looking for a car? I got some good ones."

"Maybe some other time," Nagley said. "Right now, we're interested in Ms. Pilday. Was anybody else with her?"

"Just a dog. A little guy. She carried it in one of those cages they use for pets on airplanes."

Yang held up a finger. "If she sold her vehicle and there was no one with her, how did she get out of here. Uber? Cab? Bus?"

"She had some luggage so one of my guys took her to the mall and dropped her off."

"Is that person here now?"

"No, but we can call him at home."

"That'll work."

A few minutes later Nagley and Yang learned that Pilday had been dropped off at the beauty parlor - and "she was going to Mesa, Arizona, to see her sister."

"Don't think so," Yang said. "I've seen Pilday's file. Nobody has mentioned a sister or Mesa, Arizona."

"Interesting," Nagley stood and nodded toward Kosar. "Thanks for your help. We can find our way out."

"Alrighty," Kosar said. "Don't forget. I'll give you fellows a special deal the next time you need a car."

After a quick trip to the mall, Nagley and Yang learned

that Miranda had had her hair cut and dyed. Other than that, a few people remembered seeing "the lady with the little dog," but none of them saw any accomplices or knew where she went from there.

72

When Sergeant Bramwell and Detective Roybal learned about the controversial wedding date for Jerrie Jean and Russell, they went to the lieutenant and suggested they bring the parties in for more questioning.

"What flaw?" the boss asked when hearing that there was some confusion involving the exact date of the ceremony.

"When we originally interviewed Jerrie Jean, she and Russell claimed that they were getting married at the same time as Phillip's death. But one of the witnesses insists that the wedding was on Saturday."

"What witness?"

An elderly neighbor woman. She said she wouldn't attend a wedding on a Friday because she does her laundry on Fridays."

"How old is she?"

"I don't know. Maybe seventy or older."

"That figures. Old people can get confused."

"Maybe so, but she convinced me that she knew what she was saying."

"Well, we now have stronger evidence indicating that Pilday is our bad perp. I don't have to remind you that she bolted when she had a chance to take a polygraph and clear her name. In addition to that, she has two huge motives:

namely, she thought she was getting an insurance claim. Then there is a revenge option, not to mention that she lacks an alibi.

"We think we know where she's going and we have people ready to apprehend her as we speak. In fact, I'll need you to stay close by and then go with me to return her to California. I think we can get a full-blown confession out of her before she boards the plane."

"Okay. I guess we can see how this plays out."

"Good. If that doesn't work out, we can bring in the Blackstones."

"Okay then."

73

ELMER AND ME FINALLY MADE IT to Cincinnati. We checked into another motel, unloaded our things and took a short nap followed by a long walk.

Elmer liked it when I talked to him, so I used that opportunity to figure out how I might get on the good side of the Montgomerys.

"I'm tempted to race to their home right now, Elmer. When they learn what happened to Phillip, they'll understand why I missed their party and ultimately tell me where Trevor is.

"That's why I'm going to dress nicely and be respectful and polite. I think I know where their home is, so we'll go there after their dinner. That way they won't be stressed out."

Having clarified my strategy with Elmer, I waited for the sun to get tired before putting on my dress and accessories.

As expected, we found the local school and then located the intersection that led to the Montgomerys' home. I began to tremble as I slowly drove toward their property. "I hope I can talk with Bertie," I said to myself, "because two moms ought to understand each other. Better yet, maybe Trevor will miraculously answer the door. That would be an answer to all my prayers."

Eventually, I scooted the Jeep directly across the street

from the Montgomerys' home. There were no vehicles in their driveway.

I cracked the window for Elmer, then stepped out of the Jeep and swiped a couple last-minute wrinkles out of my dress.

I marched to the porch of the home in which my son grew up. I rang the bell, but nobody answered. A second ring and a hard knock on the door proved just as futile.

Disappointed, I went back to the Jeep and wondered if I should wait or come back later.

Just then, an elderly man tapped on the window. Elmer went ballistic with loud barks and growls. I lowered my window.

"People don't ordinarily park in front of my house," the man said. "Do you need something?"

At that point I was feeling uneasy and decided to move on. "No, thanks," I said, "I was just admiring the neighborhood."

74

Unbeknownst to the Montgomerys, their neighbor placed a call to the officer who previously gave him his business card.

"She doesn't fit your description very well," the neighbor said. "She's got short, dark hair, and she was driving a black Jeep with California plates, not a white car, but she did have a little dog."

"Alright, she could be dangerous so stay indoors, where you are safe. We'll be right over."

75

Toward dinnertime, I still wanted to look up the Montgomerys. I hand-ironed my dress and stuffed Elmer and his carrier on the front seat with me.

While driving, I kept reminding myself not to piss off Bertie or Chester. That could lead to additional legal problems and likely eliminate any opportunity to meet Trevor.

At the corner of their block, I told Elmer I was going to have to leave him in the car for a little while. Then I saw some movement at the other end of the block.

Before I knew it, several police cars had converged on me and the entire block took on flashing red lights. I instantly knew that Nagley had sent them.

"I haven't done anything wrong," I said to the first officer who ordered me to put my hands on the roof of my Jeep, where I was instantly patted for a gun, but I don't like guns.

While they had me at the steady, two additional officers searched the Jeep, which Elmer didn't like.

While Elmer was going nuts a strong cop cuffed me. "We have some people who are looking for you," he said.

By that time the sidewalks had gathered a dozen neighbors.

Then another man, with a shiny preacher-like suit, stood before me and read my rights.

I glanced at the nearest lady-officer. "I'm not guilty of anything!" I insisted.

"Nobody ever is," she replied.

"You people think that I left California because I am guilty of killing my husband. But I left for the opposite reason. I'm not guilty and I knew that I'd be bullied and pressured to confess and that's happening right now. While you guys are harassing me, somebody else killed my husband. You should look for that person and leave me alone."

At that moment, I heard whimpering. "What about my dog?" I pleaded with the faux preacher. "He's too fragile for this kind of thing."

"You've got other things to worry about, ma'am."

A female officer escorted me to her squad car and cuffed me to a filthy backseat cage as if I were a wild animal. Tears dribbled on my dress while I waited and worried and the officers dispersed the neighborhood crowd.

We were the first vehicle to leave the area. "What's going to happen to me now?" I asked my driver.

She looked at me in her mirror as if she was measuring my capabilities as a killer. "We already contacted law enforcement folks in California. They'll be here in the morning. Then you'll get a free plane ride back home where you belong. Until then, you get to spend the night on a cot, compliments of the citizens of Ohio."

"What about Elmer?"

"Your dog? Somebody will take care of him."

"Are you sure?"

"Yeah. Some say, we're nicer to the four-legged critters than the two-legged ones."

I buried my teary face into my cuffed hands and prepared for a long night. "This isn't fair."

After a sleepless night, my dress was grubby. I was offered some oatmeal, but I was in no mood for food or anything else. Eventually Lieutenant Nagley rolled in with a female African American detective named Sergeant Bramwell. I didn't know her but if she was like Nagley, she could be as stubborn as a tree root. "What now?" I asked as she cuffed me.

"We flew in here late last night. I only got a few hours' sleep in a dumpy motel. Now, I'm cranky as hell and don't want no trouble, so keep your comments to yourself and I might dislike you less than I do right now."

Apparently, the woman thought that losing a few hours of sleep was a greater inconvenience than facing stern law enforcement officers who derived pleasure from sending people to prison.

At the airport, and still wearing prison-bracelets, I was ushered by Nagley to a quiet gate where we waited for boarding. Unceremoniously, we were the first ones to board the plane and went for the very last row, where the fewest number of passengers could see us.

"It's going to be a long flight," the Sergeant said. "You'd better pee now, because I'm only going to allow you one additional visit in the whole flight."

Still cuffed, I finished my business and took a center seat. After a towel was draped over my hands, everybody else was allowed to board.

During the flight instructions, an attendant stated that this would be a non-stop flight and there would be two time-zone changes. There were several mumbles and grumbles but none of those people were on their way to a small stinky room where human wolves devour their prey.

When we were at cruising altitude, I asked Nagley how they caught me. He smirked. "Your mother-in-law knew where you were going."

Technically, Juju was a grandmother in-law but I knew what he meant. "What about my Jeep?"

"A judge will probably decide, but you don't need to worry about that. Nobody has vehicles where you're going."

I shifted my attentions to Sergeant Bramwell. "I know you don't believe me," I said, "but I'm one-hundred percent innocent."

"Course you are. Everybody blows off a polygraph and trades vehicles in clandestine ways. Now shut your trap. I want to get some rest."

After a painfully long plane ride I desperately needed to stretch my legs, but we were the last ones to deplane.

At the gate, two additional detectives, one of each gender, replaced Sergeant Bramwell.

Detective Barbara Collier helped me with a much-needed restroom break, then we went for a two-hour drive to home base, where I was stuffed into a small conference room and told to sit on a folding chair in the corner.

Clearly, things were about to get a lot worse.

76

THE INTERROGATION ROOM to which I was taken had a two-way mirror and an overhead light fixture that could have lit up a state highway.

A closer look at the mirror revealed a faded red glow behind the upper corner. Clearly, they intended to record all of my statements.

With all of my wits rolling around in my head, I certainly didn't want to be interrogated. If they were to wear me out and cause me to make a false confession just to get out of there, I could go to another prison for the rest of my life.

Eventually, Lieutenant Nagley and his sidekick, Detective Yang, joined me in that little room. Nagley removed my cuffs. "Are you comfortable?" he asked in a phony, sweet tone.

"I'm sad and need some Kleenex."

"Okay. Detective Yang can take care of that. Anything else?"

"Yes, it's really hot in here. Can you turn on an air conditioner?"

"There's no air conditioning in here, but Mr. Yang can get you some water in a minute. Anything else?"

"Yes. Where's my dog?"

"Your dog? I'm sure that somebody is caring for him. Mr. Yang can look into it."

Seconds later, the lieutenant and I were all alone. "I was told that somebody advised you of your rights," he said. "Is that true?"

"Yes. Last night, in Cincinnati."

"Did you understand them?"

"Yes. I'm innocent so I won't need an attorney."

"Alright. Let's start with you telling me why you are here."

I sniffled and shook my head. "Because my husband was murdered and you guys haven't found the real killer."

He glared at me, as if I had challenged his very manhood. "I know that you raced off to Cincinnati because you have a son there. Did you expect him to hide you from us?"

"No. I've never even met him, but Phillip and I planned to go to his sixteenth birthday party. That's when Phillip was killed."

"Okay. The last time you and I spoke, you agreed to sit with a polygrapher. Do you remember that?"

"I know, but I changed my mind."

"Why didn't you call us and reschedule?"

"I told you; I changed my mind."

"Do you know what that looks like to us? It looks as if you knew that we had all the evidence we needed to charge you with your husband's death, so you bolted while you could. You can understand why we would think that, right?"

"It's the opposite. I wanted you to look for the real killer."

"But we aren't the ones who abandoned their cell phone, changed cars and left the state. Those are the kinds of things that a guilty person does so she won't be recognized. Do you acknowledge that the optics are against you?"

"I guess so, but do you admit that you can lie to me?"

"I know this: Before you were released, your husband had multiple dalliances with ladies he'd met at Wilson's bar and elsewhere. You don't deny that, do you?"

"I didn't know for certain, but I sorta figured it out."

"That must have been awfully painful for you."

"I would have preferred that he didn't do those things."

"So, he hurt your feelings, but you couldn't do anything about it until you were released. Right?"

"That's a misinterpretation."

"As we see it, you figured out that he met a lot more ladies than you expected. It was as if he'd discovered his very own oil well. He kept going back to the field, kept drilling for oil, and kept getting rewarded. That must have been hard for you to swallow."

"Not really. When we made our agreement he agreed not to tell me any of the details, so I still don't know, but I wouldn't want him dead over any of this."

"In that case, I'm betting that a non-biased person, such as a juror, would believe that you waited until you were released, then somebody you know grabbed a gun and did your bidding."

"Wrong. I wouldn't do that."

Suddenly, Nagley slapped his hand loudly on the table and scooted closer to my face. "Do I look stupid to you?"

I could smell his horrible coffee breath. I pulled back and didn't answer.

"You're not winning my sympathy, Ms. Pilday," he insisted. "Now answer my goddamn question. Do I look stupid to you?"

"I guess you want me to say, 'no.'"

He shook his head. "This isn't about what I want, Ms. Pilday. It's about the facts and your future. You've met lots of seedy characters who know lots of other seedy characters - some of whom would gladly take out a cheating husband for a thousand dollars and we both know where you could get that kind of money, don't we?"

"I don't know what you're talking about."

"Sure, you do. We already told you that your husband took out a juicy insurance policy naming you his beneficiary. Do you deny that? Yes or no?"

By that time my butt was growing numb, and I was uncomfortable, but I focused on the question at hand. "The only policy I know about was a long time ago. I told him I didn't need it, and we never talked about it again. Would you mind scooting back? You're making me nervous."

"I'll step back when you admit that you played a role in your husband's death. Then we can both relax."

"No! I knew you would do this. That's why I ran away. To be clear, I didn't kill my husband or have anybody else do it. And that's all I have to say."

"And I'm no fool, Ms. Pilday. Your husband's affairs pissed you off, so you wanted him out of the way and you wanted that insurance money."

"You're wrong," I said just as Detective Yang tapped at the outer door and stuck his head into the room. "It's seven o'clock. Anybody want some pizza?"

Nagley jumped to his feet and stomped out, as if he were pissed at Yang for breaking his momentum, but I was familiar with the good-cop/bad-cop routine.

I straightened my dress. Then, "I'm not hungry," I said politely.

On the other hand, the hot room and the bright lights were taking their toll and I longed for water.

77

After I turned down their pizza, Nagley returned with Detective Barbara Collier. "She is going to take you to the "penthouse," he said to me, "then she'll bring you back in the morning."

A short time later, I found out what a penthouse meant to them. Still wearing my formerly-nice dress I was dumped into a small dark cell that included a filthy toilet, a narrow cot, a tired dark-blue blanket and two rolls of toilet paper, one of which was supposed to be a pillow.

To keep from feeling sorry for myself I kept thinking about the time I spent two days in solitary confinement some 12 years ago in the big girl's prison.

The next morning, just before sun-up, Detective Collier awakened me. Stiff and aching, I rolled over. "What's going on?" I asked.

"The Lieutenant wants to talk with you again."

Of course he did. The man was full of testosterone and he had a dragon to slay.

Collier offered to get me a clean jumpsuit so that I didn't have to stay in my dress.

"Not on your life," I said. "The very worst dress is better than the very best jumpsuit, especially the orange ones."

When we arrived at the interrogation room, it was already

warm and getting hotter. Predictably, the red light behind the two-way mirror was recording the festivities.

Finally, Nagley slithered into the hellish space and slipped me a bottle of water before nodding to Collier. She got the message, grabbed the doorknob, and I was alone with that nasty man again.

"What's the matter," Nagley asked. "Didn't they have any jumpsuits?"

"I don't need no jumpsuit. I'm not a convict and I'm not going to be here very long."

"Good. That means you are ready to level with us about your role in your husband's demise, or are we going to have another day like yesterday?"

I shook my head. "I don't have nothing new to say."

Noticeably frustrated, the lieutenant began his litany of implications regarding motives and my lack of an alibi. When I didn't appease him, he said I was tormenting Phillip's family, who needed closure.

When that failed, he tried intimidation. "This is the only place in the building that doesn't have air conditioning," he said. "My associates and I can take turns babysitting you in here and then retreating to our cool offices. Unfortunately, you will remain here until you confess or agree to take a poly."

"I don't care what you guys do. I'm not going to confess to something I didn't do."

"Alright, I thought you might say that, so I'm going to a meeting now. While I'm gone, you'd be wise to think things over and get your mind right. Absent that, you're going to be confined to this room until you tell me what you're hiding."

Sure enough, he cuffed me to the leg of the table and left the room, leaving me alone and fully aware that his master plan was to melt me down, until I'd confess, regardless of whether I was guilty.

Nearly three hours later, I was sweating like a pig when Nagley returned with Detective Yang, who had another bottle of water for me.

While I glugged down the cold refreshment, Nagley asked me if I'd like to stretch my legs for a few minutes.

Since I had been cuffed and knotted-up for so long, I gladly accepted the offer.

Nagley had Yang uncuff me and allowed me to do some squats and march in place to stretch my back.

For the first few minutes I thought they were being kind for a change, but it didn't take long for their two-by-four to clunk me on the head. All that moving around in the excessive heat was like exercising in the desert at noon.

Sweaty and beginning to smell, I immediately plopped back in my unfriendly chair. "I should have known better," I said between deep breaths. "This is why I don't trust you."

"If you don't like it, Ms. Pilday, you could simply take the poly."

"I already told you why I'm not going to do that. Those tests are flawed, and I'd have no way of knowing if you guys are lying to me. I think you should round up your colleagues and find the real killer, and let me go."

"It's apparent to us that 'You' are the real killer, Ms. Pilday. You may have forgotten that you are in custody because you are both a suspect in a murder case and a flight risk. Ergo, I don't intend to release you until I get what I want."

Clearly, Nagley and I were equally stubborn, but there was no way that a fifty-year-old woman, who didn't get much exercise, could keep up with him and his string of younger and stronger cops.

Unable to get a confession out of me, the Lieutenant was like a manager in a baseball game. He left the room and sent one detective after the other to see who could break me.

At one point, Detective Collier spoke with me about families and moms and the pain of Phillip's family, but I had my rebuttal. "It's not my fault when stubborn law enforcement offices keep barking up the wrong tree."

Next up, Detective Yang introduced some feigned compassion. "I'm sorry if we get a little rough with you once in a while," he said, "but we have a job to do."

"And I'm sorry that you guys have to take turns sitting in this room for one whole hour at a time before you return to your comfortable air conditioned offices."

Additional attempts came from Sergeant Bramwell and her sidekick Detective Roybal.

Through all of it, my body was getting weaker and weaker, but I still had memories of prison life and I sure as hell didn't want to go back there, so I gave myself another pep talk.

When Nagley returned, he surprised me by calling a time-out for dinner. Totally spent, both physically and psychologically, I whole-heartedly agreed.

Back in the cell I was sweaty, stinky, aching and uncomfortable. I spread my blanket on the floor and laid on it and welcomed both the coolness of the cement and the relative softness of the blanket compared to the hard chair in which I'd been sitting.

After I ate, I thought we were done for the day, but out of the blue, Nagley called me back and said that he was prepared to stay until midnight if that's what it took for me to admit my involvement in my husband's death.

Then, I noticed the red light in the mirror had been turned off. That could only mean one thing: The shifty lieutenant was tired of being watched while interrogating me. Clearly, he was going to turn up the heat, both literally and figuratively; and, he didn't want any sneaky cameras looking over his shoulders.

78

After returning from Cincinnati, Sergeant Reba Bramwell helped Lieutenant Nagley interrogate Miranda. But unbeknownst to the Lieutenant, Bramwell had a card up her sleeve.

Acting on Nagley's earlier promise to revisit the notion that the wedding date was in question, Reba invited Jerrie Jean and Russell Blackstone to come to the police building, "so we can completely erase you from the Pilday suspect list."

Anxious to subtract themselves from the equation, the newlyweds whole-heartedly agreed to attend a "friendly" late-afternoon meeting.

When the duo arrived, Bramwell and Roybal escorted them to a waiting room. "I'm glad you could come in," she said to the duo. "It won't be long now. Oh, by the way, you don't have any weapons on you, do you?"

"Not me," Jerrie Jean said.

Russell shook his head, "Me neither."

"Good, then you won't mind if Detective Roybal pats you down, just to be certain."

Russell shook his head. "We already told you. We don't got no guns."

"I know," Reba said, "but we have to treat everybody the same."

"Okay, but you're wasting your time."

Detective Roybal finished the body searches. He and the sergeant escorted their unarmed guests to a short hallway near the back of the building. At the first room, Reba tapped the door. "Okay, Mr. Blackstone, you'll be in here. Jerrie Jean will take the next room."

"Wait a minute," Russell said, "Why can't we all sit in the same room?"

"If we're going to take you off the list," Roybal said, "we have to make sure your stories match."

Russell shook his head again. "Alright. Let's get it over with. We've got other things to do, you know."

"Yes, sir. We'll get started pretty quick but for now, I need to make certain Jerrie Jean is situated."

A moment later Roybal was in the hall, Jerrie Jean was alone in her room and Russell was alone in his room, which freed Sergeant Bramwell to act on the next part of her plan.

Just past the elevators, the talented sergeant entered another small office and spoke with a gentleman in a leather chair. "Alright, Minister Sullivan," she said while moving right in. "Thanks for coming in. I know it was a long ride for you, but if all goes as planned, we will get you back home in time for dinner."

"Okay. Thanks. It's times like this that I wish I'd never become a minister. It's just not worth it."

"I can understand that, so I'll get right to the point. When my partner and I were at your home, we detected a mix-up regarding the date of the Blackstone wedding."

He shook his head. "There was no mix-up."

"Do you still maintain that the wedding was on Friday?"

"It is what it is. That's all."

"What would you say if I told you we have a witness who suggests otherwise? You remember Doris Bell, I presume?"

"Of course. She likes to earn a little money, so I let her be a witness."

"She told us that she does her housework on Fridays with no exceptions. Therefore, the wedding was not on Friday. Rather, it was a Saturday."

"Oh. I get it now. She's an old lady and mistaken. She's done that before."

"So, if I were to tell you that we can prove that Russell Blackstone killed our poor victim, and that we know you covered for him by changing those dates in your book, what would you say?"

Reba watched closely while her nervous guest tapped at his shirt pocket where he kept his chewing tobacco. "If he did that, I didn't have anything to do with it."

"Don't blow smoke at me, sir. It'll just get you in more trouble. You might be interested to know that Mr. Blackstone is sitting in another area of this building right now. Poor dude doesn't even know that his head is already in our proverbial noose, along with his lovely wife, of course."

"Yeah? So? I don't know nothing about those two except that they got married at my place."

The sergeant shook her head. "You don't play fair, do ya? I'm being honest with you, but you're trying to bullshit me."

"No, I'm not. You just don't know what you're talking about."

"So, you're sticking to your story: The dates weren't changed and you don't know anything about the Blackstones. Do I have that correct?"

"Yes. That's right. Can I go now?"

"There you go again." The sergeant reached into her own pocket and retrieved a piece of paper which she handed to him. "It's a phone number, sir. Do you recognize it?"

He glanced at the paper and appeared to stiffen.

"I called your mother," Sergeant Bramwell went on. "She's a very nice woman, by the way. She even told me that you and Russell are half-brothers. What do you say about that?"

All the color left the minister's face.

"You have committed a very serious crime, Mr. Sullivan.

It's called 'aiding and abetting' or, 'accessory to murder.' Either way it's the same as if you shot the victim yourself. You'll go to prison for a lifetime, with no possibility for parole for at least twenty-five years. Now do you understand how serious that is?"

The man slowly lifted both hands to his face. "I didn't know what they were up to until it was too late."

"Yet you never turned them in and that's what makes you an accessory. Now, before you dig yourself into a deeper hole, I suggest you level with us. Things get a lot easier for you if you make things easier for us. Therefore, you have one chance and one chance only to save yourself. Admit it. You changed those dates, didn't you, Mr. Sullivan?"

After a long pause, he lifted his head. "They asked me to do it as a favor."

"Okay, then. What was their reason?"

"I didn't want to know, so I didn't ask. But they eventually told me somebody died. They seemed proud of it, but I yelled at them and didn't want to know anything else about it."

"Alright. That's more like it. For now, I suggest you work with us to tie down the loose ends. If you are one hundred percent cooperative, we can recommend that the DA show you as much sympathy as possible."

The minister nodded. "Yes, ma'am. I'll tell you anything you want to know."

"Good. And now, you are under arrest. I'll have somebody read your rights to you while I take care of something else. After that, I want you to write all this down."

"Okay. I understand."

79

With Minister Brady Sullivan under control, Sergeant Bramwell went to Jerrie Jean's room and sat across the table from her. "As you know," the Sergeant began, "we've been investigating people who may have information regarding Phillip Pilday's tragic death, and you were one of those people because you and Phillip were intimate on more than one occasion. Now I'd like to ask you a few more questions.

"For starters, when I first talked with you guys, it was clear to me that Russell was not emotionally attached to Phillip like you were. Is that true?"

"Emotionally attached? I didn't love Phillip. We just played around a little bit."

"Are you saying that your relationship with Phillip was strictly sex, not love?"

"Absolutely."

"Did he ever stay overnight?"

"Only once, when my kids stayed at their grandparents' home."

"What about the other times? Did you go to his place or a motel or what?"

"We went to his home once, but we had to work around the school schedule, so we mostly met at my place during the school day."

"How many times at your place?"

"I dunno, I'd say two or three."

The sergeant shook her head. "Are you sure it wasn't a little more than that because I've got some information here that—"

"I guess it could have been a couple more times, but what does it matter?"

"Did he ever pay you?"

"Pay me? Not really. Occasionally he brought me flowers or small gifts, but I'm not a prostitute if that's what you mean."

"I didn't think you were, but I had to ask. Did you ever do anything nice for the two of you?"

"Like what?"

"I dunno. Maybe you made a batch of cupcakes, or bought him some cologne or invited him over for a mid-night rendezvous after your kids were asleep. Anything like that."

"Yeah, I baked some cookies but we mostly just enjoyed each other's company."

"What was that like? Did you laugh and have fun?"

"Sometimes. Why?"

"Here's my point, Jerrie Jean. Generally, I don't care what adults do behind closed doors, but in my experience, the more they get together, the closer they become emotionally. They may not want to get married or live together, but they have special experiences. Were you and Phillip like that?"

"Yes. He was an interesting man. I already told you that."

"Actually, I think it was a lot more than that to you. I think you loved Phillip to some extent. But Russell had a whole different attitude about Phillip. In fact, Russell is a hot-head. He was jealous of Phillip and he drew both you and the minister into his web."

Just then, Detective Roybal slipped into the room and stood with his back to the door, like a guard. "Detective Collier is watching the hall now," he said to Sergeant Bramwell.

She nodded, then focused on Jerrie Jean again. "The last

time we talked, I mentioned your smile. Do you remember that?"

"Yeah. What of it?"

"We also talked about your love for your kids and the fun things you've done. Do you remember that?"

"So?"

"So, I've always paid attention to your body language, especially your lips. I discovered that a tiny tick is as revealing as your entire smile."

"So what? Everybody has quirks."

"But they don't act like you do when you're trying to be evasive. You can hold your lips steady but that little tick twitches all by itself and gives you away."

"That's called a 'tell,'" Roybal offered. "And, I've seen you say 'yes,' to a question while shaking your head from side to side, which indicates that the real answer was 'no.'"

Jerrie Jean's hand reached for her lips.

"In other words," Bramwell went on, "You are animated and easy to read. And there's something else you might like to know. We have surveillance cameras around here and we've been recording your reactions to all of this. In other words, you've essentially ratted yourself out."

Jerrie Jean's face went blank while the Sergeant revealed additional news.

"We also know that your wedding minister is your husband's half-brother. We think both you and Brady were drawn into this mess by your jealous husband. That is correct, isn't it?"

Jerrie Jean froze, as if she were afraid of her tells.

Bramwell leaned in and placed an arm on Jerrie Jean's shaking hand. "I want you to listen to me, now. You've got one, and only one, chance to flip on your husband. If you choose not to cooperate, we've got the half-brother cuffed down the hall. He will testify against both you and Russell. You might spend the rest of your life in prison. But if you help us net Russell, we'll ask the DA to work with you."

"Then will you let me go home?"

"We're talking about first degree murder here. It carries a life sentence, but if you're a good girl, you might be out in time to watch your grandkids enter school."

Jerrie Jean began to cry. "But who will take care of Johnny and Nickie?"

"If you don't have somebody who can take care of them, the court will probably find a foster home. Now what is it going to be? Do you want a chance to get out of prison or not?"

After a relatively lengthy pause, Jerrie Jean lifted her tear-soaked face and slowly nodded. "What do I have to do?"

"That's better. Now let's get something straight. If you're going to change teams, it has to be one hundred percent. We're going to ask you a bunch of things, but if you withhold anything of importance or mislead us in any way, we'll pull the plug on our offer and you'll spend the rest of your life in a cage. You got that?"

"Yes. I understand."

"One more thing. This offer isn't final. The DA and the court will have to approve it. I don't think we'll have a problem, but you need to know that we aren't the final voice. Got it?"

"Yes, ma'am. I understand."

"Good." Bramwell slid a writing tablet in front of the bad girl. "I want you to write a few sentences saying that Russell killed Phillip and you knew about it. Also, say that you were advised of your rights and you were not forced to make these comments. Additionally, you agree to make a complete, more detailed report, right after that."

Red-faced and wet-cheeked, Jerrie Jean sniffled. "Should I mention the GPS button-thingy that Russell used to follow Phillip around?"

With Jerrie Jean under control, Bramwell left Detective Roybal behind and scooted toward Russell's room. She and Detective Collier entered the room.

"Finally," Russell said with a scowl. "What the hell takes women so long?"

"I'm sorry, Mr. Blackstone," the sergeant said, "but it's bad news for you. Your wife is throwing you to the wolves as we speak."

"Oh, bullshit, she wouldn't do that. She loves me."

"Wrong sir, her arm might as well be half-way down your throat because she's pulling out your heart right now."

"You're wasting your time. You women can't bluff me."

"Well then, how is this? I want you to stand up and turn around and put your hands behind your back. We've got a holding cell that is just your size."

Russell looked in Bramwell's eyes, then checked out Detective Collier, who had her hand on her weapon. Clearly beaten, Russell slowly turned around and Bramwell's cuffs found his wrists.

80

AFTER THE LIEUTENANT TURNED OFF THE RED LIGHT, I knew he was in full attack mode. To begin with, we were essentially alone. I was at his mercy and only had one way out.

In legal situations, vulnerable persons could request an attorney and the request was supposed to be immediately granted, so I advised him that I wanted to call Breanne.

"You can do that tomorrow," he said.

I should have known better. The man was cagey and had backed me into a corner of sorts. "You guys have kept me here too long," I complained. "That's not legal."

"I'll tell you what's not legal, Ms. Pilday. We have interviewed dozens of other people. You're the only one who does not have an alibi. We don't have time to play who-done-it with you when we could be with our families."

"I'm sorry but I can't help that."

He stared at me for a moment, then, "Alright, let's try something else. Do you know what a grand jury is?" he asked.

"I've heard of them, but I don't know much about them."

"Let me help you. It's not a jury in the traditional sense. It's a pool of people who review multiple criminal cases to see if interrogators like me have enough evidence to charge people like you with crimes."

"Okay. So?"

"So, I have a colleague who is an expert with grand jury cases. I told him of this case and he guaranteed me that he could easily get an indictment against you. Would you like to know why he said that?"

"Not particularly."

"He said that your lack of an alibi is only strike one. Moreover, your husband's grandmother said she cannot eliminate you as the perpetrator of the crime, and she has already agreed to testify in court. My pal says that juries are inclined to believe people who fit her profile and that is strike two against you. Strike three is that you could have taken that lie-detector test but you ran for the bushes like a wild jackrabbit. Why would an innocent person do that?"

"Because she's not required to take that test and she doesn't like to be bullied. I think you enjoy pushing people around, but you should let me go and look for my husband's killer."

He scooted within inches from my face. "I'm tired of playing games, Ms. Pilday. I'm prepared to tear you down, one hour at a time if I have to. Do you understand me? You're going to stay in this hell-hot room all by yourself for as long as it takes."

"What? Please don't do that. I'm already worn out, and aching."

"I don't really give a shit. I am paid to be here, and I have an office with air conditioning. The only question is, how much misery can you endure before you give in?"

I'd met some evil men in my years, but none of them could steal a person's spirt and strength like Nagley. He clearly had all the cards and I was so exhausted I could barely breath.

Then Nagley pulled some papers from his pocket and handed me a pen. "I want you to sign here."

Undoubtedly, I had reached the end of his patience and he wasn't going to cut me any favors. I desperately wished I'd called Breanne way back when this started, but I was way too cocky. Worse, the red light was out so I knew there was no evidence of what he was doing. He was going to leave me

there until I gave in. My very survival was at risk. Bleary-
eyed, I slowly reached for his pen.

Just then, a soft knock on the door preceded the entrance
of Sergeant Bramwell. She asked her leader to step out of the
room.

81

IN THE HALL, LIEUTENANT NAGLEY learned that Bramwell and Roybal wanted to talk about Jerrie Jean and Russell.

"Are you nuts?" the boss said. "Ms. Pilday is about to sign a confession. Now, what the hell is so important that you would interrupt me?"

"I'm sorry, sir, but I took you up on your offer."

"Offer? What offer?"

"A while back, you said if you didn't get a quick confession out of Mrs. Pilday, that Chico and I could have another chat with Jerrie Jean and Russell. They are here now, along with the minister. As we speak, both the minister and Jerrie Jean are signing confessions and stating their roles in Mr. Pilday's death."

Dumfounded, Nagley swatted his forehead. "If that's true, I'm not going to release Mrs. Pilday until I can verify everything you just said. I'm going to need you and Roybal and all of your paper trails, including everybody else you've spoken with since day one. Got it?"

"Yes sir. I'm on it."

82

When the Lieutenant left the room, I didn't know what was going on, but I was weak and tempted to sign his papers, just to escape all the heat. While I waited for his return, I laid my head on the table and dreaded my fate.

While feeling sorry for myself, long minutes turned into long hours. Eventually, Detective Collier told me to sit tight until further notice. All I knew was I smelled like a slaughter house and my spirit was numb.

Eventually, I heard conversations outside the interrogation room. Ultimately, Lieutenant Nagley re-entered the scorching-hot room. He looked angrier than usual. "We're letting you go," he snapped.

At first, I didn't believe him. "Is this one of your mean jokes?"

"It's none of your damn business. Now get the hell out of here before I change my mind."

My mouth agape, I reached for the doorknob and expected him to yank me back in. "Okay," I said while turning the knob. "Thank you, but can I ask you one last question? Where's my dog?"

He slammed his hand on the table. "What the hell is the matter with you, woman? I don't give a flying fuck about your dog. Now get out of here."

83

THE FIRST THING I DID after Nagley released me was enter the lady's room and splash some cool water on my face. As if planned, Sergeant Bramwell came in and joined me.

"Congratulations," she said softly.

Considering our mutual experience when we returned to California from Cincinnati in an airplane she seemed very respectful. "Thank you. I was surprised when I was told I could leave. If you don't mind my asking, what made the difference?"

She hesitated a moment, then, "Are you sure you want to know?"

"Just the gist of it."

"Okay, I'm sorry to tell you this, but your husband had intimate relations with a fair number of women. One of them is named Jerrie Jean."

"Oh. I heard of her."

"Well, she figured out that your husband had some money in a trust and tried to blackmail him."

"Oh, my God."

"But your husband didn't fall for the extortion trap and said he was going to call the police. That scared Jerrie Jean, so she confided in her common-law husband.

"Russell is a hot-head and he was furious with her. At that

point, they both wanted to take your husband down before he could turn the tables on them. They followed him in his car, and Russell fired several shots and landed a couple. The one good thing is, Phillip died immediately. So, he didn't suffer."

"But what took so long to figure it out?"

"The Lieutenant was certain that you were the perp and he wanted to stick with it. After all, you had a criminal record, no alibi and ran from the polygraph."

I nodded. "I don't know if I'd do that again."

"It's water under the bridge now. Anyway, Russell was pretty sharp. He knew they had to have an alibi, so they went to Russell's brother, who happened to be a fly-by-night minister.

"Russell persuaded his brother to change the date on some documents so that it appeared as if Russell and Jerrie Jean were at their wedding when your husband was killed. Once we knew that they switched some dates, everything else was downhill."

"Were you the person who figured it out?"

"Well, we all work together around here."

"I've got a feeling that you're just being modest."

"And, I'm extremely impressed by your resolve and strength under pressure."

"Thank you. If I didn't stink so much, I'd hug you with all my heart."

Reba smiled, then, gently reached for me. "Two stubborn women who respect each other deserve one good hug."

After pulling away from my heroine, I asked her if Lieutenant Nagley was likely to apologize to me.

She openly scoffed. "When hell freezes over. The man is usually good at reading people, but this time it didn't go his way. He's pissed off at you and me right now, not to mention mad at himself."

"Can I ask you something else? Do you know how to get my car back?"

"It's probably in a storage lot in Cincinnati. You can go get it or have it delivered. It's probably going to cost you a thousand dollars or so. I can get you their number if you'd like."

"Thank you. What about my dog?"

"Your dog? I don't know where he ended up. Gimme a couple days. I'll try to find him for you."

"Thank you, Sergeant. You're a very kind and insightful woman. I'm glad God brought you into my life."

Following my discussion with Sergeant Bramwell, I borrowed her phone and called Phillip's sister to advise her and Juju that I'd been cleared and was ready to make arrangements to move on. "If you guys will come pick me up, we can go our separate ways," I said. "I'm so sorry for all I've put you through."

"What the heck are you talking about?" Ellen asked. *"One of the detectives called Juju and me a little while ago. They told us everything. Phillip was killed by the husband of one of the ladies he'd met. That wasn't your fault."*

Suddenly the voice changed. *"Miranda, this is Juju. You don't know how truly sorry I am for doubting you. I was unfair. Now I understand the kind of person you are. And I realize that my grandson got mixed up with some pretty horrible people, to say the least. Please say that you forgive me, or I'll never be able to forgive myself."*

I paused a moment. "If this were just about you and me, Juju, I don't know what I would say, but I do know that Phillip loved both of us, and I believe in giving people second chances. So, in Phillip's memory, I'd love to start over."

"I'd love that, too."

"Well then, would you guys come get me out of this place?"

"We sure will."

"I could also use some clean clothes and a shower."

"We'll take care of that. I want you to stay with me for the night - longer if you want to."

"I'd love that, Juju."

"Good. We'll be there as fast as we can."

84

Right after Phillip died, I held a smorgasbord of feelings. Naturally, I was deeply sad, but I was also wise enough to know that the perpetrators in murder cases are usually close to the victim. That was why Nagley came after me.

Given that I'd only been out of the Lighthouse for a few weeks at that time, I was extra skittish. My instincts screamed to "run first and ask questions later."

In retrospect, I don't know if that was a good strategy or not, but when Elmer and I were en route to Cincinnati, I loved the freedom of the open road and bonding with my little pal. None of that would have happened if I'd remained in California while the police worked things out.

My experiences with detectives hadn't been good. I knew they left a lot of destruction in their wake. They drove wedges between people and dug up skeletons and recklessly scared the hell out of people who got dragged into their investigations.

Anyway, in the end, Nagley's group managed to dig up the real perpetrators, and that's what mattered most.

Ultimately, Ellen and Juju retrieved me from the police building and Juju showered me with non-stop apologies.

After all that I had been through, I slept like a mama bear in the beginning of the hibernation season.

Eventually, I heard the doorbell. By that time, I had slept nine or ten hours and Ellen was back with a box of donuts. She made a pot of coffee and we gathered for more chitchat.

After half the donuts disappeared, Juju got a call from Breanne. Juju had invited her to come celebrate with us and she was running late.

"While we're waiting for Breanne," Juju said to me, "Phillip was always standing up for you, but I thought it was his penis doing the talking. I'm so sorry I dismissed you like that. Now I'd like to learn how you and my grandson fell in love - unless it's too personal."

Juju's question warmed my heart. "It was very romantic," I said. "It started on his trike at a truckstop. In the days that followed there was a campfire, wine, stars and his own little tail-wagger."

Juju smiled. "I remember that dog. He called her 'Killer.'"

"Poor little thing had been over-bred and abused for most of her life, so Phillip wanted to lift her spirits."

"What now?" Ellen asked.

"Well, I'm burned out emotionally for a little while, but when I get my Jeep back, I'd like to go to the cemetery and talk to Phillip for a long time. I owe him that.

"Beyond that, I want to get a job and figure out how I might meet my son someday."

"Anything else?"

"Yes. I'm looking forward to fussing over a real home as opposed to living in a jungle of bars. I'll actually enjoy simple things — washing windows and mowing the lawn – all of it."

"Those are all understandable objectives," Juju said. "I want you to stay in the rental house for as long as you wish - at the family rate, of course."

"That's half-price," Ellen stated.

"Thank you, Juju. Thank you. I promise to keep it in tiptop shape and pay you on time."

"Another thing," she said. "As you know, we went over to the rental house and confiscated some pictures and bric-a-brac. I thought that you were going to steal everything. But now I'm ashamed of myself. I want to put it all back. You can have whatever you want."

"That's very thoughtful, Juju, but I don't need very much and most of those things, especially the pictures, hold your memories of long before I entered Phillip's life. You can keep all of the original pictures, but I might want to get copies of a few of them, if that's okay."

"Of course it is. I have one more comment. When I heard about the 'special arrangement' you made for Phillip, I couldn't believe it, but now I get it."

"You do?"

"Yep. You knew that you were going to be stuck in that Lighthouse place for five years. With so few visiting hours, there were going to be times when my grandson would get lonely. Left to his own devices, he could sneak around, but that would have made him feel guilty about it, but you loved him and didn't want him to feel guilty so you took the weight off his shoulders."

"I get it too," Ellen said. "Most people have urges. If they don't have an outlet, they can get frustrated and creepy."

"Yep. I couldn't give that sweet man all the affection that he deserved. But, by allowing him to play with others once in a while, he was able to satisfy his physical needs with them, but I got his hugs and his kisses and his heart. He just ran into the wrong woman, in the end."

"Hugs," Juju said, pulling us all together. Just then, somebody knocked.

After wandering to the door, Juju called for me. "Come here, honey. You gotta see this."

Out on the porch, Breanne was holding my precious Elmer in her arms. She stepped inside and seconds later, that little firecracker ran in circles and came right to me and I knew how he felt.

I hugged Breanne, too. "How'd you find him?"

"When Juju called me about this meeting, I thought she

meant we were going to meet at her rental house to put the pictures back on the walls. It was a good thing I went there because when I was about to drive off, a delivery man drove up. He had your dog in the carrier in the back of his van."

Funny how a little pet can make a person so happy. I hugged Breanne again, then I hugged Juju, then I hugged Ellen, then I hugged Elmer. "Don't you worry, my little friend," I said. "I'll never let you out of my sight again, that is, if Juju doesn't mind you living with me for a while."

Juju patted me on the shoulder. "My grandson wouldn't want me to split you up."

We happy-talked for a while, then I filled them in on the multi-day ordeal of my interrogation. Breanne had a few words for me. "When you were brought back to California, you should have called me, or some other attorney. It would have been a lot easier on you after that."

"I know that now, but I thought I could persuade them that I was innocent."

"That brings up another matter. After all the dust settles, you might want to sue Nagley for the way he treated you, especially when he wouldn't let you call an attorney."

"I don't know, Breanne. I'm tired of all the negativity. I think I'd rather focus on positive things."

"Suit yourself. I have to admit that you have outstanding instincts. I'm just glad it all worked out."

"Me, too."

"Family hug," Juju said.

85

After I was cleared of Phillip's passing, I was talking with Ellen about Trevor's parents. Upon hearing that Bertie and Chester had blocked all of my calls, Ellen suggested I send them a certified letter. "They will have to sign for it, so you'll know that they definitely got it."

That sounded promising, so I grabbed a pen and spent hours writing a perfect letter explaining why I missed the party and to assure them that I still wanted to meet Trevor if possible.

Several days later, Chester and Bertie sent me a certified letter of their own. They didn't say whether they had read my letter, nor did they say anything about Trevor.

Instead, they included a copy of a restraining order that prohibited me from coming within fifty yards of their home. They also stated that if I were to ignore their warning, there would be legal consequences.

I sure as heck didn't have an appetite for another legal battle so I picked up Elmer, plopped my butt in a chair and realized that the only way I was going to meet Trevor was to wait until he was old enough to speak for himself. Believe me, that was a tough pill to swallow.

A while later I found myself complaining to Juju about the matter. "I understand," she said. "There is no love stronger than that which a mother holds for her own children."

"I believe that, Juju, but I've never even met my son."

"Even so, you are an extremely strong woman and God watches out for his children. For now, you have other blessings to appreciate."

That made sense and before I knew it, we were on to other topics. "That reminds me," she said, pulling some papers from a drawer. "The detectives returned the life insurance policies. Did anybody tell you what they learned about the policies?"

"Not really."

"Well, I found the file when we were going through Phillip's belongings. Lieutenant Nagley's people called the proper insurance company, and discovered that the polices of Phillip's partners were always in force, but your policy was voided because my grandson didn't pay the premiums."

"That figures. The whole time they were interrogating me, Nagley was suggesting that I killed Phillip for the insurance money, but now we know that was just another one of his dirty tricks."

"But they already knew it was void, Miranda, so why would they do that?"

"Because that could be a motive to kill my husband."

"But you must have told them that you didn't know anything about that policy?"

"Of course I did, Juju, but Nagley really believed that I was the perpetrator and that criminals lie, so he assumed that if he kept quiet about the expiration date I would think the policy was still in force which would lead me to confess to the killing. As far as he was concerned, the ends justified the means."

"Are you sure about that, honey? I've always thought the police were the good guys."

"Most of them can be pretty nice, but when it comes to solving crimes, some of them become bullies and throw the rule book away. I don't mind telling you, it almost worked."

Juju looked in my eyes. "I'm so sorry you had to endure those kinds of things."

"Me too, Juju, me too."

86

Two weeks later, and still living in Juju's rental home, I had enjoyed the typical household chores - cooking my own meals, cleaning the windows and the smell of a fresh-cut lawn.

By that time, the Jeep had arrived, and I had explored the neighborhood. I loved seeing the simple things that had escaped me for the past fifteen years, like squirrels in the trees and stars in the sky.

To show my appreciation and support for Phillip's family, I offered to paint the exterior trim of Juju's home.

Ellen and her husband pitched in and together we painted the entry door, exterior window frames plus the gutters. Juju was so happy she said I deserved one month's free rent, which I gave right back.

One day, at a gas station, a man around my age talked with me while we both filled our tanks. I was surprised when he asked me if I'd like to go to lunch with him.

My heart still belonged to Phillip, so I wasn't interested in anything like that, but it felt good to know I was perceived as a desirable ordinary woman rather than a convict.

That afternoon I visited Phillip and told him how much I loved him and missed him. When I returned home, I admired the street appeal of Juju's property and decided I wanted to spruce up the interior too.

By noon the next day, I'd managed to paint the central bath and set my sights on the small bedroom.

While removing the bedspread, I heard an unnatural 'clunk' near the headboard. A close inspection revealed a piece of a former mystery.

When Phillip died, the authorities wanted his cellphone to find out who he was talking with in the days preceding his passing - but nobody found it, so they got a court order and secured a hard copy of his phone records.

But one tug of the bedspread solved the puzzle. Phillip's phone had been wedged between the mattress and the headboard the whole time.

Anyhow, I had never imagined snooping in anybody else's cellphone. After all, some people shared intimate videos and sexy text messages via their phones. Most of those folks wouldn't want me to meddle in their private business and the feeling was mutual.

But on the other hand, that phone had become mine and I had every right to snoop. Given that Phillip was an unconventional man, he could have any number of things in there.

I held the phone to my chest while trying to decide if I really wanted to know Phillip's secrets. At the same time, Phillip could have been working on other business projects. If so, I couldn't forgive myself if I ignored his dreams.

Not yet willing to examine the contents of my husband's phone, I placed it on the end-table and went to the kitchen for a bottle of water. Elmer followed me, just in case there might be a biscuit for him but I tricked him and grabbed two biscuits.

Still debating with myself, I gave my dog his first treat and marched back to the recliner where I reclaimed Phillip's iPhone from the end-table. I held it to my chest again.

Like a tennis ball, my mind went back and forth, but ultimately, it occurred to me that no matter what I decided regarding my husband's phone, there was a good chance that I should have taken the other route.

Therefore, I powered it on only to find that the battery needed charged.

Frustrated, I retrieved my own charger and went for the outlet in the kitchen. After I set up the charger, I realized I'd need Phillip's passcode. I turned to the box of his belongings that Juju had returned to me. By the time I finally stumbled on his password folder, the phone was at 50%--which was enough for me for now.

I shuffled to the recliner and elected to focus first on Phillip's text messages.

Right away, there were a handful of messages from "QWERT." The name looked familiar, but I couldn't quite remember where I had seen it. Suddenly I realized that I held the answer right in my hands.

Those were the upper-most letters on the left side of a typical keyboard. At that point, I assumed that the QWERT message was either junk mail or a business of some kind.

I went ahead and peeked at the message to determine if I wanted to delete it. At the first glance, my eyes nearly popped out of their sockets.

QWERT was a young person who claimed to be the cousin of Trevor Montgomery.

OMG! QWERT had to be in contact with my son.

With my heart pounding, I found a number of QWERT's recent messages to Phillip. In the last one he stated that Bertie and Chester were pissed off because they'd gone out of their way to accommodate Phillip and me, yet it appeared to them as though we stood them up and never explained ourselves.

I couldn't believe it. "But my husband was killed!" I screamed to the message.

While tears of irritation rolled down my cheeks, I hoped that QWERT could put me in touch with my son.

I instructed my jittery fingers to peck out a text message of my own.

"Hi QWERT, this is Miranda. Sorry for the confusion. Phillip and I wanted 2 get 2 Trevor's party but P was murdered. It's been horrible.

Can we talk, rather than send messages? Please contact me in the morning. I'm in California, so it's Pacific Time. I'm using Phillip's phone so you have the number already. Please call."

While tears of regret blended with tears of anticipation, I wondered if and when QWERT would get my reply—and if he'd respond. I also wondered why QWERT was the one who sent the messages rather than Trevor.

With more questions than answers, I wondered if QWERT and Trevor were in London or someplace else.

With all of that uncertainty swirling in my head, all I could do for the moment was put on my sleuth hat and scroll back through the rest of QWERT's messages.

God, it was great to be free.

87

THE SHORTEST DISTANCE BETWEEN two points is a straight line, but the distance between Trevor and me had always seemed a winding lifetime away, but now, he was somewhere in Phillip's iPhone and QWERT appeared to have the password.

I hustled into the kitchen, made a cup of decaf and returned to the recliner and Phillip's phone, where I anxiously looked through the remaining QWERT messages. A few of them were about the Montgomerys and how adults didn't keep their promises.

The more I read, the more panicky I became. What if QWERT never called back? What should I say to QWERT or Trevor? Was I defying the Montgomerys' restraining order?

After a couple hours of research and second guessing myself, combined with non-stop clock watching, I essentially ran out of gas. I decided to put Phillip's phone on "Vibrate" and clutch it to my chest while I slept.

The next morning, my internal timer stirred. There were no new messages on hubby's phone, but I took some pleasure from knowing that I'd learned a couple things and successfully avoided any dirty pictures or videos.

I was just about to take a shower when a call came in. "Probably a spam call," I speculated, while actually hoping it was Trevor. If so, it would be the first time I'd heard his voice since he had cried in the delivery room.

"Hello," I said, "Is this Trevor?"

"No. It's QWERT," the caller said. *"Trevor didn't want to call you because you didn't give a damn about him or his party."*

"No. No. No." I insisted. "That's all wrong. I've always wanted to speak with him more than anything in the whole world. Please make him talk to me as soon as you see him again."

"Alright then, just a minute."

After a brief pause, "Hello," a new voice said.

OMG! It was just one word, but I instantly knew it was the voice of my precious son.

While new tears raced to my eyes, I raised my head to God Almighty and mouthed the words "thank you."

"Hello, Trevor," I said. "You can't possibly know how much this call means to me. Thank you."

"Yeah. Am I supposed to call you Miranda or Mom or what?"

"Well, if it's okay with you," I said while the track of tears continued, "let's respect your parents. Bertie has been your mom for a long time, so call me Miranda."

"Alright. I guess I can do that, Miranda."

"Are you in London?"

"What? Hell, no. That was just a scam. Do you want to know about it or are we going to lie to each other, like those other people do?"

"I don't know what you mean, but yes, let's be honest with each other."

"Okay. I'm sixteen but those other people treat me like a kid. They never bothered to tell me that they adopted me, let alone that my bio mother is a friggin' convict. That's the same as lying to me all those years."

"I'm sorry you feel like that, Trevor. I know what it's like to be misled. I never knew anything about you until you needed that liver transplant."

"That's another thing. Those other people always led me to

believe that they didn't know who the donor was. But that was just more lies."

"I know that some people can be irritating, but I'm certain Bertie and Chester always wanted whatever was best for you."

"Ah, bullshit. I can't believe anything they say."

"Hey, if your parents are so secretive, how do you know so much about me?"

He paused a moment. Then said, "You haven't lied to me so far, so I guess I can tell you."

That little bit of trust warmed me. "Go ahead, Trevor, I'm listening."

"Okay. The day before the party, my so-called parents went to church, but my dad forgot to take his cell phone. I took a free look at the text messages and discovered he'd been communicating with some guy named Phillip. Now I know, thanks to your message to QWERT, that Phillip was your husband and he got killed. I'm sorry about that, by the way."

"Thank you, Trevor. Phillip was a very nice man. I wish you could have met him."

"I'll take your word for it, because nobody else would have told me anything about it. Anyway, I got Phillip's number from one of Phillip's messages and wondered who the hell I really am."

"Well, I'm sure you don't make a habit of reading other people's texts, but in this case I'm glad you did."

"Whatever. Right after that, the party came and went with no sign from you guys. Chester was super pissed off at you. That's when I confronted them about their own deception regarding the adoption, but they yelled at me and said I was ungrateful.

"I was tired of their crap, and said I wanted to get the hell out of there. That dad person said I could never get by without him. So, I got some boxes and began packing my things in my car. We were all yelling at each other. The mom didn't want me to go. But I was pissed off too. I yelled back. She was screaming at him when I left, but at least they couldn't lie to me no more."

"My goodness. That's awful for all of you. But if you're not in London, where are you?"

"Florida. QWERT's mom and Bertie are sisters. And here's another classic lie for you. Those other people only told you that I was going out of the country so that you and your husband wouldn't butt in anymore. That's the kind of slimeballs they are."

"Well, I don't know about that, Trevor, but I want you to know that I will never lie to you."

"Yeah. We'll see."

At that moment, it sounded as if my precious son was ready to hang up, but I'd spent a lifetime looking for him so I sure as heck didn't want to scare him off. The best thing to do, I thought, was ask if I could call him the next day.

88

WHEN I ASKED TREVOR if I could call him again, he simply said "I guess so," but it sounded like a big "YES!" to me.

The next day I waited patiently for 5:00 Eastern time to tap out his number. Since he felt as if Bertie and Chester had been mistreating him, I reminded myself to ask him open-ended questions and be nonjudgmental.

To my dismay, the call went to voicemail but he soon called me back. *"Sorry,"* he said, *"but I just took a little time-out from work."*

Just hearing his voice made me grin again. "That's okay. What kind of work do you do?"

"Uncle Josh has a small fleet of big-rigs."

"Those big trucks?"

"Yeah, eight of 'em. QWERT and me clean out the trailers, then load them for the next day."

"Really, what do you haul?"

"A lot of things: hardware, food, furniture, imports. Our drivers go all over the country. After they drop off their loads, they look for shippers who want to send their cargo back this way."

"That sounds interesting."

"It's better than school. I'm sorry I wasn't more sensitive to your situation yesterday, but I get really, really pissed when people lie to me."

"Understandable. Sometimes it's difficult to know who you can trust. You said something about an Uncle Josh?"

"Yep. When those Cincinnati people and me got in a big fight, the mom person called her sister. Aunt Lori and Uncle Josh have always lived in Florida. I've been here several times on vacations and always liked them, including QWERT - he's weird but that's what I like about him. Can I ask you a question?"

"Of course."

"Why were you in prison?"

"Well, I told you I wouldn't lie to you, so I'll give you a condensed version up to the time you needed that transplant, but I want you to know I was wrongly convicted."

"Really? Isn't that what everybody says?"

"Pretty much, but sometimes it's true. Are you certain you want to hear about it?"

"Sure. I've never known a prisoner. No, let me change that. My former parents never said anything about knowing a prisoner."

"Okay, I'll tell you. First you need to know that when I was born, I had a twin brother named Mickey. If he was still alive, he'd be your uncle. Anyway, Mickey had a mental disorder from a brain tumor. He lived in various government facilities most of his life."

"Uncle Mickey, huh?"

"Yep. Now, imagine me in middle school. I blacked out while in the school play. More blackouts followed whenever I got stressed out. Eventually, I grew up and landed with a small pool of wrong people at the wrong time. One guy that I dated killed a dentist for some reason. As usual, I blacked out. Then, when I came to, two additional people had been killed. The police thought I was involved, so I got charged and convicted. I was sentenced to minimum of forty-one years."

"Holy hell. That must have been scary!"

"It sure was. Some of those ladies are just as tough as male prisoners. They formed gangs right there in prison and bullied anybody they could.

"Anyway, eight years later, while I was still in prison, Uncle

Mickey died and I started getting headaches. Eventually, a doctor found a brain tumor, which he removed, and the blackouts stopped."

"But you ain't in jail now, so what happened?"

"Two years later, a very charming young man, named Trevor Montgomery, needed me, because we shared a blood type."

"That must be when I got that transplant."

"Yep, but it wasn't easy. After the surgery, you and I were recovering in different parts of the hospital when one of my former cellmates kidnapped me out of that hospital. We made it all the way to Utah. That's when I met Phillip and his godmother who happens to be an awesome attorney. Breanne got my medical records and compared my black-out incidents with my brother's passing. She proved that I couldn't have been aware of the murders, so the DA terminated the rest of my sentence."

"That's cool, but you lost ten years of your life."

"Actually, that wasn't the end of it. The prosecutors said I had to serve some more time for breaking out of the hospital and hiding in somebody's house without their permission. That led to five years in a minimum-security facility. All of that came to an end a little over a month ago."

"Wow. That's an incredible story."

"I lost a lot of my life, but I try to focus on positive things. For instance, Phillip and I were really looking forward to your party, but somebody shot him. It took me a while to put a coherent sentence together, but when I reached out to Bertie and Chester, they wouldn't answer their phone."

I heard Trevor click his tongue behind his teeth. *"Those people are assholes."*

"In their defense, Trevor, they didn't know what was going on. Anyway, I grabbed my dog and drove from California to Cincinnati to talk with them in person. But when somebody is killed, everybody becomes a suspect, and it doesn't look good to run. The police met me right on your block, arrested me and flew me back to California until they found Phillip's real killer. Unfortunately, I never got to speak with your parents, but I did talk with the man who lives on the other side of their street."

"If he was wearing a red hat, that's Mr. Teter."

"That's him. Anyway, my favorite part of my story is, you and I saved each other's lives."

"Really? I know how you saved my life, but how did I save yours?"

"I've thought about it a thousand times. If you hadn't needed that transplant, I never would have been in that hospital, and that's what enabled me to find Phillip and his godmother, and now I've found you at last! I think God wants us to be together."

"Oh, yeah. Are you a Bible thumper?"

"Not particularly. I don't go to church much, but I believe that God has been with me from time to time. You know something? I've been dominating the conversation. That's very rude of me. I'm sorry."

"Relax. I asked you some questions and you answered them. No biggie."

"Now, let's talk about you."

"What do you want to know?"

"Do you have a girlfriend?"

"No," he said abruptly. *"What else?"*

"It sounds as if I hit a nerve?"

"I don't want to talk about that right now. Do you have any other questions?"

"I sure do. I assume you're going to school. How do you like that?"

"What for? School sucks so I dropped out."

That's not the kind of thing that a mother wants to hear, but I had been looking for him for sixteen years and I surely didn't want to chase him away. "Well, I guess you can get a GED if you need one."

"Aren't you going to lecture me about it?"

"Would that make any difference? Would you change your mind?"

"No. I don't need it for my job."

"Well, I'd rather get to know you better than criticize you."

"Really? That's sorta cool. I gotta get back to work now."

"Sure. I hope we can talk again? I want to learn all about you."

"Just don't lie to me, okay?"

"I promise. May I call you tomorrow afternoon?"

"You ain't pissed me off or nothin' so, I guess so."

When we hung up, I felt higher than a rocket. I wrote down all the relevant phone numbers just in case I lost my phone, which was impossible because I was already clinging to it as if it were a new-born baby.

89

After my first real conversation with my son, I felt as giddy as any other new mom. I could barely wait to speak with him again. When that moment arrived, I insisted that it was his turn to do the talking.

"Okay," he said, *"but before we do that, you implied that Phillip is not my biological father, so who is?"*

"Oh. I was hoping we wouldn't get to that for a while."

"Why not?"

"It's not a pleasant story, but I told you I wouldn't withhold any information from you, so if you'd really like--"

"What's the matter? Is he a jailbird, too?"

"No," I said, ignoring the unintended dig. "But it's complicated. Your father died a few months before you were born."

"It sounds interesting. I wish the people I used to live with were that honest with me."

"Don't be too harsh on them, Trevor. People who adopt babies deserve a lot of respect. They love you just as much as I do."

"Whatever. What else can you tell me about my bio daddy?"

"Certainly. I've already told you of my twin—"

"Uncle Mickey?"

"Yep. One year he and I went to a twins' convention in

Ohio. I met Don there. He was a twin too and was a nice guy at first."

"So, he's my father, right?"

"I wish it were that simple. Did you know that identical twins have identical DNA?"

"No, I didn't know that, but what does it have to do with anything?"

"I'm getting to that. Like I said, it was a twins' convention and Don had an identical twin, named Mac."

"So, we're talking about you and Uncle Mickey, plus Don and Mac?"

"Correct. I got involved with Don, but after a while, we had a squabble and Mac asked me out."

"Let me guess. You did 'em both?"

"Not at the same time, and it wasn't as seedy as it sounds. I loved both of them for different reasons."

"Oh, I get it now. One of them is my father, but you don't know which one, and DNA wouldn't help. That's pretty rad."

"That's the gist of it. As a matter of fact, they were two of the three people who were killed in that big blackout mix-up that I mentioned before. Several months later I was pregnant with you and was sent to prison. Five months after that, you came along. Since they don't allow children in prison, I had to give you up. I cried and cried."

"So, that's how you met Bertie and Chester?"

"Almost. I didn't want anybody to know that your mother was a convict, so I selected a sealed adoption. That way, neither the adoptive parents nor the biolgical mother meets each other.

"Anyway, they were in the delivery room behind a curtain, but we never made eye contact. It worked well for nearly ten years. That's when I got a call to the warden's office. I was asked to be a liver donor, which I refused, until they said it was for you.

"Later, when you and I were recovering, in different parts of the hospital, I learned your legal name. Before that, I always thought of you as 'Cody.'"

"Now that's what I'm talking about," Trevor said with a lot

of spirit. *"Why can't those other people level with me like that? I don't dislike you for any of that. In fact, it's the opposite. Thank you for treating me like an adult."*

"You're welcome, Trevor, and I'll always be grateful for what Chester and Bertie did. Now can we talk about you?"

"Sure. That's fair. What do you want to know?"

"Okay, you already said you don't want to talk about any girlfriends, so why don't you tell me about your siblings?"

"My siblings? I guess they're okay. Rodney is twelve and can run faster than me. Looks like he's going to be an athlete."

"Is that it?"

"No. I've got a scatter-brained sister."

"Tell me about her."

"Okay. In Arlene's world, everything is a crisis."

"Oh, yeah, like what?"

"Everything. The entire universe nearly exploded a few months ago when the lady-curse got to her."

"Do you mean her period?"

"Yeah, she acts like she's the only one who has to deal with that."

"How old is she?"

"Fourteen. She already likes boys."

"That's kind of normal for young ladies her age."

"It's gross, but it ain't a crisis."

I had to chuckle. "Well, you better get used to it. What about you? What was school like before you dropped out?"

"I guess it was okay. I got one B."

"Well, that's not too bad. You're probably better at some things than other things."

"That pissed me off, too."

"What did?"

"I took both Advanced Calculus and Linear Algebra in the same semester but the dick-wad algebra teacher graded me down because I had bad penmanship."

My jaw nearly dropped to the floor. "Oops. I misunderstood you. I thought you had one B in your lifetime and everything else was below that, but you meant that you have straight A's, except for one B. Is that it?"

"It's no big deal."

"Wow! I'm very impressed. I never took Calculus, let alone Advanced Calculus, and I've never even heard of Linear Algebra."

"Well, it ain't never good enough for that dad person. He thinks I should have kissed the teacher's ass so that I'd get straight A's again. But I'm tired of his barking at me. Now I've got a job, and I can get by without them."

"What about your Aunt Lori? Do you get along with her?"

"Yeah, whenever QWERT and I aren't loading trucks, we are painting her house and landscaping it. She and Uncle Josh say I can stay here as long as I want."

"Oh, really? You and I have something in common. I used to run small painting crews in the prison. You'd think it would be easy to paint bars, but the trick is to paint with a mitt instead of a brush or roller."

"That's pretty rad. I wouldn't have thought of that."

"There's not a lot to do in prison, so it broke the monotony, and we made a little money to buy a few things from the prison store – we called it the 7-Eleven."

"That's cool, too. You said that you've never heard of Linear Algebra, but I never knew much about criminals. Can I ask you something else along those lines?"

"Of course."

"You said that Phillip was killed. What happened to him?"

I would have preferred to hear more about Trevor's past, but I'd also told him that I would always be honest with him, so I gave him the information he'd requested. Eventually, he was intrigued by the hot interrogation room and all of the bullying that went on. *"Wow,"* he said. *"Remind me not to double-cross you. You're a badass."*

"Not really. I just stood up for what I believed in until they found the real bad guys."

"That's another thing you and I have in common. I'm standing up for myself too."

"I guess we both have a stubborn streak."

"So, who did it? Who was the perp?"

"One of Phillip's former lovers and her husband. They tried to blackmail Phillip, but when he said 'no,' they thought he might go to the police. I miss him a lot."

"Sorry for bringing it up."

"Don't worry about it. I try to stay positive."

Suddenly the mailman stepped onto my porch and my four-legged partner went nuts.

"What's going on?" Trevor asked.

I chuckled. "It's Elmer. I got him from a shelter. He thinks he's a tough guy, but he only weighs fifteen pounds."

"Oh, yeah? I like lizards and snakes. But my silly sister hates them."

"You know something?" I said. "We should send each other a few pictures."

"Okay. Including our scars."

I actually laughed out loud and agreed to his request. Then he paid me the compliment of a lifetime.

"I don't care what anybody says, I'm glad you got out and found me."

Naturally, when we hung up, I cried, but this time it was happy tears.

90

BACK WHEN I GAVE BIRTH TO TREVOR, I had nobody to take care of him so I selected a sealed adoption, in which the parties never would see each other.

But when my boy needed a chunk of a compatible liver, the sealed envelope was opened. Bertie and Chester were grateful that I'd saved his life so they agreed to send me a thumb-drive full of pictures of Trevor as he grew up.

However, they still wanted to keep the adoption a secret to protect Trevor, and I was obligated to go along with it.

But when QWERT and Trevor found me, that changed everything. Among other things, Trevor wanted to speak with me, and I wanted to see any and all of the pictures that he had taken on his cell phone.

I quickly discovered that his pictures were more creative than most people's. He had a picture of his sister drooling when she fell to sleep watching TV. He also had a close-up of dog poop and an extra-bright full moon. One of his best impromptu pictures was of QWERT when he was thirteen years old and had to clean a toilet on Thanksgiving. Apparently, they all got to laughing about it and QWERT's mop-top hairdo added to the humor.

Naturally, I loved my son's ability to draw outside the lines. But my pictures were very limited. After all, I'd been in prison for a long time and there were no cellphones or cameras in there.

Nonetheless, I sent him some pictures of Elmer, plus Phillip and me at the lawn party and at the redwoods. Finally, I took a couple selfies and one of my scar to fulfill his request. He responded in kind.

Our pictures begged for explanations, so we talked back and forth about family, and school events and holidays behind bars.

"Those big trees are rad," Trevor said of the redwoods.

"They're beautiful. Phillip took me there for a mini-honeymoon right after I was released. The funny thing is the town is in Miranda, California and you have to go through Phillipsville, California to get there."

"No shit? That's funny."

"Yeah. You can look it up if you want to. Those trees were spectacular, but the best part of that little journey was about the open road. After being herded around for so many years, I cherished driving. Phillip bought me a car of my own. I still cry when I think of him."

"That's okay. I know that girls cry a lot."

I actually got a chuckle out of his reply. "Thanks for that. Where were we?"

"I don't know," he said, *"but I've been wondering if you have a job."*

"Good question. I've been snooping around, but some companies won't hire anybody with a criminal record."

"Why not? You paid your dues, didn't you?"

"Sure did, but it depends on the crime. A person who commits a money-crime wouldn't get a job as a cashier, and somebody who was drunk and violent might not get a job in a bar."

"Are you having any luck?"

"I was completely exonerated regarding the original crimes so that slate is clean. My only other problem was breaking out of the hospital when you were born, but I wouldn't have done that if I was never wrongly charged with the big crimes."

"I see what you mean. Somebody ought to hire you."

"I haven't had a chance to apply for any jobs yet, but I'm going to get more serious about it in a little while."

"If that's the case, you should come down here. There are lots of jobs."

I didn't know what prompted his question but I didn't want to be rude. "Me? I've never considered leaving California."

"Why not. You ever been to Florida?"

"A long time ago."

"Well then what's stopping you. You would like Aunt Lori. You both talk a lot."

I had to giggle again.

"Why are you making noises?" he asked.

"You say some cute things. Anyway, I'm flattered that you'd invite me to see you, but it's a wacky idea."

"No, it isn't. I already talked to Aunt Lori about it. I can put her on the phone right now if you want."

Partially stunned, I needed more information. "Are you serious?" I asked.

"Sure. It only takes five hours to fly from Los Angeles. If you can't afford the ticket, my aunt could tell you how to get a cheap flight. She's good at that too."

"It's not that."

"What then?"

"I thank God that you don't know what jail is like, but being confined in an airplane is almost as bad. If I were to come, I'd probably drive the whole way."

"I guess I can understand that. So, do you want to talk with Aunt Lori or not?"

Whoever said that God works in mysterious ways was wise. One of the greatest wishes in my entire life was to meet my son, but every single one of my countless efforts had been thwarted by obstacles of some type. But suddenly, it appeared as if the opportunity of a lifetime had simply dropped into my lap. All I had to do was verify my son's comment.

A short moment later, his aunt was on the line. It happened

so suddenly that I didn't know what to say so I just blurted it out. "Hello, Aunt Lori. This is Miranda. Trevor said that I could come visit, but I had to hear it for myself. Are you really okay with something like that?"

"Hi, Miranda. It's a pleasure to chat with you. Trevor has been excited ever since he heard from you, so we'd love to meet you."

"Are you sure? Bertie won't even talk with me. I don't want to drive a wedge between two sisters."

"Nonsense. My sister can be a little uptight sometimes but she was willing to let you join Trevor's party a while back, so I can probably explain everything to her. Besides, you're Trevor's biological mother, and you both want to meet the other."

"That's so kind of you. If I were to come there, I'd want to bring my little dog. It might be better if I stay in a motel."

"You can do that if you want to, but it's no problem; our little Collie would love to have a playmate."

"It sounds wonderful, but there's one final thing. I hope you are sitting down."

As it turned out, she already knew about my colorful past - but Trevor hadn't told me that Aunt Lori was one of those people who sees the good in everybody.

91

I'D WAITED WELL OVER HALF OF MY ADULT LIFE to embrace my only child, so a three-day, cross-county trek should have been a walk in the park, but in the beginning, I was so excited that everything and everybody seemed to be in slow motion.

Before I departed, Juju pointed out that my Jeep had a ton of miles on it, so I opted to rent a car for a couple weeks.

Eventually, I packed some clothes and snacks plus my ever-trusty four-legged buddy. Then, off we went, a lot like Dorothy and Toto.

Along the way, I treasured the freedom to make my own decisions such as when and where to eat and sleep. There were occasions when I could see for miles at a time, unlike being in a sterile ten-by-ten room of bars.

I also cherished the privacy, especially after living in packed quarters for so many years.

Throughout it all, there was plenty of time to deal with pent-up emotions and child-like enthusiasm for a future that would surely include Trevor in some way.

Ultimately, Elmer and I were closing in on Miami, where a few final twists and turns led us to the very last block, but an unexpected set-back arose. We were among a group of huge warehouses rather than a residential neighborhood. Something was clearly wrong.

I was about to call for better instructions when a petite, pony-tailed lady on a bicycle waved at me. Elmer growled while I lowered the window.

"Are you Miranda?" she asked, smiling. "I'm Lori."

Lori's tan face and legs guaranteed she had spent a lot of time outdoors in the proverbial Sunshine State.

"Yes. I'm so pleased to meet you," I said just as she came to a stop.

"Thank goodness. QWERT gave you the wrong address. Our home is a half-mile away. You can follow me. We'll be there in a few minutes."

As she pulled away, I noticed a lovely tattoo of a surfer on her upper arm and her muscular calves. I grinned uncontrollably because I knew that Trevor had to be nearby.

Several minutes later, we pulled up to the curb of Lori's stucco home. The yard had been xeriscaped and there was a tarp covering some bushes, which confirmed Trevor's previous comment about painting their home.

I'd barely stepped out of my car before Lori and I shared a heart-felt hug. Then the door from their home swung open and a small collie escorted two young men outside. The first youngster sported a mop-top hairdo; the second one was the son of either Don or Mac, two identical twins that I once loved.

Surprisingly tall, Trevor might as well have had a halo glowing over his sun-bleached hair. He wore typical beach attire: sandals, shorts and a tee shirt with C2C on the front. Trevor beamed a happy white grin at me, a lot like my own.

As he scooted toward me, I couldn't help crying. We hugged and I hugged him again. Then we pulled apart and he wiped my tears from his cheek. I was in love, like never before.

The remainder of that day was used up with Uncle Josh's barbecued hot dogs. He was handsome, with thick, dark hair nearly to his shoulders and a well-groomed mustache.

The afternoon was consumed by hours of glorious stories and kindness. It was the single greatest day of my life.

Around midnight, we were all pooped but for different reasons. My hosts were accustomed to a different time zone and had been awake for four extra hours.

As for Elmer and me, we had endured a long drive and all that concentrating made a person want to rest her mind and clean up. Elmer slept with me in a back bedroom.

In the middle of the night, Elmer stirred a bit, which caused me to pause and remind myself where I was. I smiled my way back to sleep.

The next morning, QWERT and Trevor went to work at Uncle Josh's shipping warehouse. I eventually rolled out of bed and Lori made a nice breakfast of yogurt and sourdough french toast. After we cleaned up, I was invited to tour the warehouse. Everybody, including me, was required to wear a "C2C" tee-shirt.

"It stands for Coast to Coast," Lori told me. "We only have eight trucks but we're doing well and getting another one very soon."

It was very clear that they all took pride in the family business.

Thereafter, I watched my son and QWERT clean out the back of a semi. Then they used an electric Pallet Jack to begin loading the cargo area for its next haul. All of it was new to me, but it was like a movie. I loved every minute of it.

A couple days later, QWERT and Trevor were loading a truck when Uncle Josh nearly knocked me off my feet.

"Since you like to drive and could use a job," he said, "would you consider driving a big rig? We've got a new one coming in. Tall Bob has been with us for six years so he has seniority, but that leaves his truck up for grabs."

I felt like I'd just been tapped on the head by an angel. "I'm super-honored," I said, "but I don't know anything about driving big trucks."

"No problem. We can train you."

"Why wouldn't you hire a man? They know more about these things than I do."

Lori scoffed. "So what? There are lots of lady truckers."

Uncle Josh nodded. "You'll be required to take a written test, but before that, you'll go out with other drivers until you learn the ropes. The toughest thing is backing up. By that time, you'll know if you really like the trucker's lifestyle. If so, we need a driver and you can have the job."

"I've never thought about anything like that," I said. "Besides, I have a criminal record."

"We respect your honesty, but you got shafted, so it's no problem for us. Ain't that right, Lori?"

"He's right, Miranda. You'll typically be on the road for six to ten days at a time. In between runs, you can stay with us. That way you won't have to fund an apartment, but if you'd prefer a motel, there are plenty of them around here or you can simply sleep in your rig. Either way, you can keep Elmer with you."

Josh nodded. "If you are wondering how much it pays, our best people make something in the neighborhood of seventy thousand dollars."

"To get that kind of money," Lori said, "you have to be on the road nearly all the time. You'd probably be better off working a little less and settling for fifty-five thou. That will leave you with some extra time so that QWERT and Trevor can teach you how to surf with us."

"That's a good one," I chuckled. "I don't even know if I can still swim."

"Well then, you'd probably like walks on the beach and sunbathing."

"Now that's more my style."

"Like Josh said, we have an opening and would like to fill it. All we ask is that you give it some serious thought."

"Well, I do love to drive."

92

After a week with Trevor and Aunt Lori's family, I felt like a full-blown family member. Among other things, they offered me a job that fit me like fresh air.

There would be plenty of time to deal with my loss of Phillip and fifteen years, but most importantly, my son would be a part of my life.

The only bad thing involved my wardrobe: With no closet, I'd be forever adorned in jeans and C2C tee-shirts.

Overall, the pluses outweighed the minuses by a trucker's mile and I was inclined to accept their proposal.

At about that time, Trevor wanted to take me to dinner. "Just you and me," he said.

I didn't know what he had in mind, but I cherished any time with him. At an Italian restaurant, we placed our orders, then he looked me in the eyes and said, "Remember when you asked me if I have a girlfriend?"

"Of course, I do," I said. "In fact, I was surprised that you didn't have girls dripping off each arm."

"Well, there really is somebody. Her name is Shelly. She's back in Cincinnati. We send lots of text messages and talk every day."

I grinned. "That's exciting. Why didn't you say so?"

After a small pause, "Because I wanted to see if I could trust you."

"Trust me? About what?"

He nervously tapped at this fork, then, "Shelly is pregnant and we don't know what to do."

I felt like I was hit in the stomach with a bowling ball.

"Shelly is freaked out," he added. "She doesn't know how to tell her parents. I suggested she come down here and stay with me, but she's too scared to leave home."

"If you don't mind my asking, how old is Shelly?"

"Fifteen."

My stomach tightened and my appetite disappeared, but my son needed me, and I wanted to help him. "I'd love to see her. Do you have any pictures of her?"

As we cruised through several cellphone pictures, I said polite things, such as "she's cute" and "she has pretty hair," but all the while I was thinking that she looked as if she still liked dolls.

"I may be wrong," I said, "but I doubt if Shelly's parents will let her move away. And Aunt Lori and Uncle Josh wouldn't want the responsibility. Do Chester and Bertie know about this?"

"Hell, no. I wanted to tell them, but they've been yelling, nonstop, at me lately."

"What about Aunt Lori? Have you told her?"

"I was going to tell her first, because she could be a mediator, but when you said you'd come visit us, I wanted to hear what you'd think because you won't get hysterical either."

"I can understand that. Do you know when Shelly is due?"

"She thinks she's in the sixth week. We wanted to talk to somebody who wouldn't blow up. Now we know that you're real good with people."

"Well, thank you. What do you want to know?"

"I love and respect Shelly. I know that her voice counts more than mine. If she wants to keep the baby, I'll work real hard until I'm eighteen, and then we can get married. But we want to know what we should do next."

Dumbfounded, I'd always expected that my initial meeting with Trevor would be some sort of child-like fairytale, but I didn't expect that my sweet young son was entangled in a Romeo and Juliet relationship. Clearly, he was correct when he said he needed guidance. "I'm sorry honey," I said, "but it wouldn't be appropriate for me to stick my nose in everybody else's business. I can tell you this: Shelly needs to see a doctor very soon. Other than that, you and Shelly have to face your respective parents, back in Cincinnati, starting with her folks."

"I was afraid you would say something like that."

"Just remember, honey, you're not the only persons who has been in this situation. Nearly everybody gets through it, but the important thing is to be honest about it. If you do that, there's a better chance of a good outcome."

"Do you think I should tell Aunt Lori, first? She would be a good ally, just like you."

"I think you can level with her, but ask her to keep it hush-hush until you can speak with the others."

"Then what?"

"Well, if you really want my opinion, a baby is a huge responsibility, even for somebody who is prepared for it. But you guys are so young it could ruin your entire lives. Given all of that, I think you should talk with Shelly's parents and see what they suggest."

"Yeah. That makes sense. All I know is, they are very religious. Shelly said they wouldn't want an abortion."

"In that case, somebody has to raise the child. That's an enormous undertaking and it's very expensive. Your other parents could confirm that for you."

"If they'll do that, I'll work really hard to pay for everything."

I have to admit that the mom in me was impressed by my son's sense of responsibility, albeit after the fact. "That's very noble of you," I said, "but it might not be the best thing for the mother or the baby. Either set of parents might offer to raise a baby themselves, or they can consider adoption. That's how I learned of Bertie and Chester."

Trevor smiled for the first time since we placed our orders. "Thank you for helping me. You've convinced me to go back to Cincinnati and talk with the adults, face to face. At least they'll know I'm not going to run out on Shelly or the baby."

"I'm glad to hear that, Trevor, and the sooner the better. Now, I'd like you to do a favor for me, if you don't mind?"

"Sure. What is it?"

I hesitated a moment, then looked him in the eyes. "When you go back to Cincinnati and tell Bertie and Chester about the baby, they will be shocked at first. It might get sticky. But remember this, parents want the best for their children. So, when things slow down a little bit, maybe you can ask Chester to help you get back in school. You are such a smart person, you deserve to have a great career in science or business or aerospace, but you can't do that by washing out the cargo area in big rigs."

He actually chuckled.

"What's funny?" I asked.

"Aunt Lori has said that exact same thing. To tell you the truth, it sounds pretty doable. I only have to make up one semester, but first I have to face Shelly's family. Then I'll have time for myself."

"That's an excellent plan, Trevor."

He nodded. "Okay then, it's my turn to ask you for one last favor."

"Yes. Of Course. You can ask me anything,"

He tilted his head off to the side then back. "Would you mind if I call you Mom?"

I put my hand over my mouth and quietly nodded my head.

93

I don't know what pleased me more, Trevor calling me "Mom," or knowing that I could become a grandma.

I was still staying with Aunt Lori and Uncle Josh when Trevor leveled with them regarding the potential baby. After the initial shock, Lori called Bertie and plans were made for my son to fly to Cincinnati where he would face both the Montgomerys and Shelly's parents.

I later learned that when my son reached Cincinnati, he and Shelly visited Shelly's folks first. Apparently, her parents were angry, disappointed, and well aware of the financial responsibility, but they were also very religious and forgiving people who prayed about the matter and agreed to help raise the baby if necessary.

After that, there was a discussion about living arrangements. Shelly insisted that she and Trevor were in love and wanted to stay together, but that idea got shelved when Shelly's mom pointed out that the most important thing at the moment was to see a doctor.

Under the circumstances, Trevor was satisfied with the first meeting, but he hadn't yet met with Bertie and Chester. He hoped they would be of a similar mind, but he doubted it.

As it turned out, Chester had a difficult time with Trevor's news. Red-faced with anger, he made true-but-hurtful comments about naïve young people, irresponsible behavior, and the cost of raising families. But then something different caught Trevor's attention.

While defending himself from Chester's onslaught, Trevor noticed a faint smile on Bertie's lips. Clearly, his adoptive mother was imagining her first grandchild and that gave Trevor hope.

While Trevor was occupied in Cincinnati, I too entered a new world. I held a lot of respect for Lori and Josh, so I decided to accept their offer and become an over the road trucker.

Uncle Josh said I could begin right away, but I preferred to return to California with Elmer for my limited belongings and to say a heart-felt thanks to Juju and Ellen. We'd been through a lot together and I considered them my West Coast family. I especially liked it when they referred to me as "Phillip's wife," and when Ellen's kids called me "Aunt Miranda."

94

After I said my good-byes to Juju and Ellen, I returned to Florida and Trevor called me from Cincinnati. He said that he had talked with the other adults about me. He claimed that if they kept the baby, I too would become a grandma, and ought to be part of his or her life.

Shelley's parents were open to that notion, but Chester hesitated and grumbled. Nonetheless, my son held his ground and insisted that babies shouldn't be torn from their mothers. Naturally, that made we cry, but the whole conversation was premature because there were still four to five months to decide if they were going to keep the baby or put it up for adoption.

Beyond that, after six weeks of on-the-job driving with three different partners, I went on my first solo trip, called "the cherry."

Some six-hundred miles later, carrying a load of outdoor toys and sporting goods, Elmer and I pulled into a decent truckstop. I got cleaned up, watched a little TV and slept in the cab.

I'd already earned four thousand dollars, so I sent half of it to Juju as back rent.

Overall, Elmer and I loved the open road, which was the antithesis of our former lives in our respective cages.

A couple months later, Elmer and I were cruising down a highway in Tennessee when a call came in from my former attorney. "Hi, Breanne," I said. "It's nice to hear from you."

"Are you sitting down?" she quizzed.

"Sort of. I'm driving a big rig."

"Oh, yeah. Juju told me about your job. Congratulations. That must be exciting."

"It's also soothing."

"I can imagine. Can you pull over somewhere? I need to talk with you for a little while."

"Sure. Is everybody okay?"

"Definitely. Everybody is fine. I just need to ask you some questions regarding a business matter and it might take a while."

"In that case, let me look for a good spot and I'll call you back."

A while later, I pulled into an open area just beyond the shoulder of the road. I removed Elmer from the cab and stretched my legs. Then I called Breanne. "So, what's on your mind?" I asked.

"Before we get into that, I understand that you are going to be a grandmother. Is it a boy or girl?"

"They had an ultrasound. It's a boy."

"How nice. I bet you're thrilled."

"I wish it were that simple."

"Uh-oh."

"As you know, raising a baby is difficult enough, but Trevor and Shelly are just kids. I think they've figured out that it's not realistic to get married either."

"What are they going to do?"

"They considered putting the baby up for adoption."

"That makes sense. Trevor's folks know a lot about that."

"True, but Chester and Bertie are still raising Trevor and his siblings. That leaves Shelly's parents. They're enthusiastic about taking the baby, but Shelly's father got a transfer to the North Dakota oil fields. That produced a set of logistics about visiting and finances and the like. That's about all I know for now about that matter, but there is one additional bit of good news."

"Tell me about it."

"Sure. Since Trevor was only one semester behind in school, he and Chester persuaded the principal to let him do independent study and catch up. That way, he can still graduate high school and get into college. I'm thankful for that because Trevor is a very smart young man, with lots of potential."

"That's wonderful, Miranda. Perhaps I can add to your good fortune."

"Huh? What do you mean by that?"

95

After I brought Breanne up to date, she had a message of her own.

"If you're wondering why I called," Breanne said, *"I was contacted by another attorney who is representing Phillip's partners."*

"Craig and Allen?"

"Yes. After several years of working on Phillip's app, they are very close to finishing it and they've received a strong offer to buy you guys out."

"Buy me out? What do you mean. Is this a joke?"

"No. I'm as serious as a heart attack. When Phillip passed away, his share reverted to you."

"I heard that before, but I didn't know what that meant."

"You'd better brace yourself because the offer is for twenty-two million dollars. Craig and Allen get a little over five million each. Your share comes to over eleven million, before taxes."

"Oh, my God, Breanne. Are you joking me?"

"Nope. There are a lot of more-valuable apps than yours, but it's still a nice one."

"Oh, my God!"

"If you are wondering," she went on. *"you can accept the offer, reject it, ignore it, or make a counter-offer."*

"Really? Why would I ignore it?"

"It's a negotiation tactic. Some people get nervous when they don't get an answer to their offer. So, if you just ignore them, they might offer more."

"I don't think I want to play games. To tell you the truth, after those guys got their insurance money, I thought they wouldn't want to sell for years, if at all."

"Could be, but when there is a lot of money on the table, people are known to change their minds. Anyway, they want to accept the deal and move on to other endeavors, but you have fifty-two percent, so you are the final decider. It's all up to you."

My heart pounded as if it wanted to escape the question. Then, I said, "What would you do if you were me, Breanne?"

"Well. You might get more money if you wait another year or so, but if a competitor should come up with a similar but better app than yours, you could lose everything. The choice is yours, but I'd take the deal."

"Sounds like it. How much are the taxes?"

"Around thirty-five percent. That's about four million dollars, but that would leave you with seven point six million after taxes."

Stunned and quivering, I said, "Gosh, Breanne, maybe I should talk it over with the partners or Josh and Lori."

"That's certainly one of your options, but remember, if you take too long, the buyer can withdraw the offer."

"Oh, in that case, I think Philip would want me to take the deal."

"Okay. Good choice. The buyer has agreed to pay you in sixty days, that leaves a little time for Craig and Allen and everybody else to take care of loose ends. In the meantime, the buyer put up a non-refundable good-faith deposit of one hundred thousand dollars."

"What's that?"

"You get to keep it, even if they back out. It proves they are serious. Your share is fifty-two thousand. I can wire that right away."

"Really? Fifty-two-thousand dollars for me? I've never had that much money."

"You'll have it within twenty-four hours. I just need an account number."

"Oh my God, Breanne. How can I ever thank you?"

"Well, now that you ask, I never did get all of my fees when we got your prison sentence revoked. That was five years ago, and we've had other legal discussions since then. I wouldn't mind catching up on that."

"Of course, Breanne. Of course. How much is that?"

"Well, a lot of attorneys would charge you twenty-five percent or more of what you are getting. That would be almost two million dollars. But I don't have as much overhead as the bigger firms, so I'd be thrilled with five hundred thousand dollars. The first twenty-five thousand will be paid tomorrow morning after your wire comes in. The rest is payable when you get your big check, in sixty days. After all of that, you'll still have over seven million dollars."

"Wow! Okay, Breanne. I don't mind telling you that I'm shaking like a leaf in a breeze."

"That is why I had you pull over. So, what are you going to do with all your money? Retire?"

"I don't think I'd do that for a while. I really do like driving, but I might be able to help Trevor's family."

"Well, you'll have sixty days to figure all that out. After that, I know some financial planners who can help you invest your money wisely. For now, I gotta notify everybody that you've accepted the deal and wire that deposit into your account."

"Okay then, thanks a lot, Breanne. I love you."

"I love you too. For the time being, stay close to your phone in case I need anything."

She could count on that. When we hung up, I turned to Elmer. "Guess what, buddy? We are going to be millionaires."

Predictably, Elmer didn't care, so we returned to the cab where I blasted the horn, yelled several extra-loud YAHOO's and aimed my rig down the open road.

ABOUT THE AUTHOR

Like most Americans I liked my career of several decades but I have to admit that I didn't always approach the mornings with wild enthusiasm.

But then, I retired and discovered something I never would have guessed: When the day is mine, I love to get up even earlier. Now I'm the guy who wakes up the rooster. I still work as much as I ever did, only I now work on things that bring me a different form of compensation. Like writing books.

Some have asked me where I get my ideas, but it's no mystery. I had a storied youth with six sisters and a wild family. When I wasn't engulfed in that world, I spent a fair amount of my time wandering the alleys and streets of our neighborhood. A fellow learns a lot from all of those people even before he arrives for his first day of school. If he has the ability to recall the characters and the activities in which they engaged, and blend that with a dash of make-believe, there's a goldmine full of fodder from which to draw his inspiration.

AWARD WINNING BOOKS
BY THIS AUTHOR

NON-FICTION

Instant Experience for Real Estate Agents

Stop Flushing Your Money Down the Drain

FICTION

Three Deadly Twins

Monday's Revenge

Grandma's BFF Does Coke

Zero Degree Murder

Miranda in the Wind

All books available in paperback or ebooks

**Books may be ordered from
Amazon or other online bookstores**